"Jake Wilder?"

"Yes," he said cautiousl[y] [...] unfamiliar woman's face.

She emerged from the shadow of an overhanging oak and stepped into the moonlight. "I'm—"

"Maggie Flannagan," he said softly. "Bea's granddaughter." In the brief pause that followed, Jake studied the face he knew so well from photographs, focusing on the mouth he'd privately declared the most kissable he'd ever seen.

"How'd you know?" she asked, clearly bewildered.

"Well, I..." He closed his mouth. In the two years he'd lived in Broken Arrow, he'd heard all about her from Bea. Suddenly something came back to him. He and Bea had been standing by his barren flower beds when she'd mentioned leaving him a legacy. When he'd asked what she meant, she'd smiled and said there would come a time when he would just have to look to see it. With the proper care and nourishment, she'd promised, it would give him enough pleasure to last a lifetime. He'd wondered then if she'd planted something in his flower beds, but now...

Well, he was looking, all right. And what he saw was Maggie Flannagan.

Dear Reader,

Welcome to the Silhouette **Special Edition** experience! With your search for consistently satisfying reading in mind, every month the authors and editors of Silhouette **Special Edition** aim to offer you a stimulating blend of deep emotions and high romance.

The name Silhouette **Special Edition** and the distinctive arch on the cover represent a commitment—a commitment to bring you six sensitive, substantial novels each month. In the pages of a Silhouette **Special Edition**, compelling true-to-life characters face riveting emotional issues—and come out winners. Both celebrated authors and newcomers to the series strive for depth and dimension, vividness and warmth, in writing these stories of living and loving in today's world.

The result, we hope, is romance you can believe in. Deeply emotional, richly romantic, infinitely rewarding—that's the Silhouette **Special Edition** experience. Come share it with us—six times a month!

From all the authors and editors of Silhouette **Special Edition**,

Best wishes,

Leslie Kazanjian,
Senior Editor

SAMANTHA QUINN
A Promise Made

Silhouette Special Edition

Published by Silhouette Books New York

America's Publisher of Contemporary Romance

To Ms. B. Hamilton, Ms. P. Bly
and Ms. K. Compton,
my stalwart critique group.
Thanks for sharing the frustrations
as well as the fun.
Thanks, too, to my husband, Ted,
for always being there when I need him.

SILHOUETTE BOOKS
300 East 42nd St., New York, N.Y. 10017

ISBN: 0-373-09551-1

First Silhouette Books printing September 1989

Printed in the U.S.A.

SAMANTHA QUINN

says imagination has always been a part of her life. She made good use of it, first in theatre, then in art, before she finally found the perfect creative outlet through writing.

A native Oklahoman and mother of three, she says, "My family keeps me grounded in a reality that bears an uncanny resemblance to Erma Bombeck columns." Samantha adds that her husband's unfailing support has been an immeasurable ingredient in her success. When possible, the family enjoys "getting away" to Grand Lake and going sailing.

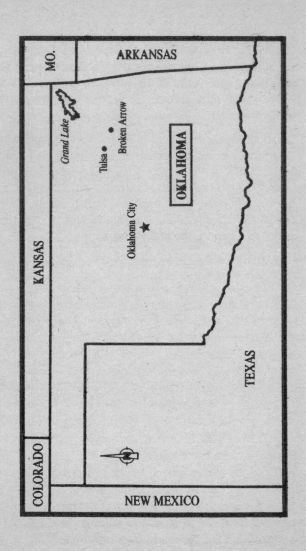

Chapter One

Y ou could've told me, you know.''

The comment, as much as the fact that the car had slowed to a stop, opened Jake's eyes. "Told you what?" he asked, returning the bucket seat to its upright position.

Frank McKinley turned toward him and rested his elbow on the steering wheel. "No wonder you weren't in the mood to jam with the guys after their concert," he said with an air of omniscience. "But God forbid you say something as direct as, 'Hey, Mac, I've got a lady waiting for me. Let's split.' No, instead you just kept your mouth clamped shut and acted itchy as hell.''

Lady? Jake eyed his friend, totally at a loss. The cracks about how private he was he understood, having listened to them for more than ten years. But the rest of it? "Want to clue me in about what you're talking about, or do you just intend to keep up a running monologue?''

Mac paused as if he was considering the question, then grinned. "As much as I'd like to needle you a bit longer, it's my guess she's been kept waiting long enough." He nodded toward the house and Jake followed his gaze, sure his friend was playing one of his practical jokes.

He wasn't. Though midnight cloaked any real recognition, the figure that rose from his stoop was definitely female in form. The glow of a cigarette brightened as she took a puff, and Jake raised a brow. Teresa Wilson had smoked, but she'd left town six months ago. She also had waist-length blond hair and stood nearly as tall as his own six-two. The woman on the steps was petite, with hair that blended into the night.

"It really would be a lot more fun having a bachelor for a friend, if said bachelor would divulge his carryings-on."

Jake gave Mac a smirk, knowing his friend was far too happily married to care about vicarious living. "Your imagination has always been far more exciting than my life," he said, smoothing his shirt into his jeans. "As for the lady, I don't have the slightest idea who she is." He grabbed his leather bomber jacket and white scarf from the back seat. "But I'm about to find out." He ducked out of the car and shrugged into his jacket. "See you Monday," he said, waving his friend on, then faced her.

Surprises, he mused. Oklahoma was famous for them in late April, but they usually came in the form of tornadoes. Tonight the sky was clear, the air crisp, and the only surprise around was the lady of mystery. Clad in jeans and a windbreaker, she came toward him with purpose-filled strides.

"Jake Wilder?"

"Yes." He said cautiously, attempting to search the unfamiliar woman's face.

"I'm really sorry to intrude on you at such a late hour." She emerged from the shadow of an overhanging oak and into the moonlight. "I'm—"

"Maggie Flannagan," he said softly. "Bea's granddaughter." In the brief pause that followed, Jake studied the large eyes he knew from photographs to be a dark moss green, the barely tip-tilted nose and the mouth he'd privately declared as the most kissable he'd ever seen.

She stopped before him and slipped her long, brown braid behind her shoulder, her expression bewildered. "How'd you know?"

"Well I . . ." He closed his mouth. In the two years he'd lived here, Jake had seen photographs and heard about her from Bea. He knew almost everything, from her fall at age seven out of a sycamore behind her grandmother's house, to the recent breakup of her engagement and subsequent loss of her job. Not sure how she would feel about the extent of his knowledge, he hedged with a smile, trying to decide what to tell her.

In the midst of thought he found himself distracted, suddenly wishing she would smile in return. Would the dimple on her right cheek be as winsome as it had appeared in pictures?

"What's wrong?" She swiped at her cheeks. "I've got something on my face, right?"

"No, of course not." He dipped his hands into his pockets. "You surprised me, that's all. Of course, I knew you'd be coming sometime."

Her eyes narrowed suspiciously as she combed through her bangs with her fingers. "That still doesn't explain how you knew I was me."

"Uh, Bea's gallery," he said, finally thinking of a nonincriminating answer. "I swear, she must have more than fifty family pictures on that one wall alone." The slightest frown and raise of her chin reminded him that her pain was still fresh. "I'm sorry. That was thoughtless of me."

"There's nothing to be sorry about. It's just me and..." Her gaze shifted with a faraway thoughtfulness to the white, two-story Victorian house next door. Wisps of hair danced at her cheeks, set into motion by a breeze. "It seems like only yesterday when Gran and I got that idea, but I was twelve. She'd just bought a new camera and said she was tired of having to drag out photo albums every time she wanted to look at pictures.

"In some ways it doesn't seem real to me that she's gone," she continued quietly. "I've found myself glancing at the house all night, half expecting the glow from the television to light her bedroom window upstairs."

How many times had he done the same thing in the past three weeks? "Yeah, I miss her, too. She was very... special."

A smile lit her eyes. "I know she thought highly of you." She looked down at her cigarette. The end no longer glowed. "Darn things go out most of the time before I can even finish them." He watched as she conscientiously walked to the curb, tossed the cigarette into the gutter, then headed back.

"I saw the note on your door." She slipped her hands into her back pockets, a smile teasing her lips. He found the flicker of her dimple irresistible. "All I can say is, if the past few hours have been your idea of 'just a minute,' I'd hate to wait for what you'd define a long time."

Jake lifted his brows apologetically and raked his fingers through his dark hair. "Sorry. The note was for Mac, the man who dropped me off. If I'd known you were coming..."

"Originally I thought I'd drop over just to let you know not to be concerned when you saw a light on in Gran's house. But when my key didn't turn..." She looked at him questioningly. "Did you change the lock?"

"No, of course not."

"That's odd." She shook her head. "Oh, well, if you'd be so kind as to let me have the spare. Mom said you were checking the house once a week and watering the plants. You do have the spare, don't you?"

"Sure, but what about your key? Could your mother have given you the wrong one?"

"I don't think so. She marked it with yellow tape." Maggie held it out to him. "See?"

Jake took it and nodded toward his house. "Let's go get mine and compare."

"Yes, please. I'm rather anxious to get into Gran's," she said, falling into step next to him.

She was shorter than he'd expected. Five-three maybe? Four at most, and as slim as a willow. Maybe that was why he felt inexplicably protective toward her. That, and knowing how much she'd been through recently. The death of her grandmother alone had to have been a horrible blow. Though Bea had loved all three of her granddaughters, it was Maggie with whom she'd had a special bond.

Jake approached his porch steps, where items spilled forth from an open tote bag like a cornucopia. "Come on in," he said, maneuvering around them. "It won't take a minute."

"No, that's okay. I'll just wait out here."

Already halfway up, he looked back. "You're sure?"

"Yes." She gestured to the bag. "I need to pick up my mess." If he hadn't been watching so closely, he would've missed her near-imperceptible glance toward Bea's before she pulled a cigarette and lighter from her pocket. "Besides, I enjoy being outside."

From what Jake could see, Maggie didn't look as if she was enjoying anything. It was nerves, he thought. It had to be. Entering her grandmother's house was something she would obviously do with mixed emotions. She tried to light her cigarette three times with a less than steady hand, but the lighter refused to cooperate. He moved down the stoop.

"May I?" He took the slim lighter from her.

She nodded. "This is my last one. Normally I don't smoke, but flying makes me nervous."

Jake didn't bother to point out that she was on the ground, but stroked his thumb over the small wheel. A flame appeared obediently on the first try, and he shielded it with his hand.

"Thanks." She leaned forward and took the light, then exhaled quickly. "My whole day's gone like this. My first plane had a delayed takeoff, so I missed my connecting flight, my luggage is stranded somewhere east of the Mississippi, the key to Gran's door won't work, you weren't home—not that you should've been," she added quickly.

Jake slipped the lighter into Maggie's free hand and instantly felt guilty for not being home sooner. "Oh, great. Your mother mentioned how you'd almost been hospitalized with the flu at the time of the funeral, and now your hands are cold. I hope you don't get sick again because of me."

"I won't." Her voice was quiet, her eyes determined. "I refuse to."

Jake's gaze lingered on her upturned face. The beginnings of warmth and awareness swirled within him, and something else he couldn't quite name. He thought of the restlessness that had hit him shortly after reaching the Assembly Center in Tulsa, and the way he'd been anxious to cut short the visit with his old friends after they finished their concert. Was it possible that on some level he'd known she was here?

He quickly discarded the notion as ridiculous. "Still, it would've been better if I'd been here. I'm sure you're as exhausted as you are chilled."

"As a matter of fact, I can think of nothing better than getting settled and taking a long, hot bath."

Jake steeled his mind against the provocative image. After all, she was Bea's granddaughter. "I'll get the key and be right back."

Once inside, he flicked on the porch light and walked into the living room. Maybe it was best she hadn't come in. Music books lay scattered on the floor; sheet music shared space on the coffee table with the remains of a sandwich, two glasses and a half-filled cup of coffee; five guitars—three on stands, and two more in their cases—added to the chaos.

He wound his way through the room, pausing to scoot the piano bench back into place before going into the kitchen. No maybe about it, he decided, surveying the core of disaster central. She'd definitely had enough trauma for one day. He grabbed the key from the rack and stopped briefly to compare it with the one she'd used.

He frowned. The keys lined up perfectly. Puzzled, he strode to the front door and opened the screen. Maggie stood at the far end of the porch, her purse over one shoulder, the tote over the other. The nerves were back again, this time in full force. Turmoil radiated from her straight posture, and she bounced lightly on her heels, no doubt gearing herself up.

He should know what to say, Jake thought. He'd had social amenities drilled into him long ago. He could be charming when it suited him, as long as a relationship stayed on a purely social or business level. Yet when it mattered, really mattered like now, his mind went blank. Wishing he knew what to say to make the next few moments easier for her, and regretting that he didn't, he let the door close behind him.

Maggie turned instantly, her expression expectant. "Bad news," he said. "The keys match, so that leaves us with the question of why yours didn't work."

"It wasn't from lack of trying, believe me. The darn thing simply wouldn't turn at all." She walked toward him. "Maybe I'll have better luck with yours."

Jake reached for her tote bag. "Why don't you let me take that and—"

"It's fine," she said, clamping her fingers around the strap. "Besides, I've put you out enough and—"

"You haven't put me out at all." He let his hand fall to his side, recalling how stubborn Bea had said Maggie could be.

"It's nice of you to say so, but if you'll just give me your key, I'll be on my way."

He looked down at her extended hand, then up to her eyes. "First of all, I don't say things to be nice. Ask Mac. He says I don't say anything at all. And secondly—" he slipped both keys into a pocket "—nope."

The lift of a single brow eloquently illustrated her thoughts on his audacity.

Jake smiled. Maybe she wouldn't let him carry the bag, but he would be damned if he'd let her go over there alone. He held his ground, sure Bea would have wanted it that way. "Look, Maggie, if your key didn't work, chances are mine won't, either. It's been nearly a week since I last went in. Maybe some kid has jammed the lock. I might as well find out now."

After a moment's consideration, she relented with a nod. Side by side they started across the dew-laden lawn.

Though small in stature, Maggie had a natural long stride that kept up easily with his own. He liked that. Women who took prissy little steps drove him nuts, as did women who felt constant chatter was a necessity. Watching her, he smiled inwardly. Maggie, he decided, would be a good neighbor.

"It's a marvelous old house," he said, glancing up at the dark, lonely windows. "It should never be empty."

"Mmm. Gran always said it was made for kids. She'd hoped to see it filled one day with her great-grandchildren. I guess if she's watching, she'll have to settle for someone else's."

Apprehension tensed muscles in his neck. "What does that mean?"

"There are a few things I want to get started first, but then I'll be putting the house up for sale as quickly as possible." She glanced over at him. "You look surprised."

"Well... I kind of thought you'd be staying."

She frowned. "Unfortunately, it's not feasible." She stopped and dropped her cigarette, then ground it out with her toe. "I'm moving from L.A. to Pacific Grove after I take care of things here. I've recently invested in a bed-and-breakfast inn that a couple of my friends own. After Gran's house sells, I'll be able to become a full-fledged partner."

Despite her words, when she looked up at the house Jake thought he saw a shade of reluctance about her decision. "Sounds like you've got everything all figured out."

Maggie started walking again. "I think it's what Gran wanted. One of her favorite sayings was, 'God never closes a door that he doesn't open a window.' Well, in the will she said something about the house being my window, a fresh start, a legacy from her to me."

Legacy. It all came back to him. They'd been standing by his barren flower beds when Bea mentioned leaving him a legacy. When he'd asked what she meant, she'd smiled and said there would come a time when he would just have to look to see it. With the proper care and nourishment, Bea had promised it would give him enough pleasure to last a lifetime. He'd wondered then if she'd planted something in his flower beds, but now . . .

Well, he was looking, all right. And what he saw was Maggie Flannagan.

Jake rubbed the back of his neck. He was being absurd. It *had* to be something like flowers. Not even Bea could *will* one person to another. It had to be the craziness of the night, the full moon, the eerie sense of needing to get home earlier . . . a charming old woman repeatedly saying, "You and my Maggie would be perfect for each other."

"Jake?"

He glanced up, surprised to see that he'd stopped at the bottom of Bea's porch steps. "Sorry, I was just thinking." He moved up the stoop quickly and pulled out the key. "May I?"

"Be my guest."

Jake fit the key into the lock and turned it. When the bolt slid back without hesitation, he stepped aside with a flourish. "Voilà!"

Maggie wagged her finger in disbelief. "Those keys may look exactly alike, but yours works and mine doesn't."

He pulled the other key from his pocket and did a double take. There was no telltale yellow tape. "Maggie, this is my key. *Yours* is in the lock."

"It can't be!" She dropped her belongings and plucked the key from his hand. "It doesn't make sense!" She stared accusingly at the lock, then back at him. "Lord, you must think I'm a flake. I'm not, really. I swear, I must've tried that key at least twenty times! I pushed, I jiggled, I cussed . . . it wouldn't turn!''

"I don't think you're a flake. Promise," he added sincerely, though he did think it odd that the key hadn't turned. From the distress in her eyes, however, he didn't think she needed to hear it. "Maybe it was the weather. Maybe the humidity made it stick."

She gave him a long dry look. "You know as well as I do that humidity makes *doors* stick, not locks." She sighed deeply and picked up her things. "I don't know what to think. I guess I'll just lump it in with the rest of my wonderful day." Her smile was tired, but genuine, as she extended her hand. "Thanks for your help, and I'm sorry you tromped over here for nothing."

"Nothing, Maggie?" Her hand fit perfectly into his.

Perfectly? Was that more of Bea's programming? he wondered. Or something more basic, more elemental, like the need of one man for one certain woman? Now he *really* was being absurd. Releasing her hand, Jake covered his conflicting emotions with a smile. "After all, we met, and I get a chance to be chivalrous."

"Pardon?"

"There's no need for you to go into a dark house alone. I thought I'd just go in with you and—"

"I'll be fine. I'm used to walking into a dark apartment." Her tone seemed a little too casual, her smile a little too bright. "Thanks again, and good night."

"Night." He hesitated, but then, so did she, as if she wouldn't go inside until he left. "If you need anything—"

"I promise I'll call."

Jake turned away slowly and went down the steps. He heard the creak of the door as it opened and—

"Oh, my God!"

In the moment he took to get up the stairs, she'd backed out, slammed the door and dropped her belongings. When she turned, she went into his arms without hesitation, her body shaking with something much stronger than mere nerves.

"What is it? What's wrong?" he asked, taking hold of her shoulders. He bent down slightly, trying to get her attention. "Maggie, talk to me."

"The stench...oh, Lord..." She lifted her face, her eyes brimming with distress. "It smells like...like...something died in there!"

Air from the opened door drifted outward like a vaporous cloud. Realizing she hadn't exaggerated, he moved them back discreetly where the air wasn't tainted. Maggie was still shaking and he moved his hands up and down her arms, hoping to relax her.

"You don't suppose a...a...band of killer rats or something have gotten in the house, do you?"

"Killer rats?"

Though smiling, she still clutched repeatedly at his jacket. "I guess that *is* a bit ridiculous," she murmured. "It was the first gross thing that popped into my mind." Her gaze wandered to her hands. "Sorry," she said, backing away. "I seem to be saying that a lot tonight. The smell just took me by surprise. I'll be fine."

He admired her pluck, but didn't believe her. "Why don't you have a seat on the steps and I'll go inside and—"

"Oh, no, I—"

"Independence is great in a woman, Flannagan, but you're carrying it a bit far," he said firmly. "Sit."

"Sit?" The dark porch hid the indignation that no doubt blazed in her eyes, but couldn't disguise her tone of voice. "Do I look like a dog?"

"Now it's my turn," he said quickly, holding up his hands. "I'm sorry. I didn't mean for it to sound like that."

A chuckle was the last thing he expected to hear. "Me, edgy? Never!" She ran a hand through her bangs, then rubbed her chin. "Tell you what, how about a compromise? I'll go in, but I'll let you go first."

"You're all heart." He started for the door, then glanced back when his imagination conjured a gang of rats standing on their hind legs waiting inside, complete with tattoos on their arms. "Stay close, okay?"

"Like a shadow," she whispered.

Jake paused, took a deep breath, then turned the knob. Maggie's hands rested lightly at his waist. Entering, he flicked the light switch and searched for the source of the foul smell. Sheets covered the furniture like ghostly shrouds, but gave no hint as to the possible offender. When he was sure there was no imminent danger, he pointed to the windows. "You open those and I'll get these."

"What do you suppose it is?" Her voice sounded suddenly nasal.

"You got me." A glance revealed that she held her nose. All in all, a good idea, he decided, doing the same. Despite such precautions, he could tell the stench grew stronger as they walked through the dining room. "It's my guess it's coming from the kitchen."

Jake opened the swinging door, confirming his suspicions. He fought a desire to bolt outside for fresh air and turned on the light. Nothing was amiss, and yet the longer he stood in silence, the stronger he felt something beyond the obvious wasn't quite right.

Maggie moved from behind him to the sink. Leaning over it and going on tiptoe, she pushed the window up with her free hand. "I wonder—"

"Listen."

"What?" she asked in a whisper.

"The refrigerator. It's quiet."

"So?" She headed into the nook and began raising windows there.

"Since I first knew Bea, it's always had a loud hum."

"That's right," Maggie groaned. She turned slowly and stared at the silent white appliance. "And Mom mentioned that she'd stocked it for me before she and Dad came back to California, which means . . ." She didn't finish the sentence. The smell alone said enough.

"I think it means I owe you an apology." Jake shook his head. "I'm sorry, but when I was here last week, I thought something didn't smell quite right. I figured the house was musty from being closed up. Obviously it was the beginning of—"

"Hey, it's no big deal." She turned back to the windows. "I probably would've thought the same thing."

"Maggie, why don't we allow the house some time to air out, then come back in the morning?" Jake walked to where she struggled with the final window and added his strength to hers. "You can stay with me tonight and—"

"No! I mean, no," she added softly as the window gave. Cross ventilation pushed at the white half curtains. She glanced at him, then back at the opening. No words were needed.

They both dropped to their knees and pressed their noses to the screen in search of clean air. Arm to arm, they gasped several times in unison before Jake's gaze met hers, careful not to get too far away from the screen. Sharing the moment, they both began to laugh. It was a hell of a situation, yet because of Maggie, almost pleasurable.

"I appreciate the offer," she said, her voice normal, "but I think I'll stay and clean up. Gran would die if I—"

Maggie closed her eyes with a succinct curse, then opened them again. Her smile was wry. "Ever notice how many times you use the word *die* when someone already has?"

"Human nature."

"Let me amend myself," she said, looking out into the night. "Gran'll *haunt me* if I leave her house without taking care of the problem."

Maggie's photos, Jake decided, didn't do her justice. There was something about her eyes. Deep green and expressive, they had small yellow flecks that seemed to brighten or dim with her mood. The photos hadn't shown that, nor the way she blushed at times, her face fragile pink. Because he couldn't help himself, he stroked her cheek. "We wouldn't want that, would we?"

Whether it was puzzlement at what he'd said, or the way he'd touched her that made Maggie look at him, he wasn't sure. Her lips were parted slightly, her eyes wary. He suppressed a desire to kiss her and smiled in reassurance before standing bravely, determined not to hold his nose.

Hers wrinkled. "How's the smell?"

"Gross. Am I green yet? No, don't tell me." Her wariness faded, and Jake took off his jacket and hung it on the back of a chair.

"What are you doing?"

He unbuttoned the cuffs of his white shirt and started rolling up his sleeves. "She may have left you the house, but I was in charge until you arrived." He opened the back door to aid in airing the room, then retrieved a box of black plastic trash bags from beneath the sink. "That makes me responsible, so I'm going to help."

"Oh no, I couldn't let you—"

"Hey, your grandmother was someone I didn't want angry with me when she was alive. That goes double now.

I'll bet she could put on one hell of a haunt if she wanted to.''

Gratitude curved her lips, punctuated by the capricious twinkle of her dimple. ''Tell me, Wilder, do you have a strong stomach?''

''I guess we'll both find out.'' He placed his hand on the freezer handle as she stood. ''Ready?''

In the weeks since Gran's death, Maggie had dreaded the moment when she would walk into the house without her grandmother in it. Though that time had come and gone, Maggie knew she had yet to face the reality. Tonight there had been no chance for her heart to accept what her mind knew.

Her pensiveness receded as she padded barefoot down Jake's hallway, fresh from a hot bath and bundled up in his full-length, terry-cloth robe. The smell at Gran's had permeated the house, and after working with rancid remains for two hours, she'd been more than happy to accept his invitation to stay at his house for the night. Rounding the doorway of the dining room, she smiled. Most people would furnish the room with a table and chairs. The presence of the baby grand piano was another assurance that Jake wasn't most people.

Soft soothing strains of classical music from the living room contrasted with the clatter of dishes in the kitchen. She'd told him not to bother with straightening up the house for her benefit; he'd promised he only planned to do a little.

The man lied; the room was no longer deserving of the ''disaster-area status'' he'd apologized for earlier. She wondered how he'd managed to do so much in so little time. The couch was made up like a bed, the coffee table cleared, except for two music magazines, and the instruments had been put into cases or on stands, lining the walls. Her gaze moved to the two ceiling-high bookshelves that flanked the fireplace. Filled to capacity, they held books about music as well as bound sheet music and all the essentials of Jake's sound system, except the speakers. She smiled, studying the room. Was this what was meant by a house filled with music?

She settled on the couch, tucking her feet and the extra length of the robe beneath her. Gran had said Jake was a nice man, and Maggie had to agree. How many other men would have helped her tackle that mess? How many would have laughed with her as they dashed outside, gulped clean air, then took bets on who could last the longest inside before another return trip? How many other men would have drawn her a bath, given her a friendly shove into the bathroom, then waited in the hallway to take her clothes to wash the smell out of them?

Very few, she thought, stretching her arms over her head with a yawn.

Yes, Jake was a nice man and—how had Gran put it?— a real looker. She smiled at the remembrance but wondered what such a paragon was doing playing nursemaid to her on a Saturday night. Her gaze skittered over the variety of guitars and banjos. She knew he'd lived here for two years and had a business in Broken Arrow. Gran had said he dealt in stringed instruments ranging from the inexpensive to collector's items. She knew, too, that he played them as well.

Was music his only passion?

Primary? Maybe. Only? Never! Besides good looks he also had an easygoing nature and a ready smile. Women, no doubt, had a place in his life. Droves of them probably waited patiently, willingly for him to call and—

Maggie settled her arms around her waist and closed her eyes, letting her head fall back against the sofa. Whom Jake called wasn't her business. He'd been kind. She was grateful. That was it. They were neighbors... temporarily, at least. And, she told herself, she was relieved there wasn't a chance for anything beyond that. Men, no matter how nice and good-looking, simply weren't on her priority list just yet.

When her thoughts strayed to Brad Taylor, she opened her eyes and sat forward. "Speaking of lists..." She hummed along with the music, took the leather-bound notepad from the table, and opened it to the page she'd been writing on when Jake had arrived. With the demise of the refrigerator, the list would have to be lengthened considerably. She rubbed her nose, wondering if the house would be habitable by tomorrow.

The house. Maggie dropped the notepad, then stood. Lifting the robe's hem to keep from tripping, she sidestepped the coffee table and headed for a window. Had they remembered to turn out all the lights in their hurry to leave? Had they—

"I thought you said you wanted to take a *long* soak in a tub. Well, I heard the tub draining more than ten minutes ago, so you could hardly have soaked for even five."

She was being chastised, she thought, giving Gran's house a quick glance. "I, uh—"

Attraction stole her words as she faced him. The jeans and white shirt had been replaced by worn, golden cords and a casual black V-neck sweater. Sleeves pushed up to the elbow, a kitchen towel draped over his shoulder, he stood six feet away, a scowl on his face to match his hands-on-hips stance. Though she'd just spent a couple of hours with him, it was as if she'd never really seen him.

Now she did.

There was an unashamed sensuality to his mouth, an arrogance to the straight line of his nose, an intensity in blue eyes made more so by the contrast of dark lashes and well-defined brows. And his hair... enviably thick and black as night, it swept back from his face, adding a touch of drama and abandon to the precision of his sculpted features.

Her observations had taken no more than a few seconds, yet with them the earlier comfort she'd felt was gone. Hoping to regain it, she opted to tease him with a speculative look. "Hmm. I hadn't pegged you as the type to listen at keyholes."

"I didn't," he said quickly. "The plumbing is old and you can hear—"

"I see." Still holding up the hem, she took a step forward, careful to keep her expression serious. "You feel it was a waste of your hot water?"

"No, I...." A grin cracked his stern expression. "Okay, smarty. But if you'll remember, the idea was for you to relax, and I still contend five minutes was hardly long enough."

"I did relax, then I started thinking of everything I have to do tomorrow, rather today, and I wanted to write them down before I forgot." She nodded to her notepad. "Really, the bath was wonderful, but I don't think I'll be able to truly unwind until I'm settled in at Gran's. Surely you can understand that."

Though the scowl was gone, the directness of his gaze remained. She'd never seen eyes of a blue so deep. No mere window of his soul, she felt they saw beyond her facade—beneath the robe, and even more disturbing, past her defenses.

She lifted a brow. "Then again, maybe you can't understand."

"Of course I do." His gaze softened with a whisper of a smile. "I was just noticing how you look in my robe."

Maggie ignored the flutter in her stomach and moved to the couch, sitting as she had before. "Cute, huh?" She knew how she looked without makeup and with her hair wavy from the braid, its ends slightly damp. "Like something the cat dragged in, threw in the tub, then tried to hide under yards of terry cloth."

"Actually I was thinking that you looked—that the *robe* never looked so good."

"Chivalrous to the end, eh, Wilder?" Maggie hoped her laugh was light and airy. "Look, don't let me keep you tied up any longer. I'm sure you're beat." She grabbed her pad and pen, then looked up. "And thanks for everything. I—"

"You were serious?" he asked, the scowl firmly in place again. "You're going to make notes at two in the morning?"

"It won't take me long and it'll help me wind down."

He mumbled something as he stalked toward the kitchen, but she couldn't be sure what. Maggie sighed with relief at his departure and tried to tell herself such awareness was really a healthy sign. After all, since her break with Brad she'd decided to make some changes in herself. And the fact that she could already find a man appealing was really a step forward in the make-over of Maggie Flannagan.

She grinned as her gaze wandered to the notepad on her lap. Well, she thought, some habits were hard to break. Inherently organized, she'd been making lists for as far back as she could remember. Her jobs at Taylor Development Corporation for the past eight years had merely honed the habit to a skill. From her start as a secretary to her final position as project manager, Brad had always admired—

What Brad had admired didn't matter anymore. Her love for him had faded into nothingness. Her feelings for his children, however, weren't as easily forgotten. Maggie closed her eyes against the swelling sense of loss, wondering how long it would take before— "Here. I want you to drink this," Jake said, striding into the room.

Needing a moment to compose herself, she faked a yawn. When she opened her eyes, she kept them carefully directed at the jelly glass he held out to her. An inch of amber liquid was in it. "What is it?"

"Brandy. Mac broke my last snifter a month ago."

"Thanks, but I'm not much of a drinker."

"Take it anyway. It'll go a lot further in helping you to unwind than that list you're not making."

"I was, too," she said, taking the glass. "I was just...thinking." She downed a quick swallow, then wished she hadn't. The heat was a shock to her system, and her gaze flew accusingly to his.

"Never had any before, huh?" He crouched down and pushed her hair back, touching her cheek in the process. Another wave of heat washed over her, more intense than the first. Awareness was one thing, she thought, but such sensitivity was ridiculous. "Trust me. You really will sleep better if you finish it."

"If it doesn't finish me off first."

"I brought you this, too." He laid a blue cotton shirt across her knees. "The oldest rage in nightwear. I figured if you tried to sleep in the robe you'd go nuts."

Maggie fingered the Ivy League shirt, while attraction and gratitude eddied into confusion. She took a larger swallow of brandy, this time welcoming the burn. Come tomorrow, she would be able to think clearly. "I don't know what to say. You've been so kind. You've helped me—''

"Don't say anything. Please. I'm glad I was here for you . . . eventually, at any rate."

She lifted her gaze to his. "But—"

He stood abruptly, stealing her notebook in the process and tossing it on the table. "Hey, I'd be glad to tuck you in, or even help you get into my shirt." There was a playful gleam in his eyes as he walked to the stereo and switched off the music. "Buttons can be awfully tricky, you know."

Given space, she felt a degree of ease return and was able to smile. "I think I can manage."

"Well, then, I guess I'll go back to my room. Holler if you need anything, and be sure to finish the brandy." She lifted the glass to her lips and choked down the last swallow. "Good night, Maggie."

"Night."

In a matter of moments Maggie had turned out the light, traded Jake's robe for the shirt and slipped under the covers. Silence surrounded her. Moonlight streamed in through the windows, bathing the room in a soft glow. She took a deep breath, welcoming the fresh scent of clean sheets. Achingly exhausted and deliciously warm, she yawned and stretched, then snuggled deeper. Sleep would be no problem. . . .

If only her eyes would stay closed. If only the quiet didn't magnify the tick of an unseen clock. If only visions of sugarplums danced in her head instead of refrigerators!

Maggie groaned and sat up, planting her feet on the floor, her elbows on her knees, her chin in her hands. She stared sightlessly at the table. New refrigerators were far too costly, secondhand ones could be unreliable, and ice chests were too small. Frowning in concentration, she stood and began to pace the length of the living room.

There were so many decisions to make, and her funds weren't unlimited.

She stopped at the window, leaning her shoulder and head against the wood frame. It was five years since her last visit, but even then she hadn't been all that familiar with the area. Tulsa was only minutes away, but the problem of unfamiliarity remained. Her frown deepened as she ran a finger across the dusty sill. There would be so much to do come morning, so many problems to handle. Not only the refrigerator, but she would need to buy food and God knew what else. And she could do none of it until she heard from the airport about her luggage.

Jake might be able to give her some ideas of where to purchase a secondhand refrigerator, she mused. He could even draw her a map of how to get there, and to the store, and . . .

Maggie's gaze lifted toward her grandmother's house. He could also tell her where the cemetery was located.

She slid her fingers up the cool pane of glass. "Dammit, Gran," she whispered. "Why couldn't you wait for me? Why'd you have to die?"

Emptiness was an ache inside her. Her throat tightened with tears she knew wouldn't form. If only she'd been able to come to the funeral with the rest of her family, perhaps Gran's death might have seemed real rather than like a nightmare she couldn't awaken from. As it was, real acceptance had been held at bay. Tears had been nonexistent.

Maybe once she stood alone in Gran's house, once she woke up there without the smell of sausage tempting her from bed, or passed the empty dish that Gran had always kept filled with candy orange slices, or saw what the dining room table looked like without a jigsaw puzzle cluttering it . . .

Sorrow swept over her body with hard chills, and unshed tears burned her eyes. It all seemed so impossible. Gran just couldn't be dead. She'd been too vital, too loving, too giving for death to claim so quickly. Oh, how she missed her. More than anyone else, Gran had seen the best in her, Maggie thought, brought out the best.

With macabre fascination, Maggie realized how cold she'd become, how her body shook, how her breathing was more a jerky spasm. Though she'd never fainted, she thought it would be a blessing and even began to pray for the release.

Then suddenly there was warmth at her back. "Maggie?" Gentle hands were at her shoulders, turning her around.

She lifted her gaze to Jake's, searching his eyes. "She's really dead," she whispered shakily. "Isn't she?"

"Yes."

The knot in her stomach tightened and she crossed her arms over her waist and held tightly. "She wanted me to come back with her, but I didn't. I told her I would after I got back from Pacific Grove, but then I got sick and she . . ." Maggie squeezed her eyes shut. "If only I'd come with her, maybe she wouldn't have died. It's my fault—"

"No, Maggie. It was simply her time."

"No it wasn't!" she insisted. "We had things to do! We—" She lowered her gaze, torment twisting inside of her. "I—I should have been with her, but she died. Oh Lord, she died *alone*."

"Didn't your parents tell you?"

"Tell me what?"

He cupped her chin in his hands and lifted her face. "I was there."

Chapter Two

If she wasn't in shock, she was close to it. Dread curled in the pit of Jake's stomach. If only she hadn't looked so vulnerable... But standing in front of the window, dwarfed by his shirt and her hand outstretched against the pane of glass, she'd looked so forlorn and alone that he'd come to her without a second thought, wanting to console her.

He'd hoped the news that Bea hadn't died alone would help. It seemed only to have made matters worse. Maggie stood before him, her eyes blank, her body incredibly still.

"Maggie?" he whispered.

She lifted her face from his touch. "You were with her?" Her voice was quiet. Too quiet. "Why didn't you help her? Why didn't you *do* something?"

Jake reached for her. "I—"

"No!" She pushed his hands away. "She trusted you, and you let her die!"

The condemnation in her eyes as she whirled away triggered inner panic. He grabbed her arms, desperate to make her understand. "It wasn't that way. I—"

"It was! It was!" she cried, fighting against him. "She wouldn't have left me otherwise! She would've waited. She would have, I tell you!" Wanting to escape, Maggie glared up at him in her struggle for freedom, then froze. His stricken expression was more effective than a slap in bringing her to her senses.

What had she been doing? *What had she been saying?* For weeks she'd bottled up frustration and guilt, then moments ago it had exploded . . . all over him. Filled with shame that she could have been so unfair, the threat of tears blurred her vision. "Oh God," she whispered, laying a palm on his chest. "Forgive me, Jake."

Maggie waited for him to yell at her, push her away, tell her to leave. She deserved all of that, and more. Instead, he stepped forward. Hesitantly, as if expecting rejection, he closed his arms around her, cloaking her in tenderness.

"There's nothing to forgive," he murmured. "I think, maybe, it's time to let the tears come."

With his words of encouragement, Maggie felt the last frayed bond of restraint break. Her tears came in torrents, and with them the memories of all the times she'd meant to call, to write, to visit. Remorse echoed in her sobs, perhaps more keenly felt with the remembrance of Gran's never-failing understanding.

Through it all, Jake held her, comforted her and even sensed the moment before she felt she would crumple to the floor. He carried her to the sofa and, still cradling her, sat down.

Wrapped in the shelter of his arms, her weeping grew softer as memories ran sweeter: the warmth of summer, the light lavender scent of Gran's perfume, the never-ending supply of chocolate chip cookies, the fun of working late into the night over jigsaw puzzles. With each cherished memory came the knowledge that as long as Gran lived so vividly in her heart, she could never be truly gone.

Drained, but serenely so, Maggie wiped at her eyes and nose with a handkerchief Jake had given her. Grasping for words of gratitude, she gazed at him, only to have the cruelty of her accusation stab at her anew. Moonlight illuminated quiet tears of guilt glimmering in his eyes.

"Maggie, I—"

She pressed a finger to his lips. "No, please. I was wrong. So wrong." She framed his face with her hands and kissed his eyes. "I'm sorry."

His torment still shone brightly, and she eased the line between his brows with her fingertips. "Please understand, I didn't know what I was saying," she whispered, scattering soft kisses over his face, wanting only to mend the damage she'd done.

It felt natural when her mouth found his. His lips were warm and responsive, their touch a balm of forgiveness to her heart. Without forethought she slipped her fingers behind his neck and pressed closer. Here there was no pain, only the sweet purity of healing as she gave herself to his kiss, and in the giving, received.

For weeks her body had been numbed by stress. But now strong hands ranged warmth over her back and tangled in her hair, releasing tension with but a touch. Her lips parted on a sigh, inviting, accepting a small celebration of life itself.

Need stirred a kindling passion. Not only to be completed emotionally, but physically as well.

Maggie broke the kiss, her body well warmed and willing, even if her mind wasn't. She slid her arms from around his shoulders in amazement. Such easy intimacy wasn't like her. Maggie's gaze fell to her bare legs stretched out on the sofa, and she immediately tried to get up.

Jake didn't question his reluctance to release her, but kept his arms loosely about her waist. "Stay." He felt the surprise that stiffened her posture as she tugged at the long shirttails. Smiling to himself, he pulled the blanket up and over her legs. "Please?"

"You don't have to hold me any longer, really." Hair slipped across her cheek, hiding the innocence of her silhouetted profile. "I'm fine."

"I'm not," he admitted. She glanced toward him. "We need to talk."

"About the . . . the kiss?"

"No." He smiled, stroking her cheek with the back of his fingers. "The kiss pretty well spoke for itself. And I know," he added quickly, "that you didn't mean for it to, uh, go quite the way it did. Neither did I."

Maggie fussed with the blanket's satin border. "Are you always so understanding?"

"Rarely," he admitted with a chuckle. His reward for honesty was a sniffle and a smile. "Actually, I wanted to explain about Bea, about that last night, if you think you're up to it. It might help."

"Yes, I'd like that," she said softly, nestling against his chest.

"First of all, I want to assure you that Bea died peacefully. You see, we'd had dinner here, then dessert at her house. We did that sort of thing about once a week." He played his fingers through the silky length of her hair. "She was in particularly high spirits that day. She mentioned that she'd seen her lawyer to make some changes in her will—"

"Did she say why?"

"No. Just that she was very satisfied that everything was in order. Anyway, after we'd made a sizable dent in a pie, she asked me to play my guitar. I didn't think anything of it, as she loved to sit in her rocker and doze while I played. I kidded her like I always did, saying my playing bored her so much it put her to sleep. Bea denied it, of course, claiming she always heard every note.

"After I'd been playing a while, she fell asleep. Since that was normal, I went through a few more songs, waiting for her to snore as she invariably did. When I finished, it dawned on me that she never had." Jake swallowed hard, wanting to keep his voice even for Maggie's sake. "I called her name a couple of times, and when she didn't answer, I went over to her. She looked very serene. A smile was on her lips. . . ."

Voices from the back of his mind broke through to consciousness. Maybe if he'd watched Bea more closely he would have noticed something. After all, he hadn't been sitting far away. Anxiety sped his heart and tightened his chest. Surely Maggie would feel the same and wonder—

The touch of her lips to his cheek was soft and full of absolution. "Thank you."

"For what? Maybe if I'd noticed—"

"No!" She sniffled emphatically and pulled back to look at him. "It was her time, like you said. She was ready."

Though her affirmation was passionate, uncertainty swamped him. "Do you really believe that?"

He saw the answer in her eyes before she spoke. "Yes."

Awed, Jake didn't move, but knew she would pull away any moment. After all, the crisis had passed, her need was fulfilled. He should wish her good-night and go to the solitude of his room. Maybe there he could allow the relief that she hadn't blamed him to sink in.

Maggie moved, but not away. She slipped her arms around his neck and rested her cheek against his shoulder.

A hug. Such a simple gesture, yet one he cherished. He moved his arms slowly, unsurely, then held her near, not wanting to examine whether he was doing it for her still, or accepting it for himself.

The fact that he'd held her for more than two hours after she fell asleep had nothing to do with anything sexual. In fact, there'd been something immensely peaceful about it, soothing really. Jake poured his third cup of coffee and leaned against the kitchen sink, recalling how those feelings had carried over, even after he'd gone to his room. He'd lain awake until after seven, oddly reluctant to surrender to sleep.

As well he should have been. Maggie Flannagan wasn't just any woman, he reminded himself, fixing his gaze on the house next door. She was Bea's granddaughter. She was coming off a broken engagement. She wasn't really even his type.

He scowled, recalling the half-drowsy, half-aroused state he'd awakened from after only two hours. He could recite that list to himself all he wanted, but logic hadn't kept dreams at bay. Maggie was a woman who appealed to him on more levels than he'd expected.

Legacy, ha! He took a sip of hot coffee and narrowed his eyes. For all his wishing Bea had been talking about flowers, the more he thought about it, the surer he felt she'd meant Maggie. Jake pushed away from the sink, directing his scowl upward. "What in the hell were you thinking of, Bea?"

He set his cup on the table and dropped onto a straight-backed chair. His track record with women showed no talent for enduring relationships. In his late teens and early twenties, he'd had no inclination to be serious with anyone; as he'd grown older, life on the road had been too hectic. Relationships of any sort had been few and far between. Then, a couple of years before the band broke up, he'd met Claire. Quiet, interesting and far from the madding crowd, she'd been a friend to him before she'd even known who he was.

Jake encircled the warmth of the ceramic cup with his hands. A friend, he mused, taking a sip. He'd lived twenty-eight years before making the discovery that a woman could be one. Then, mistaking the novel feel of it, he'd convinced Claire to marry him within two weeks. Between his persuasiveness, and the fact that she was rebounding from a broken relationship and in need of affirmation, she'd agreed. The marriage lasted almost two years. Had it not been for an unplanned pregnancy, it wouldn't have made it even one.

His stomach jolted with another onslaught of nerves. Come August, Christopher would turn four. Come August, the child would live with him for six months, as he and Claire had agreed. Jake pulled his wallet from his back pocket and fished out a picture taken a month ago. A young boy with curly hair the color of his own and laughing blue eyes looked up at him. *His* child... and he felt as if he hardly knew him.

A fact he would change when August came, he vowed. Though Christopher was blessed with a loving family—Claire, her husband, Evan, and Chris's baby half sister, Audrey—Jake felt it was important for the boy to know his father loved him as well. His eyes closed as his jaw clenched in determination. *His* son would never have to wonder if—

"That coffee smells like heaven."

Jake stood abruptly, pushing back memories and erasing all emotion from his face as easily as he slipped the child's photo back into place. Maggie had paused in the doorway, notebook and pen in hand. She looked as fresh as spring sunshine. The apricot sweater she wore brought a glow to her cheeks; freshly laundered jeans hugged her body like a lover.

Something stirred deep inside him at the thought and he quickly controlled it. "Don't let the smell fool you."

Maggie smiled and slipped her braid over her shoulder. "Sit, please." She took a mug from the rack. "May I?"

"Help yourself." He sat, then watched her pour the coffee. "How'd you sleep?"

"Like a baby apparently. I rarely sleep past six at home." She glanced at him over her shoulder. "Do you have any cream?"

"Will milk do?"

"Fine."

Jake got the milk, then handed her the carton and leaned casually against the counter. "Spoons are in the drawer in front of you."

"Thanks." She closed the drawer with her hip and poured a dollop of milk.

Last night he'd wondered if her size had added to her vulnerability. She was no taller this morning, yet all hints of vulnerability had been replaced by sure competence. Standing as close as he was, he caught a faint whiff of her perfume. Both innocent and sexy, it tempted. Were she another woman he would have leaned over and kissed the bared curve of her neck. But this was Maggie and—

As she mixed the coffee, her hips swiveled ever so slightly. He watched in fascination and quickly labeled the "something" that had stirred only moments before as desire. Only now it wasn't as subtle as a stirring. In defense, Jake retreated to his seat.

"About last night..." Maggie returned the milk to the refrigerator, trying not to think how appealing he looked in casual gray chinos, a pink henley shirt and burgundy suspenders. It was a look she'd always labeled "contrived casual." On him it didn't look contrived at all, but as natural as his bare feet.

"Yes?"

Maggie faced him with a smile. "I just want you to know how much I appreciated everything. Walking into Gran's today will be much easier now. Not only because of the smell, but..." Retrieving her coffee and notepad, she seated herself across from Jake. "Well, you helped me over a rough spot and for that I'll be eternally grateful."

His modest shrug stretched the cotton shirt across his broad shoulders, emphasizing their width. Maggie took a quick sip of coffee, welcoming the caffeine jolt. "You're wrong," she said over the mug's rim. "It *is* heaven."

He smiled, but barely. Considering how easily he'd talked last night, she found his near silence unsettling. Of course, some people didn't talk much in the morning. She bit the inside of her lip, recalling the intensity of his expression as she'd approached the kitchen. He'd looked upset. She thought they had straightened everything out last night, but maybe there was something else.

His gaze lowered to the newspaper, laying sinfully long lashes against his cheeks. Maggie picked up her pen and doodled nervously on the corner of the pad. "Look, I'll be honest with you. The last thing I remember about last night was thinking I'd just close my eyes for a minute. Did I say or do something—"

"No. You just went to sleep, and pretty fast at that."

"I hope I wasn't too much of a bother."

Last night? "None," he said honestly, lifting his eyes. Since then? Definitely. He sipped his coffee, hoping to scald some sense into himself. Instead, the coffee was warm and welcome, as was her presence. "How about some breakfast?" he asked, grateful for a reason to leave the table.

"No thanks," she said, "this is fine." Jake settled once more, though somewhat reluctantly, as she turned back a page in her notebook. "After I finish this I'll leave you in peace. In the meantime, would you mind answering a few questions and making me a map?"

"No problem." Even as he said the words he was aware how quiet the house would be when she left. How still. Growing up, he'd spent most of his time alone, the silence filled by the music he'd made. As an adult, he'd found he preferred the solitude. Suddenly, it didn't seem as appealing. Without pondering the implications, he added, "In fact, I'd be glad to take you where you need to go and—"

"No thanks. Since I'm going to be living here for a few weeks, I might as well learn how to get around on my own."

By the time she finished her coffee, Maggie had two maps. One that gave her the basic layout of Broken Arrow, the other detailing the key places she needed to go to in Tulsa. Jacket on and ready to leave, she paused at the front door. "Thanks again for everything."

"You're sure you don't want me to come along?"

"It's not necessary. These maps are great."

Jake slipped the notebook from her grasp and opened it. "In case you make a wrong turn, here's my number." He scribbled it quickly. "Feel free to call for help."

"Let's hope I won't have to," she said, reaching for the notebook.

The transfer, Maggie realized, should have taken place with no problem. It didn't require a touch, yet somehow, they did. The moment turned timeless as two fingers lingered over the exchange. One long and square-tipped, the other slender. In the dark of night she'd been cradled in his arms, had even shared a kiss that had hinted at intimacy. She'd told herself it was the emotions of last night that had allowed it to happen. Now the room was bright with the cold light of day, and yet . . .

She raised her gaze in curiosity and found in his eyes the same awareness that licked through her veins. Temptation bade her to step closer, test the moment. Wisdom curled her arm to her chest and forced a platonic grin to her lips. "See you around."

"Bye, Maggie."

Maggie walked briskly out into the sunshine, relieved to take a safe breath as she crossed the greening lawn. Though Jake Wilder was a good neighbor to have, she recognized that without a doubt he could be a complication as well. A complication she wasn't up to handling.

Her pace slowed at the porch as she was reminded of Gran's love for irises and the way she'd planted early-, middle- and late-blooming ones to keep them around as long as possible. Stands of them flanked the steps, their blossoms open to the sun, their scent sweetening the air. Behind them were azalea bushes in white and pink, adding to the beauty. The flower beds had been her grandmother's pride and joy. As a child Maggie had helped weed them.

Would new owners take similar care?

Not dwelling on the question, Maggie walked up to the door and put the key in the lock. She paused, thinking how much Jake *had* helped her over a rough spot. Yesterday when she first stood here, she'd been a mass of suppressed anxiety and guilt. Though sadness remained in her heart, it was natural and something she could deal with now.

Inside the air was chilly but relatively fresh, thanks to the attic fan and open windows. Opting to keep her jacket on temporarily, she set her belongings by the door and surveyed the room. White sheets hid all familiarity, and Maggie whipped around, quickly ridding the room of its ghostly reminders.

She dropped the coverings on the floor beside the ancient rocker, then lowered herself onto its petit-point-stitched seat. "I'm home, Gran. A little late, but I'm home." Though her father had retired from the Air Force when Maggie was in her late teens, and her family had then settled in Los Angeles, this house was the one place she'd ever really thought of as home.

Maggie didn't fight the tear that ran down her face, but rocked back and forth, feeling oddly comforted. "Remember my telling you about Monarch Inn? Well, I've done as you suggested and invested in myself. I took Pam and Kathie up on their offer and put a chunk of my savings into the bed-and-breakfast. It's a lot riskier than a company job, but I think it's going to be a lot more fulfilling, too.

"If only I didn't have to sell the house to get the rest of the money," she whispered. Maggie's gaze drifted to the gallery wall over the sofa and she sniffed, wiping at the dampness on her cheek. "I know, Gran. 'Look to the future and do what must be done.'" She rose, seeking her favorite picture. Gran's smile was mischievous, her eyes challenging. Age might have turned her brown hair to silver, but it hadn't diminished the strength she radiated.

Absorbing that strength, Maggie smiled and let her eyes sweep over the arrangement of family photos before settling on one of herself and her sisters. Even at age eleven, Colleen's dark beauty had held the promise of elegance that was so like their mother's. Kelly, the youngest at nine, had both their father's red hair and his flamboyance. Though she'd always been proud of her sisters and their later successes—Colleen's as a jewelry designer and Kelly's as a prominent West Coast talk-show host—there'd been a time as a child when Maggie had felt woefully plain and had been sure she'd been adopted since she favored neither parent. It was Gran who'd quieted her insecurities by pointing out that the person Maggie took after was her.

Family and tradition. Both had been important to Gran; both were captured in photos of black and white, and later color, lovingly hung—

Her gaze stopped on a more recent addition, and she moved closer. The picture had been taken here, obviously at Christmas. She had no trouble imagining Gran setting the time delay on the camera, then running around it to pose. It was whom she stood with and that the picture should be up on the "family" wall that surprised her. Jake stood beside Gran in front of the tree. He held what looked to be the white scarf he'd worn with his jacket last night, while Gran displayed a muffler, gloves and matching hat. Maggie's brows raised. She knew Gran had thought Jake was special. What she hadn't realized was *how* special.

Pensive, she wandered into the dining room and pulled the dustcover from the table. Memories flooded her mind as she ran a hand over the cool, polished wood. "It really doesn't look right without a puzzle, does it, Gran?"

She looked around the room, and her heart sank at seeing the places where faded wallpaper had begun to peel away. "I'm going to fix that. I'm going to fix it all, just the way we planned," she vowed. It might not be practical, she thought, but that didn't matter. What *did* matter was that the redecorating was the last thing Gran had asked of her. Maggie neither could, nor wanted to, do less.

Buoyed by a spirit of anticipation, she smiled. "By the time I finish it, Gran, it'll be exactly the way we wanted it. I'll put new paper in here and the kitchen. Maybe even the bathrooms, too."

Excitement took hold and she ran to the stairway, then took the steps two at a time. A quick peek in the first bedroom told her what she already knew...no room would be exempt from her refurbishing efforts.

The next room she entered was the one she'd always claimed as her own. As she freed the room of its protective coverings, her gaze rested on the bed. The spread was white chenille, the throw pillows handmade. Maggie picked up one of them and held it to her chest. Thoughts of yesteryears flowed into her with the warmth of the summer evenings she'd lain on the bed or sat on the window seat, wishing on the night's first star.

Life had been simpler then, she thought. And she'd been impatient, ready to throw herself into life and love. When she promised to give Gran thirteen great-grandchildren to spoil, her grandmother hadn't laughed. Instead, she'd given her a hug and said she hoped she would have enough energy to keep up with all of them. Maggie's smile was poignant, the memory bittersweet. Her life had turned out considerably different from her childhood dreams.

Maggie set the pillow on the bed reverently, then crossed the hall to the master bedroom which ran the full length of the house. Sheets snapped in the air as she removed them from the old-fashioned white wrought-iron-and-brass bed, a chaise longue, a dressing table, a chiffonier and finally the photograph-covered dresser. The room was pure Gran, Maggie thought, looking at the childish paintings framed like treasures on the wall—filled with and decorated by love.

Her gaze journeyed slowly around the bedroom. Legally, Gran's estate had been dispensed—Colleen had Gran's jewelry, except for the wedding rings given to their mother; Kelly had Gran's beloved china and collection of elephant figurines; their mother had received the pieces of furniture she treasured from childhood; and both sisters as well as their parents had received shares of stock and money. All that was left was a final, sentimental sorting through.

Maggie thought of the clothing in the drawers and behind the closet door. Some items she would keep as valued pieces for her vintage purse and hat collection, an endeavor Gran had started her on; some she would send to her mother or sisters; others she would keep simply because they reminded her too much of Gran to part with. What remained would go to her grandmother's favorite charity, the one where she'd actively worked for years.

A glance at the clock sent Maggie downstairs. Nearly forty-five minutes had passed since she left Jake's. Having gotten such a late start on the day, she had a lot to make up for. The first stop would be the cemetery. Though she wanted to put some of Gran's beloved iris on the grave, she realized the visit would be little more than a formality.

This was where Gran would always be. Here, in the house where she'd lived for almost fifty years. Here where her spirit and vitality were reflected from every wall to every flower in the garden.

Maggie retrieved her notepad from the living room and went into the kitchen. The bright square of linoleum where the refrigerator had sat brought to mind both her and Jake's groans as they moved it out on the back porch.

Lord, how could she have made it through last night without him?

"I met your neighbor last night, Gran," she said, jotting down items as she searched a cupboard. "He was nice." She paused mid-word in her list. "Okay, more than nice. I'll even admit to feeling a vague sort of attraction to him. But who wouldn't have? I was in need and he helped. I would've been drawn to anyone who exhibited that kind of sensitivity."

Maggie started writing again, then stopped. "Okay, maybe I was drawn to him for more than that. And yes, I'll admit to feeling something again this morning. But that's all; it goes no further." She glanced up at the yellowed ceiling. "I'll start on the house right away and get it on the market next week. Once I'm finished with the work, I'm out of here. And that means no more visits with your very attractive neighbor. I appreciated his help last night, but I can handle everything else from here alone. You got that?"

Her gaze lowered by degrees when she realized she was waiting for an answer. Maggie shook her head and laughed into the silence. All she needed was someone to see her and call the nearest funny farm. "Forget the damn list," she mumbled and went to retrieve her purse.

After a call to the airport that confirmed she would receive her luggage that evening, Maggie added Gran's car keys to her own key chain, picked some flowers, locked up the house and headed for the one-car garage near the back of the property. The sight of the homemade swing suspended from the sycamore curved her lips. Though Gran had always sworn she'd put it up for her grandchildren, Maggie remembered Gran using it as much as they had.

Her smile lingered as she undid the heavy padlock and pushed back one side of the wood door. With its screech of protest, her eyes lifted toward Jake's place. He didn't seem the sort to live in a little one-story house tucked away in such an old neighborhood. Then again, there was a genuine quality about him that didn't quite fit the slick condo image in a swinging singles' community, either.

Contemplation furrowed her brow, and she leaned against the door. What was he doing now? she wondered. Had he gone back to bed? Did he have a date this afternoon?

She wouldn't give him or what he was doing another thought. Maggie turned and pushed back the other door. Heaven knew she had enough to think about.

Sunlight glinted off the bumper of the twenty-year-old cream puff. Gran had bought the car the summer Maggie was ten and had always bragged how it never gave her a lick of trouble. Maggie walked beside it, trailing her fingers over the chrome molding. The baby-blue paint job looked almost new. And the interior, she thought, opening the door—

A rush of Gran's flowery scent filled her senses, making Maggie gasp. Eyes wide, she glanced about, the eeriness of the sensation jogging her memory. She'd smelled it just yesterday when she tried the front door key for the first time. Or rather, Maggie corrected herself, she'd *thought* she smelled it. At the time she'd been sure she was imagining it. But this? How could the scent be so strong unless . . .

"Gran?" she whispered, her heart beating rapidly.

This time Maggie made a full, inspective turn. As a child she'd gone through a period when she worried about her grandmother dying and leaving her. Gran had sworn that if she did, she would find a way to watch over her until she was grown and happily settled. Surely Gran couldn't really—

Maggie spied a lacy handkerchief lying on the seat and sighed in relief. No doubt Gran had put perfume on the hankie, so of course the scent was strong. Maggie slid inside, promptly picked up the handkerchief, folded it and put it in her purse...not wanting to chance a testing of her logic.

Grinning at her foolishness, she slipped the key into the ignition and turned it.

Nothing happened.

Maggie gritted her teeth and turned the key again and again, yet the car never made so much as a token groan. "Dammit, Gran," she muttered. "For someone who's supposed to be watching over me, don't you think you're falling down on the job a bit?"

Five minutes and several failed attempts later, Maggie surrendered. She could look under the hood, but she wouldn't have the slightest idea what to look at. She could call a garage, and be charged a king's ransom for a tow job to find out what was wrong. With a final sneer and a whack at the steering wheel for good measure, she got out of the car and left the garage. Though she would have to swallow her earlier resolve, she knew what she was going to do.

Chapter Three

By the time Maggie topped Jake's front porch, her mood had been transformed from frustration to enchantment. Though she didn't know a lot about guitar music, she did know what she liked. The melody was expressive and haunting, yet soothing in its simplicity. Gran had said Jake could play, but Maggie hadn't imagined he would be so good. She stood, a willing captive until the piece's end, then rang the bell.

As Jake opened the front door, his eyebrows lifted in surprise. "Is something wrong with the house? Does it still stink?"

"No, the house is fine," she said dismissively, then she shook her head in admiration. "You play wonderfully."

He opened the screen and motioned her inside. "You heard?"

"I couldn't help but." Last night she'd been too preoccupied to notice much of anything. Now she focused her gaze with new appreciation on the instrument in the stand. "Is that the one you were playing?"

"Uh-huh."

Maggie studied the polished top and ran her fingers lightly over the strings. "I don't know much about guitars, but it's beautiful."

"Isn't it?" He stepped beside her and lifted the guitar from the stand. "The top's a fine-quality spruce, the back and sides—" he turned it over "—Brazilian rosewood. This particular guitar was made in the thirties by Domingo Esteso."

"And that's good?"

As he nodded, warmth and good humor shone from incredibly blue eyes. "That's good."

"Why?"

"Esteso gained renown making flamenco guitars, but he also produced fine classical instruments. Far fewer in number, the classicals are considered uncommon." He shifted the guitar into playing position. "And their sound..."

The spell he cast was woven with notes, and she was powerless to do anything but stand in awe. His concentration was total, the music evocative. Maggie felt drawn into the piece, lured to a place where nameless wishes grew stronger with unfulfillment. Mesmerized, she watched the play of his fingers over the strings and the corresponding flex of muscles in his forearms. Too vividly she remembered the touch of his strong, sensual fingers roaming her back. Too much she found herself wanting it again.

"Such depth," he murmured, still playing. "Such sweetness of tone. Can you hear it?"

More than was comfortable, Maggie thought. She swallowed hard and flicked her tongue over her lips, willing an evenness to her voice. "You do it justice."

Silence filled the room as he raised his gaze to hers. His eyes were intense, omniscient; for a moment she feared he knew what she'd been thinking, what she'd been feeling.

He grinned suddenly, breaking the spell as he replaced the guitar on the stand. "So much for Guitar Appreciation 101. You'll have to forgive me. I get a little carried away sometimes."

He got carried away? "No," she said. "I enjoyed it." She picked up a tuning fork from his music stand, struck it against her palm, then replaced it. "How many guitars do you have?"

"Personally?" At Maggie's nod he rubbed the back of his neck. "Oh, about fifteen of various styles and types." He glanced back at the guitar he'd been playing. "That one, unfortunately, isn't mine. I'm showing it to a prospective buyer tomorrow."

"You know," she said earnestly, "instead of selling guitars you ought to consider playing professionally."

His eyes gleamed with—was it amusement? "Thanks, but I'm very happy here."

In that instant, Maggie envied him. He had what he wanted: a home, a business, a life filled with the things he enjoyed. Her gaze drifted to his bookshelves, then stopped, zeroed in on a picture flanked by a metronome and a row of books. She took a step closer, studying the young boy in the photo. "You have a son?"

"Yes. That was taken when he was around two and a half. He's nearing four now."

She steeled herself from wondering about his marriage and why it had evidently ended, concentrating once more on the child. "He favors you around the eyes, and the hair color, too, of course."

"You think so?"

The wistfulness in Jake's voice caught Maggie's attention, reminding her things weren't always as they seemed. "More than a little," she assured him. "Are you teaching him how to play?"

"Not yet, though Claire says he does display a bent toward music." His grin was irreverent. "Of course, all he'd have to do is bang on a few piano keys and she'd think he was Mozart."

"What do *you* think?"

That quickly, the look in his eyes grew guarded. "I haven't really been around him enough to think anything. Claire and I have been divorced since his first birthday."

"I'm sorry. I wasn't trying to pry."

Jake wasn't sure if it was guilt at knowing so much about her personal life without her knowledge, or the beginnings of trust that pushed him to divulge more. "The divorce was amicable, but she moved to Seattle and I moved here, so I haven't been able to see him as much as I should." He looked beyond Maggie to the picture. "That'll change in August. I'll have custody for six months."

"Are you excited about it?"

"Well...sure. But I've never been around kids much, except Mac's. And that's hardly the same as raising them."

How well she knew, Maggie thought. Brad had been lost when Sharisse not only divorced him, but left their children behind as well. Never having taken an active role in their raising, he'd relied on Maggie heavily. At the time, she hadn't considered the consequences of becoming so physically and emotionally involved with a ten-month-old and a three-year-old. Because she'd learned her lesson the hard way, she was glad she wouldn't be around in August.

"Hey," Jake said, stooping to transfer the guitar to its case. "We kind of got off track. I'm sure something other than my playing brought you to the door."

"I'm sorry." She pressed her fingers to the bridge of her nose and gave him a wry smile. "You're right. I was wondering if—do you know much about cars?"

"A little." The latches closed with successive clicks, then Jake stood and slipped his hands into his pockets. "Is the Ford giving you trouble?"

"It won't start. It won't even try. Does that tell you anything?"

Dark brows ruffled with his frown of contemplation, then smoothed. "Well, yeah." Maggie looked at him expectantly. "It, uh, won't start."

"Cute, Wilder," she said. "Real cute."

"Tell you what—" he walked to the couch and went down on his knees "—let's take a look under the hood. A wire could be loose, or maybe the battery's dead." He ducked beneath the coffee table. "If it's the latter, I've got a battery charger we can hook up to it, then you can give it another go in the morning."

"*Morning?* I can't wait that long. I've got a list a mile long of things to do. Couldn't you just jump it?"

"I'd be glad to, but I can't." Jake sat back on his haunches, a scuffed pair of docksiders in his hands. "For starters, it's a one-car garage, so I can't pull in next to it. Secondly, the garage is on a slight, downward slope... hardly enough to notice, but plenty to keep me from being able to push the car out."

That wasn't what she wanted to hear. Maggie started to pace, her head bowed in thought. Taking a taxi from place to place, when she wasn't even sure how many places she would have to go, would be an extravagance. That left her with two choices. Either go ahead and call a tow truck to take the car to a garage, or just wait until tomorrow and hope the charger did the trick.

"My offer still stands, you know."

"Huh?" She raised her head.

His shoes were on and he'd retrieved a lightweight jacket from the entry closet. "I'll drive you around."

"Oh, no. I've imposed on you enough."

"Nonsense." Jake closed the front door and turned the lock. "The only thing I had on tap for today was doing laundry and paperwork. Both of which you heard me diligently putting off when you came to the door."

"But—"

Jake shrugged into his windbreaker and walked past her. "We can go out the back and stop by the garage for my charger, just in case." Aware that she wasn't following him, he stopped to face her. The stubborn glint was in her eyes again, only this time he wasn't going to give in. She needed him, and for reasons he didn't want to pursue, he was enjoying it...enjoying her. He closed the distance between them and caught her hand. "Time's a-wastin', Flannagan."

Her first steps were slow and reluctant, then he heard her sigh. "I owe you for so much already."

"I'll just put it on your tab."

"There are just a couple of sacks left. I'll go out and get those and you can start putting this stuff away."

"Good idea." Maggie set a bag on the kitchen counter.

At the sound of the back door closing, she began rummaging through the bags, then fished out a package of devil's food cookies. Though she and Jake had gorged on pizza little more than an hour ago, her mouth had been watering for a chocolate fix since buying the cookies at the store. She grabbed two, one for herself and one for Jake, having discovered they shared a mutual lust for the delights of chocolate. Kicking off her loafers, she slumped against the counter, closed her eyes, then took a bite of heaven. Yet it wasn't the taste she concentrated on, but Jake.

He'd been wonderful, she thought. He'd hooked up the battery charger for the car, been quietly supportive at Gran's grave, helped her choose a used refrigerator at a good price and driven her all over Tulsa and Broken Arrow. He'd also driven her crazy. A delightful sort of crazy, she amended with a smile.

Where Brad had always complained about shopping and lauded her for keeping to her list, Jake had relished making her laugh and veering her off into side trips at every opportunity. Maggie opened her eyes with the realization that while he'd done a lot for her in the past twenty-four hours, most of all he'd been a friend when she hadn't even known she needed one.

"Hey, where's the doorman?"

She rushed to the back porch and opened the screen. Her gaze was drawn immediately to the narrowed blue eyes peering at her over an armload of groceries. "Sorry, I was—"

"I know." He brushed past her, a playful scowl on his face. "You were taking the time to kick off your shoes and feed your face, thoughtlessly leaving the help loaded down like a pack mule."

"Now that you mention it," she purred, catching up with him and sticking a cookie in his mouth, "there *is* a slight resemblance." The phone rang, and Maggie laughed, scooting quickly out of the way to avoid his backward kick.

Jake set the groceries on the table and swallowed his mouthful. "Call me a mule," he grumbled. "How ungrateful can you be? Do I still get that cup of hot chocolate, too?''

"Turn on the fire, the teapot's full." She picked up the receiver, a smile lingering on her lips. "Hello."

"You certainly sound in good spirits."

The smile died, and Maggie turned toward the phone's base on the wall with amazement. Brad sounded as if those fateful last days in February had never happened. "I . . . *was*."

"Oh." His tone held disappointment that she wasn't going to put on an equally forgetful front. "I tried to call you at your apartment all day yesterday, then finally called your parents. Your mother told me about your grandmother. I'm sorry."

"Yes, it was quite a shock."

There was a long pause, as if he'd expected token sympathy to break the ice. "How're you doing?"

"Fine."

"How long will you be in Broken Arrow?"

"Two, three weeks. However long it takes to get things organized."

"Then it shouldn't take long. You were always so good at that."

For two years compliments like that had warmed her, spurred her to work harder. Now it simply made her skeptical. "What'd you call for, Brad? Aimless chitchat isn't like you."

"Now, Maggie, don't give me a hard time. It was a mistake to let you leave. Things have been an absolute disaster. Jeffers wasn't ready for the promotion, and Milligan isn't, either."

So that was what this was all about. "Jeffers can be a fine project manager if you show him a modicum of patience and don't expect him to know everything right from the start.''

''It's not just that....'' Dramatic pauses, she mused. He'd always been good at those, too. ''Jonathan and Amy miss you.''

The pain was sharp and swift. ''That's not fair,'' she managed flatly, holding her temper. Had he always been manipulative? ''I think we'd better end this conversa—''

''Fair or not, it's the truth. I miss you, too. I need you, Maggie.'' She didn't doubt the truth of his honest pleading. It simply didn't reach her anymore. ''Please, won't you come back to work when you get finished there?''

Maggie's eyes widened with her rising blood pressure. ''Sharisse would just love that, wouldn't she?''

''My business life doesn't concern her,'' he said abruptly. ''To be truthful, letting her have a say in that wasn't my first mistake.''

''Well, this call was a mistake, too. I'm not job hunting anymore. I've bought into a bed-and-breakfast in Pacific Grove, and I've got a great new life waiting for me. So do me a favor. Don't call again. I'm not interested.'' Maggie hung the phone up quickly, then picked it back up and slammed it down for good measure. ''Of all the nerve—''

''Are you okay?'' Jake asked, laying a hand on her shoulder.

Startled, Maggie turned around. ''Well now, if *that's* not humiliating! I'd forgotten you were here!''

''There's nothing to be humiliated about.''

''Oh, I suppose not,'' she said, her voice rising with the wave of her hand. ''You were such good friends with Gran that you probably know all the gory details anyway!'' Maggie clutched her hands beneath her chin in an imitation of her grandmother and pitched her voice high and sweet. '''My poor little granddaughter. Her fiancé's ex-wife returned and he reconciled with her a week before he was supposed to marry Maggie, then suggested she find employment elsewhere to boot.'"

Jake remained calm in the face of her fury. "You knew Bea well enough to know that isn't the way she told me."

Of course she did, but she didn't want to listen to the voice of logic or reason right now; she wanted to rail, and she knew her grandmother would have understood perfectly and forgiven her less-than-true parody. Pivoting away from Jake, Maggie paced. She'd been through shock and sorrow before coming to accept Brad's calling the wedding off, but she'd never allowed herself to be really angry. Now that she was, it felt damn good!

"You know what galls me? I mean, what really galls me." She stopped in front of Jake. "He didn't have to *suggest* anything. I would've quit on my own!"

Maggie whipped around to the counter, pulled a package of paper napkins from the sack and pointed to the phone with them. "Want to know why he called? He *needs* me and wants to rehire me. Can you believe it?" She slammed down the napkins. "The louse even threw in that his children miss me."

The threat of tears was swift, and Maggie closed her eyes to ward them off. Amy and Jonathan had been blameless, but no amount of anger or acceptance toward their father could lessen the pain of having had to leave them. She shuttered her mind against her last memory of the children, forcing herself to think of Sharisse instead.

When her eyes opened, she stared at the pecan cabinet doors in front of her. "I guess I was a bit of a fool," she said, her voice quiet. "Sharisse is very beautiful, you know. Even before she came back there'd be times when Brad would get a faraway look in his eyes that made me wonder if he still loved her. I asked him once, point-blank. He said he didn't.''

The control it took for Jake to keep his mouth shut was considerable. It wasn't his place to tell her what a jerk the man had been. She seemed to be working toward that conclusion on her own.

She gave him a quick glance. ''Want to know what's funny about this whole mess?'' Despite the fact that her voice was almost calm, there was an edge to her chuckle and a brightness to her smile that revealed a lingering hurt and confusion. ''I wasn't the one who pushed for a relationship outside of work. I wasn't the one who asked to get involved with his children. And I sure as hell wasn't the one who brought up marriage and pushed to have a date set!''

She shook her head and reached back into the sack. ''Before I ever got involved with him, all I wanted in a man was someone I could love and who'd love me in return. I don't need diamonds, a ritzy house in the hills or three cars. All I want is a man who thinks *I'm* the neatest thing to come along since...since...'' She pulled out a jar of Peter Pan. ''Since peanut butter!''

Maggie laughed then, soft and warm. Though the storm had passed, the color was still high in her cheeks and there was a sparkle to her eyes. All in all, Jake couldn't recall having ever seen a woman look more appealing.

''Men,'' she muttered, sauntering across the kitchen with the jar. ''What do *they* look for in the women they marry?''

''Well...''

She shelved the peanut butter and turned toward him quickly, her braid coming to rest over her shoulder. ''The question was more rhetorical than actual, but yeah.'' She closed the distance between them in three easy strides. "Tell me." She folded her arms casually under her breasts.

Her eyes were darkly green and serious. Full of curiosity, they prevented him from giving a less than truthful answer. Jake raked his fingers through his hair, knowing she would find his truth woefully inadequate. "I'm, uh, not a good person to ask."

"You're male."

"Yes, but..." He straightened one of his suspenders needlessly, then shrugged. "I'm not cut out for marriage."

Her lips curved, but he wouldn't have called it quite a smile, even though her dimple dented. "What's the matter?" she asked, moving her hands to her hips. "Is it too...limiting? Do men just want endless variety?"

Jake swallowed—hard. Maybe the storm *wasn't* quite over. Her eyes blazed, compelling him once more to reveal something he rarely did: something personal. "I don't know about 'men,' I only know that somehow I'm just not good at it. The fault lies in *me*."

She rocked back and forth on her heels. "That sounds like a standard male cop out."

"It wasn't," he said frankly. "But, okay." For the first time since his divorce, he opened his mind to the fantasy of happily-ever-after and what he would want in a woman. His eyes closed in thought, he said, "If I were looking, and if I were good at relationships, I'd want a woman who spoke her mind, who stood on her own two feet, who was intelligent and didn't play games and who showed an interest in what I do, yet was happy on her own." He glanced at her with a grin. "And if she were easy on the eyes..."

Maggie's smile could have frozen hot water at ten paces. "Oh, I get it," she said softly. "Just your—" she took a step toward him and Jake braced for all hell to break loose

"—*basic woman*?" Instead, she remained calm and merely walked her fingers up his suspenders. "Someone with the brainpower of a card-carrying Mensa member, the independence of a Gloria Steinem and the looks and figure of...shall we say, a statuesque, overly endowed centerfold?" Smirking, she flicked her fingers against the burgundy straps and started to turn.

"Whoa!" Jake caught her hands, preventing her escape. "*I*," he began with equally soft emphasis, "didn't say anything about being a genius or a Steinem double. As to centerfolds..." Though Jake had always more than appreciated the type, he began to wonder why. Maggie's makeup was minimal—a little mascara, a bit of blush, bare, temptingly stubborn lips. "Some men are attracted by a more natural look, and short can be nice." His gaze lowered, touching her sweater where her breasts pressed innocently against the angora softness. Arousal that had been building steadily beneath the surface pushed at him with more force. Jake tensed against it and cleared his throat. "And as far as overly endowed goes, quite a few men prefer gentler curves."

The detached observer tone was getting harder to pull off. He was standing too near, looking too closely. His gaze returned to hers, hoping for respite. Instead he found himself pulled in deeper by green eyes filled with a sort of confused amazement. He knew he'd gotten too personal. He could see that in her eyes as well. Still, maybe it was for the best. Maybe she hadn't realized her own appeal.

Careful to keep a tight rein on his own desire, Jake relinquished one of her hands and picked up her braid. Her hair was brown, spiced by cinnamon fire. Playing the ends between his thumb and forefinger, he was fascinated by the way sunlight from the window brought it to life.

"What do men want, Maggie? Ask ten of them and you'll get ten different answers." He caressed her cheek. "I *do* know one thing. The man was a jackass not to see how special you are."

The confusion left her expression slowly, and she squeezed his hand. "You know, you're really very sweet, and great for the ego, too." She kissed his cheek as if she were his maiden aunt—quick with no body contact. "Thank you, Jake."

Want had pulled his muscles tighter than a bowstring, and she thought he was simply being sweet? Evidently the jerk had done more damage to her self-esteem than he'd thought. Frustration that had little to do with need drove him to take that final half step forward, bringing their bodies within an inch of each other.

"I'm not sweet, dammit!" He guided her arms around his neck, then lowered his hands to the small of her back. "You're a very desirable woman!"

Jake initiated the kiss to prove his point; he lingered when he hadn't intended to because what he'd said was true. From the first touch of his lips to hers, he knew he was in trouble. Desire sped through him, fierce and fast. He tried to tell himself to be content with a simple kiss. To be content with the petal-soft feel of her lips beneath his, with the tantalizing brush of her body. But then her lips parted slightly with the smallest of moans, and suddenly what was supposed to be reaffirming for her, undid him. Abandoning all thoughts of noble intentions, he slid a hand up to cradle the back of her head and deepened the kiss.

She tasted of chocolate and sunshine, of moonlight and madness, even in the full light of day. Still, there remained an innocence in her response, in the way her body moved hesitantly against his, so full of fire, yet small and delicate. It was madness, to be sure, he thought as her fingers entwined with the hair at his nape. Her scent surrounded him, filled him; her warmth beguiled. It was as if he'd never been kissed before, and greedily, he wanted more.

As though privy to his thoughts, Maggie pulled away abruptly, keeping her eyes downcast as she brushed at her bangs with a trembling hand. In much the same condition, Jake stood stock-still, willing his body to relax.

"That, uh..." She lifted her gaze. Her eyes were clouded and her cheeks flushed. "That wasn't good."

She could have decked him and not surprised him more. "No?" he asked, reminding himself to handle this lightly. "Wanna give me a second chance?" He grinned. "I'll try harder."

"No," she said quickly, taking a step back. "And I wasn't talking about the kiss."

"Then it was?"

She massaged her temple with a fingertip. "What?"

"Good." For reasons he didn't stop to think about, he found it important that she admit it. "You enjoyed the kiss?" he prompted, shoving his hands into his pockets to keep from pulling her toward him again.

"Do you think I would've let it go on like it did if I hadn't?" Maggie wrapped her arms tightly around herself, wondering how long it would be before she felt as if she was on solid ground again. "But that's not the point. The point is, it can't happen again."

"Why not?"

Maybe *he* was used to receiving unrestrained responses, but *she* wasn't used to giving them. Though she'd wanted to effect some changes in her personality, absolute turnabouts weren't what she'd had in mind. And certainly not with someone she'd known less than twenty-four hours!

Honesty being the best policy, she commanded her pulse to slow and gave him a level look. "It would make things...complicated, and I can't handle that now. I've got enough complications as it is."

Complications weren't exactly his cup of tea, either. Yet somehow when he was kissing her, he'd forgotten. Feeling it was best to downplay what had happened, for her sake, he smiled. "It was just a kiss," he said gently. "One that we both enjoyed, sure, but there's nothing for you to worry about. I promise."

Embarrassment made her ears burn as the rumble of water in the teakettle warned of its imminent whistle. She turned gratefully and opened the cabinet. She'd overreacted. The man had given her a simple kiss, and she'd blown it all out of proportion.

"Oh, great," she said, grabbing two cups and crossing the kitchen. "You must think I'm some emotional cripple, who goes around looking for reasons to get upset." She switched off the flame under the kettle and searched through the overhead cabinet for instant cocoa. "Last night over Gran, today over Brad, then now over... over..."

Damn! Her hands were trembling again! She faced him, clasping her hands behind her. "Normally I'm—"

God, maybe she *had* become an emotional cripple! He stood mere inches away, his eyes full of understanding, his hands coming to rest on her shoulders, and all she could think about was...things she shouldn't think about!

"You're a strong person, Maggie. A strong person who's had to deal with a lot of upsetting things lately." He brushed his lips against her forehead, then looked deeply into her eyes. "You're also one hell of a good kisser." Giving her a quick wink, he turned away.

Maggie leaned back against the stove for support and watched him walk to the table, pick up his jacket and slip it on. She should have felt relief, yet she didn't. "Don't you want your hot chocolate?"

"I better pass." Jake sensed it would be a long time before he tasted chocolate in any form without recalling the kiss they'd shared. "It's a lot later than I thought it was, and I really do have to start that laundry and paperwork."

"Oh, of course." Maggie swallowed past her disappointment and pushed away from the stove. "Hey, and thanks for your help today. I suppose I could have let it wait until tomorrow, but—"

"Nonsense. It was my pleasure," he said, heading for the back door.

Maggie followed him. "What about the battery charger?"

"Leave it on until morning, then disconnect it like I showed you." He opened the screen door and moved down the steps, pausing at the bottom. Wind whipped at his black hair, accentuating his rakish appeal. "If the car doesn't start, give me a call. If it does, leave the charger in your garage. I'll get it eventually."

"Okay."

"See you around," he said, starting to walk.

"Yeah. See you around." Maggie headed for the kitchen.

"Hey, Maggie?"

In a second she was back at the door, pushing it open. "Yes?"

His smile was infinitely tender, warming her from the inside out. "Trust me. The man *was* a jackass."

Chapter Four

Not again!"

Maggie frowned, searching through the clutter of boxes and folded clothing in Gran's room for her marking pen. For the better part of the two previous days, she'd sifted through the clothing, linens and keepsakes of the second story, cherishing memories before sorting the various items into boxes bound for California or the thrift shop. She'd also had to look for the tape dispenser three times, and the marking pen twice. If she was absentminded by nature, the misplacements wouldn't seem odd.

Since she wasn't, they did.

A breath of spring pushed at the open priscilla curtains, distracting her, as if nature itself was coaxing her to forget her work. Resolute, she allowed herself only a deep breath of its sweetness before resuming her search.

Discipline, Maggie thought. A personality trait that had kept her to schedules and helped propel her career, now

kept her packing when she would have preferred working
in the garden. She dropped to her knees and flipped the
dust ruffle atop the quilt before her gaze strayed to the
window. Robins and cardinals sang the praises of May;
sunshine glinted off newly leafed trees; responsibilities
nagged at her.

Last night she'd made a brief call to Marilyn Henshaw,
the woman in charge of the thrift shop. Marilyn expected
her to drop off a few boxes at the shop before they opened,
which meant Maggie had no time to lose.

Palms against the cool, wood floor, she ducked her head
and looked under the bed for her marking pen. Dust bun-
nies scampered across the slick floor, pushed by her breath.
Her gaze swept the length of the area—

The slam of a back door and a familiar whistle made
Maggie want to sit up. She curled her fingers against the
floor to prevent it, but could do nothing about the quick-
ening of her heart. She no longer needed to look to know
Jake would be locking his back door, filling the birdbath
with water from the hose, then taking seed to a tree stump.
She hadn't meant to watch him Monday and Tuesday.
She'd just happened to be by a window. Happenstance or
not, she wouldn't watch him today.

The whistling stopped far too early, pricking her curiosity. She waited a moment for her discipline to kick in.
When it didn't, she rose slowly, stopping when her gaze
inched beyond the sill to the yard next door.

Maggie's heartbeat scattered. Though Jake stood before the birdbath, it was as if he looked, not only at Gran's
house, but into the window at her. Logic assured her that
he couldn't see her. She was kneeling a good four feet from
the window. Yet his gaze held her captive.

What went on behind those eyes? Those all-knowing,
all-seeing eyes of his? Like a two-way mirror, they permit-

ted him to look out, without allowing anyone else to see in. He was an enigma, she thought. Though he seemed friendly and open on the surface, she'd witnessed his ability to mask what he was truly thinking on more than one occasion.

It was only when he returned his attention to the over-flowing water that Maggie realized she'd been holding her breath. She exhaled on a frustrated sigh, turned away from the window, then sank back on her heels. After their last kiss, he'd promised there was nothing to worry about.

There wouldn't be, she vowed. She thought of the cookies she'd made him as a small token of appreciation, and frowned. Given her preoccupation with the man and the effect he had on her, maybe she should wait another day before she took them to his house.

Better yet, she could take them by his shop. By nature, homes were intimate and casual, whereas a place of business was more formal, structured . . . safer. It wasn't cowardice, she decided, but good sense.

Pleased with her decision, Maggie slipped her fingers into the back pockets of her jeans, then exhaled a curse. She pulled the missing pen from her pocket and laughed. "Maybe I *am* getting absentminded," she muttered.

A glance at the clock put her back into motion, and she labeled the last of the boxes. Within minutes she had them loaded into the car and was headed for the thrift shop on Main Street, a few blocks away.

There was an ambience about a small town—the way trees arched over neighborhood streets, the way one could hear a train whistle amid the dark of a quiet night, the way neighbors introduced themselves with coffee cake. Though this was only her fifth day here, she'd gotten a taste of what Gran had called "community life," and she liked it.

Maggie parked in front of the shop called Friends Helping Neighbors, then got out. Ignoring the Closed sign on the door, she went inside as per Marilyn's instructions. "Hello," she called. "Can anyone hear me?"

"I'll be out in a minute. I'm in back."

"I'm in no hurry." Maggie wove through the rows of tables, pleased to have her preconceived notions about a thrift shop obliterated. Though the clothing and household goods might have had previous owners, there prevailed a feeling of pride. Walls gleamed a freshly painted white; eye-catching displays showed less-than-new things to their best advantage. She paused to straighten a row of shoes, then moved to the counter.

As a child she'd always felt as if she belonged in Broken Arrow. It was odd how easily that feeling returned, how easily the feeling suited her. Maggie bit her lower lip, reminding herself not to get too comfortable. Pacific Grove was a small town. In fact, it was a much smaller town than this. And it was, after all, her future home.

"I had a hunch I should've stayed in bed this morning. Fool that I was, I got up anyway." The brunette who hurried toward Maggie rolled her eyes. Attractive and in her mid-thirties, her short-cropped hair emphasized large, dark brown eyes. The woman stopped before Maggie, a clipboard and small gray box in hand, and gave her a quick once-over. "You *are* Maggie, aren't you?"

Maggie nodded and extended her hand. "Marilyn?"

"The one and only." She glanced first at Maggie's hand, then her eyes before embracing her in a quick hug. "I'm not one to stand on formality," she said, stepping back. "Especially since I feel as if I already know you. Bea was not only my best worker, but a dear friend. She was also the closest thing to a grandmother I ever had. I figure that sort of makes us related."

Marilyn's eyes sparkled with a sincerity and friendliness that invited instant kinship. Touched, Maggie smiled. "Sounds good to me. I've never had a cousin."

"Great." Marilyn walked past her and around the counter to the back. "Now that we're related—" she crouched behind the counter, momentarily disappearing "—feel free to call on me for anything while you're here. What I can't help you with, chances are Danny, my husband, can." She appeared again, a pencil clamped between her teeth and papers in hand. She attached them to the clipboard and set it down. "I also have a couple of boys, ages nine and twelve. They're great for slave labor." She slipped the pencil behind her ear. "That's what they call yard work."

Small-town hospitality. Though she intended to do the work at Gran's on her own, Maggie felt warmed by the genuine offer. "I'll keep that in mind. Thanks."

"Let me do this first, then I'll help carry in your boxes. So," she said, opening the cash register, "what are *you* doing for the next four and a half hours?"

Maggie watched Marilyn transfer the money from the box to the register. She worked quickly, assuring Maggie she was the kind of woman who could do ten things at once. "Well, I'm running a couple of errands, picking up paint, then heading home to mask woodwork."

The petite woman looked up, wrinkling her nose in a frown. "Oh, busy, huh?" She sounded disappointed.

"Do you need me to do something?"

"We-ell," she drawled, "now that you mention it, I do usually work with a couple of volunteers. Frances won't be in on Wednesdays for the next several weeks because she just had a baby. And my other helper called right before you came in to tell me she'd broken her leg late last night." She closed the cash drawer with her hip and slipped her fingertips into her pockets. Her brows lifted hopefully. "Is there any chance you could fill in the nine-to-one slot on Wednesdays while you're in town?"

Maggie thought of all she had to do, but knew she'd already decided. "Have I been conned?"

Marilyn grinned. "By the best." Her gaze met Maggie's earnestly. "Really, don't let me steamroll you. I just figure it never hurts to ask. If you don't have time—"

"Let's get the boxes," Maggie said, heading for the door. "You've got a lot to tell me if you're going to open at nine."

"Great!" In a flash Marilyn caught up with her. "You know, even though we didn't talk long last night, I told Danny that I had a feeling you were my kind of person."

Still dazed from the call he'd just received, Jake hung up the phone and stared absently at the assortment of computer brochures scattered over his desk. "And I thought *this* was a problem," he muttered, pushing at the pamphlets. He propped his elbows on the arms of the chair, rested his chin on steepled fingers and willed the tightness in his stomach away.

Responsibility. Real responsibility for another human being. What did he know of it? Other than being in a band, which was a different sort of responsibility altogether, his excursion into matrimony had been his only short-lived try at it.

As far as Christopher went, paying child support was easy, and Jake's occasional visits had been fun. Having custody, however, promised to be more complex. At the time of the divorce, he and Claire had agreed that once Chris turned four, he would have the boy for six months. Thereafter Chris would spend the summers and some holidays with his father. At the time it hadn't sounded as if it would be difficult. Now he realized he should have upped the age to twenty-one.

The excitement Jake had felt over the upcoming custody had been clouded by fear. What did he know about taking care of a child? Sure, he'd been around Mac's kids and occasionally played horsey and bought them ice cream. But what did he *really* know? What did they do all day? What did they eat? What did you do when they got sick? Jake loosened the collar at his throat. It wasn't that he didn't have any experience with children, it just suddenly didn't seem like he had enough.

Jake bolted out of his chair and paced the confines of his small office, repeatedly raking his hands through his hair. Not only did he not have the simple answers to the everyday questions, the room that would be Chris's was filled with assorted sound equipment and boxes he had yet to unpack from his move two years ago!

The immensity of how unprepared he was sank in, and Jake stopped. He didn't even have a bed for the kid!

The urge to talk to Maggie swept over him from nowhere. She'd been on his mind for days, sneaking up on him without provocation. He would imagine her laugh, see her dimple when she smiled, remember how soft her hair had been in his hands, how easy it had been to be with her, how hard it had been to restrain himself from going beyond a mere kiss.

He shook off the last thought and paced some more, yet Maggie's image stayed with him. More than once Mac had commented how much help Brenda was when he had a problem to work out. While that was okay for Mac, Jake had been raised to solve his own problems, not impose them on others. Knowing that, believing that, didn't prevent him from wishing he could simply talk to Maggie.

A soft knock on the door put an abrupt halt to his pacing and he frowned. Dipping his hands into the pockets of his khaki pants, he commanded composure. "Come in."

Jake clamped his jaw to keep his mouth from gaping. As if in answer to his wish, Maggie entered his office and stood just inside the doorway. The pink of her tucked-in T-shirt reflected on her cheeks.

"Hi!" Her smile faded by degrees into the silence. "I...uh...brought you something." She held up a colorful round tin. "I made some chocolate chip cookies last night, and knowing how much you like them..."

She pressed her lips together, then strode to his desk and set the tin on a clear corner. "Well, they're not much in the way of an appreciation gift, but I thought you might enjoy them." She pushed at a brochure. "Computer shopping, huh?" Their gazes met before she started backing toward the door. "Sorry for the interruption."

As she groped for the knob behind her, Jake realized his frown was still in place and that he hadn't said a word. "Wait! I, uh...thanks." He grabbed the cookies off the desk, then before he could think better of it, took her arm. "Do you like limeade?"

She looked perplexed. "Yes."

"How long's it been since you had a *real fountain* limeade?"

"I don't know."

"That's too long." He opened the door and propelled her down the short hall and into the showroom. "Mac, did you meet my neighbor, Maggie Flannagan?"

Jake's partner stood behind the counter, beneath one of the twin arches that Maggie suddenly realized were teller windows from a turn-of-the-century bank. "Do I look like the kind of man who'd let a beautiful woman go by me without an introduction?"

She took the compliment, though she knew better than to believe it. "Hello, again."

On the way in, her nerves had been wound so tight she'd only vaguely noticed the hodgepodge of antique touches mixed with the display of stringed instruments. Now that she wanted to linger for a closer inspection, Jake was hustling her toward the door.

"If Redman calls about his appraisal, it's on my desk. And I haven't been able to catch Wise. His secretary said call after two. Do you mind? I'm going to take Maggie to Petrik's."

"No sweat," Mac replied.

The bell overhead jingled as Jake opened the door, pausing long enough for Maggie to recognize that the listing of various guitars, violins and cellos was on an old depot board from a train station. "Oh, and Peterson was supposed to drop by with—"

"I know, Jake. I work here, too."

"Right."

"Bye, Maggie. Come again sometime when he's not in such a hurry to scoot you out."

"Thanks, I will. You've got an interesting shop..." she said brokenly as Jake pulled her outside. Squinting against the strong sunlight, she dug her heels in and slipped her arm from his grasp. "Whoa, Wilder. First you look at me as if I'm from outer space, then the next thing I know we're moving down Main Street like we're in a Chinese fire drill. So what's with you anyway?" His long study of her diffused her annoyance and sped her heartbeat.

"You know, you and your sisters don't look at all alike."

Though she couldn't say why, that particular comment hurt, coming from Jake. She'd always been very aware of the differences between her and her sisters. Maggie lifted her chin. "So I've been told," she managed evenly.

"The tall one doesn't look as if she'd budge for anything less than Dom Perignon, and the redhead looks as if that would be too conventional." Maggie's hurt faded as quickly as it had begun. "That's what I like about you. You look—"

"If you say cute or wholesome, I'll think you terribly unoriginal," she warned, trying not to smile.

"As I was about to say, you look like the kind of woman who'd appreciate a really good limeade."

Maggie grinned and snapped one of his red suspenders. "Just goes to show you don't know everything. All three of us Flannagan women would walk a mile for one."

Jake presented his arm. "How about a block and a half?"

"What are we standing here for?"

Main Street was predominantly lined with one- and two-story buildings. Awnings provided shade, stenciled glass fronts displayed wares. Older buildings lent charm and warmth to the street, and traffic moved slowly between the few stoplights. Though the town had grown far beyond Main and had several small shopping centers in various locations, this was the area Maggie liked best.

The honk of a horn had her looking toward the street. Mrs. Irving, her neighbor to the west, waved at them. Both she and Jake waved in return at the older woman and her husband.

"I take it you've met the Irvings?" Jake asked.

"Yes. They and Mrs. Lacey across the street brought me a coffee cake the other morning and stayed for a visit. They seemed very sweet."

"They are."

As Maggie and Jake walked down the sidewalk, it occurred to her that she should have told him she was too busy. The morning at the thrift shop had really thrown her behind. She could still plead a pressing schedule, but she didn't.

When they walked into Petrik's, Maggie felt transported back in time to a drugstore of the fifties. The soda fountain at the front of the store was authentic, from the age-old malt machines and chalkboard menu to the swivel seats at the counter. Round tables and ice-cream-parlor chairs invited cozy chats, while the antique pharmacy counter at the back of the store fulfilled more serious requirements. The aroma of hamburgers and onions wafted in the air, making her hungry as she spied an old jukebox.

"Does it work?" she asked, turning to Jake.

Their drinks on a table, he stood patiently behind a chair, holding it out for her. "One play for a dime or three for a quarter." He dug in his pocket and brought out a coin. "Go for it," he said, flipping it neatly to her.

After choosing a mix of old and new tunes, she sat down, a smile on her lips. "I'm glad you brought me here."

"Yeah, I really like it. It's gained quite a reputation. Not only locally, but it's even been written up in newspapers as far as the West Coast." He watched her expectantly as she took a sip of her drink. "Well, what do you think?"

Maggie sighed her approval. "S'wonderful!"

"Wait till you taste the hamburgers and fries. I hope you don't mind, but since I hadn't eaten I took the liberty of ordering us some lunch."

"If the food is as good as the atmosphere is authentic, it'll be great." She looked up at the ceiling fans, knowing they were the real things instead of popular replicas. Maggie took another drink, then leaned forward slightly.

"Speaking of atmosphere, where did you find all the old pieces in your store?"

"When Mac and I bought the place from Bill Sipes, the teller setup, the cash register and the depot board were included in the price. Most of the other pieces are things Brenda, Mac's wife, has found."

"I love antiques, and they certainly give your store a unique setting."

"Yeah, thanks." Jake's eyes had lowered to where he fiddled with a napkin on the table, turning it first one way, and then the other.

Though Maggie didn't know him well, it was apparent something was on his mind. The same something that had made his expression so intense in his office? Maggie took another sip, then asked, "Thinking of buying a computer?"

"Thinking's right. Mac and I are considering expansion. If we do, we'll need one, but trying to make heads or tails out of those brochures is like reading Greek to me. I know next to nothing about them."

"The computer you choose depends on what program you need to work with, which depends on what kind of work you plan to do. Since I have a fair knowledge of computers, I'd be more than happy to help you."

"Thanks," he said, still concentrating on the napkin. "I may take you up on the offer."

Despite his words, she could tell he never would. She frowned, wondering what had him so preoccupied. As he creased the paper napkin repeatedly, her gaze was drawn to his hands. Talented, strong, capable, completely masculine, yet exquisitely fluid in their movement. She'd seen a demonstration of their expertise with the guitar, and had felt their magic as they roamed her back over the barrier of a shirt. What would they feel like against her bare skin?

"Maggie?" She looked abruptly at his face and gave thanks that he wasn't psychic. His eyes were darkly serious and full of questions.

"Yes?" Unwillingly, her lungs refused to draw another breath, though she felt certain the question wasn't of a personal nature, since they'd agreed on no complications.

The intensity of his gaze broke as he leaned back in the chair. "So, how have things been going?"

Maggie inhaled then, fighting a smile. Whatever he'd planned to ask, that wasn't it. "I got my luggage back late Sunday, the refrigerator was delivered Monday and, thanks to you, the car's been running fine." She propped her chin on her palm. "I've made a lot of headway packing things upstairs, and this morning I went by the thrift store to drop some things off." She laughed lightly in remembrance. "I ended up volunteering to help out on Wednesday mornings."

"It certainly sounds like you've kept yourself busy."

"Uh-huh."

He shifted in his seat, this time planting his forearms on the table. His shirt sleeves were rolled up, revealing muscled forearms dusted with dark hair. She curbed the impulse to reach out to him, and sat quietly.

"Maggie..."

"Still here," she said softly.

He looked up at that and cracked a smile. "I—"

"Here you go, Mr. Wilder." A fresh-faced teenage girl set two basket specials on the table. "Made yours just the way you like, with extra pepper." She smiled at Maggie. "My name's Tricia. If you need anything, give a holler."

"We will, Tricia." Jake smiled. "Thanks."

Maggie turned her attention to the food. At first bite, she found herself sighing once more with approval. Jake, she noticed, did little more than push French fries around on his plate. After taking a second bite of the burger, she dabbed the corners of her mouth with her napkin. "What were you about to say when Tricia brought the food?"

"Oh, nothing."

"Never try to lie under oath, Jake. You're lousy at it." He raised his head, denial in his eyes. She popped a fry into her mouth. "You can tell me it's none of my business, but don't say it's nothing."

She saw the twitch of nerves in his jaw as he hesitated. "Christopher is coming. Early."

"That's great . . . isn't it?"

"Well, sure it is." He grabbed the ketchup and began squirting it on his plate, his gaze locked with Maggie's. "I couldn't be happier about it. Really. I'm thrilled."

His eyes were earnest; his French fries drowned. "I believe you." She took a drink of limeade, then played with the straw. "Do you love ketchup?"

"Sure. Doesn't everyone?"

"Probably not as much as you."

A curse mixed with Jake's laughter. "I wasn't all that hungry anyway." He shoved the plate aside and opened the cookie tin. "Besides, why bother with lunch when you can skip straight to dessert?"

If the ketchup was an indication, it was his son that had had him so preoccupied. "How early is Chris coming?"

"Three months." He popped a cookie in his mouth and brushed the crumbs from his hands. "I leave tomorrow night for Seattle. We'll get reacquainted, then fly here on Wednesday."

"That *is* early."

"No kidding." He took another cookie, but only stared at it. "Evan, Claire's husband, has been the manager at a swank restaurant in Seattle. Last week Skeffington's of London gave him an offer he couldn't refuse. After a year of training and observing their operations there, they want Evan to run the restaurant they plan to open in Dallas. So that's why I'm getting custody now, rather than having Chris make an extra transatlantic flight." His eyes met hers. "I got the call right before you popped in."

"How close are you to being ready for him?"

"Real close, if he likes to sleep in boxes and play with amplifiers and sound boards." He put the cookie in his mouth.

Maggie's eyes widened. "You've got a problem."

"Nothing I can't handle," he answered quickly. Too quickly, judging by the way she'd immediately focused her attention on her hamburger. He hadn't meant to sound sharp, but realized he had. Jake rubbed the back of his neck. What harm could there be in asking her for a few suggestions? He tilted his head, getting her attention. "Any recommendations on beds? And I guess he'll need a dresser and…toys. What kind of toys do almost-four-year-old boys like?"

"You're going to need a lot more than a couple of pieces of furniture and some toys." She put a French fry in her mouth and frowned in concentration. "Sheets, bedspread, curtains. It probably wouldn't hurt to buy him some clothes, too. Boys run through them like water in the summer."

"I hadn't thought of that." He pulled a pen from his pocket and a small piece of paper that looked like a cash register receipt, then began writing. "What else?"

"Plenty." Warnings flashed through her mind. She didn't want to get involved with him or his son. But damn, he obviously needed help.

Maggie wiped her fingers on her napkin and tossed it on the table. She *wouldn't* get involved. She would simply

help out a little. Surely that was the least she could do after all he'd done for her.

She stood, stealing a cookie from the tin before closing
it. "Lucky for you, you know someone very well versed in
little boys who happens to have a free afternoon on her
hands. What's your budget?"

"A free afternoon?" He looked adorably doubtful.
"Five'll get you ten you have a list in your purse that says
different. Really, if you'd—"

"Oh, I get it." Maggie narrowed her eyes and put her
hands on her hips. "As long as it's *you* helping *me*, it's
okay. But if the tables are turned it's another story."

Though her dimple winked with her teasing, he'd seen
the flash of history replaying itself in her eyes. That she
would still offer, despite it, made Jake determined to keep
their time together "uncomplicated." "The budget's no
problem. Time limitations are."

"I'm not the one still sitting at the table."

If Jake listened hard enough, he could make out Maggie's voice singing along with the Carly Simon CD she'd
chosen to play. Damn if she wasn't an easy woman to be
around—intelligent, enjoyable, appealing.

Jake scowled, realizing it was the appealing part caus-
ing him trouble. He set the last amplifier in his living
room, then placed his hand at the small of his back and
stretched. His eyes closed, he could see Maggie the way he
had minutes ago. She, too, had been stretching. Arms
above her head, her T-shirt had pulled covetously over her
breasts before she bent and touched her toes.

His eyes opened on a sigh of restraint. All-American,
wholesome looks laced with unexpected sexuality. He
hadn't realized how provocative unlikely combinations
could be... how seductive.

Jake shook his head to clear it of such fanciful thoughts. "Hey, Flannagan, what's taking you so long? I told you just put the box by the basement door and I'd take it down later."

"I'll be out in a minute."

Jake slumped on the couch, propped his feet on the coffee table and laced his fingers behind his neck. The weariness in his muscles as well as the clock on the table said it was nearing midnight. His mind spun with all they'd accomplished in one day. Maggie had been untiring. She'd thought of everything Christopher would need from rods for the curtains to books for bedtime stories. Then, after they'd dragged in late from the shopping, she'd insisted on helping him clear out the room.

The music ended, filling the house with an unsettling quiet. The silence spawned a tension in his muscles that had nothing to do with exhaustion. Jake put his feet on the floor and sat forward. He'd been crazy to accept her help. Not that he'd had much choice, but he should have found a way, should have insisted at Petrik's that suggestions were help enough, should have tactfully blocked her from coming inside tonight. For with her leaving, he knew, the house would feel a little emptier.

Survival, he'd learned, meant depending on no one but himself. It was easier that way, less complex. In the past—

"Got a headache?"

Jake looked up as Maggie plopped on the couch. "No," he said, then took a deep breath. "Look, Maggie, I, uh, really appreciate your help this evening and I'd like to pay you for—"

She sat upright. *"What?"*

Jake rubbed his jaw. "I said—"

"I know what you said, I just find it hard to believe!" Irish heritage blazed brightly in green eyes. "In fact, it's darn close to insulting. I returned a favor, Jake. You helped me when I first got here, remember? I was happy to do something in return." She shook her head, then snatched her purse from the table. "You're not in debt to me if that's what you're worried about. The favor's returned. The slate's clean. And I'm out of here."

He grabbed her before she could stand. "Wait a minute!" He released her when Maggie glared pointedly at his hand. "Look, I'm sorry. I didn't mean to insult you." He pressed his finger at the headache forming between his brows, searching for words. "I guess, uh, I'm not very good at saying thank-you."

She folded her hands atop her purse, her eyes downcast. "You can say that again," she muttered.

Jake lifted her chin. "Thank you, Maggie."

Slowly the stern line of her lips softened. When her dimple slipped from hiding, he felt relieved. "You're welcome, Jake."

Though it was foolhardy to allow himself to relax even a little, he did. As he smiled, her expression grew quizzical and she tilted her head. Suddenly self-conscious, Jake sat a little straighter. "What?"

"You don't look like there's anything wrong with your mouth," she said, setting her purse on the floor.

He wiped his lips. "Is there?"

Maggie leaned back against the couch, trying very hard to keep a straight face as she rested her feet on the table. "Apparently you have a very subtle case of tight lip."

"Tight lip?"

"Uh-huh." She grabbed one of the small throw pillows and trailed her finger along the cording. "Remember my being so impressed with your music the other day that I said you could play professionally?" Jake nodded. "Your answer, as I recall, was that you were very happy here."

"I am."

"You fink," she said, thwacking his shoulder with the pillow. "Why didn't you tell me that you had?"

That quickly, the look on his face grew wary. "How'd you—"

"The last box. When I picked it up, I got poked by something, so I opened the box to rearrange the stuff inside. Naturally I saw the awards and some of the pictures." She folded her arms over the pillow and studied him, fascinated that after the life he'd led he would end up here. "I can't help but wonder why someone like you is living in Broken Arrow, Oklahoma."

"Why not?" He looked away and she thought he was going to leave it at that. "Look, you said the other day that you didn't care about having three cars and living in the hills of L.A. Well, I quit trying to live the way people wanted me to long ago. I came here at first because of Mac. After our band split up, he came back here with his wife to visit her family. He stumbled onto Strings for Sale. The original owner was wanting out, so Mac gave me a call. I came to check it out, then stayed because I liked it." He faced her. "Does that answer your question?"

"Yes." Brad had always concerned himself with image. Jake apparently didn't give a damn. Admiration welled inside her, pushing her liking of him up another notch. "I still say you could've told me, though." She smiled, hoping to ease the guarded look in his eyes.

He frowned. "What was I supposed to say? Brag that we'd even played Carnegie Hall?"

She'd touched a nerve. Some people wore fame like a badge, while others preferred to keep their public and private selves separate. Had some people treated him differently because of his past? Wanting desperately to prove to him that it made no difference to her, she decided to diffuse the tension in the air with humor.

Maggie moved closer. "Modesty becomes you, Wilder." She grinned mischievously. "Almost as much as your once shoulder-length hair."

The wariness in his eyes receded slowly. "Are you making fun of me?"

"Hey, what can I say? Someone has to. Besides, I'm jealous." Her exaggerated pout earned her a small smile. "Your hair looked better than mine ever has."

"There's nothing wrong with your hair." He wrapped the strand at her cheek around his finger, brushing her skin in the process and sending a chill of delight up her spine.

Maggie held very still, willing the teasing tone of her voice to continue. "Spoken by a person who never had to contend with stick-straight locks." She eased her hair from his grasp. "Tell me, did you perm it? Or did it have that bit of curl naturally?"

"I'm warning you, Flannagan." His eyes narrowed with the threat. "Don't push me."

"Aw, come on, Jake." She touched his hair as if considering the texture. "Tell me your secret. Hot rollers, right?"

"Mag-gie," he drawled, leaning toward her with menace.

Maggie watched his eyes in true gunfighter tradition, waiting for the change of his iris to signal his move. One moment led to the next, then a third. Just when she figured she'd stared him down, he grabbed her arms with a growl.

Laughter bubbled free from inside her with his look of revenge. "D-don't get mad—"

"I don't get mad," he said. "I get even." A grin quirked the edge of his mouth, but he fought it off well. "Tell me, Maggie, are you ticklish?"

"No, don't, that's not fair," she pleaded as she giggled, trying to squirm from his grip. "Really, I hate it." Her eyes widened when he deftly captured both of her wrists with one hand, freeing his other for torture.

In a bid for freedom she tried to turn and pull away abruptly. He thwarted her move with one of his own, and she lurched backward onto the couch, determined to escape. What she got was Jake on top of her and a new twist to their game.

Though he'd braced himself by releasing her hands and planting his by her shoulders, the pressure of his body against hers was still very male, very intimate. Maggie knew she needed to think of something clever to say and quickly, but the way his breath kept fanning her ear fogged her rapidly overloading mind.

Jake half pushed himself up on his hands and gazed down at her. Maggie's lips were parted, while the look in her eyes was uncertain at best. He knew what he should do, but desire built through accidental touches of the evening and the kindness of the day combined with his remembrance of their last kiss, drawing his mouth to hers.

In the moment he paused, she'd had a choice—and she'd made it. Opening up to him seemed so natural that Maggie spared little thought to how out of character she was acting, but let the pleasure, wild and delicious, sweep over her. She told herself it was only a kiss, and reveled in his dark seductive taste and the feel of his legs entwined with hers.

His mouth moved to her jawline, nibbling and scattering kisses along the way. She kneaded his shoulders as his lips journeyed downward, steeping her in sensations.

Pulses throbbed in places they shouldn't and, for the briefest of moments, Maggie considered surrendering to the need mounting between them. But as his hand covered her breast and she felt her heart leap up to meet it eagerly, protective instincts made her stiffen.

"Stop, please," she whispered. She felt both the tremble in his body as he froze, and the ache of longing in her own when he backed off.

Maggie took a deep breath and somehow got to a standing position. Her legs were weak and she prayed they would hold while she straightened her shirt. The silence between them was deafening. She retrieved her purse and kept her gaze lowered. "I'll leave now."

"I'll walk you home."

Not having the strength to argue, she nodded. Outside the dark sky was bright with stars and the air was refreshingly chilled. While it helped physically, the coolness could do nothing to clear the chaos in her mind. Operating on automatic, she put one foot in front of the other until she stood on Gran's porch.

"I know you volunteered to let the delivery men in, but perhaps you would rather have someone else do it."

Maggie lifted her gaze as far as the key he held. "Don't be silly. I don't mind at all." When she extended her hand, palm up, he pressed the bit of brass into it, then curled his fingers over hers.

"I told you the other day that you didn't have anything to worry about. To tell you the truth, I think we *both* do."

"I know," she whispered, raising her gaze to his. Obviously she didn't have a patent on confusion, for in his eyes she saw the very same things she felt.

Not sure if she or Jake had taken the first step, Maggie accepted the warmth and tenderness of his arms around her, resting her head against his chest. Though it made no sense to feel safe, she did.

It might have been five seconds or five minutes before he lifted her chin with his finger. "Perhaps rather than worry, we might consider the possibilities."

Maggie opened her mouth, but before she could say what she knew deep inside, Jake gave her a quick kiss and strode away, leaving her more confused than ever.

Chapter Five

Consider the possibilities. The advice was logical; what it proposed was not. Despite her conflicting emotions, she'd known what her answer would be the moment he made the suggestion. Still it hadn't kept her mind from entertaining the thought. Tempting as it was, it left her with the final problem—how and when to say what she should have said a week ago.

Maggie peeled the last bit of backing from a brightly colored dinosaur, smoothed the decal onto the wall and forced her mind to the subject at hand. She hoped Christopher would like the room. The furniture was sunny yellow; various kinds of dinosaurs in different colors romped across the bedspread and curtains. She smiled, pushed up the sleeves of her UCLA sweatshirt, then tucked her fingers into the back pockets of her jeans. The two four-foot dinosaurs she'd put on the wall added just the right touch.

For a woman with no real artistic ability, she'd always prided herself on being able to create a comfortable room attuned to the person who would inhabit it. Not enough of a flair to make a living at it, but enough to enjoy doing it. She thought of her own apartment, the quilts framed on the wall, the comfort and character of weathered woods and old-styled furniture.

The charm and history of antiques had never appealed to Brad. To him they were simply old, and decorating in general, he'd said, should be left to professionals.

Maggie dismissed the remembered prick to her vanity, and realized why she liked Jake's house. Though it was definitely in need of attention as far as decorating went, what was there definitely reflected who he was.

Not wanting to dwell on Jake in any form, she pulled a drawing pad and box of crayons from Chris's bookshelf and placed it open and waiting on the child-size table. All the room needed now was a pair of scuffed tennies and dirty socks on the floor to make it look lived in.

Satisfied, Maggie began picking up the backing paper that littered the floor and stuffing it into a trash bag.

"What's all this?"

She gasped and stood straight, facing Jake. He'd stopped in the doorway, exhaustion—and was it worry?—etched into his features. Her heart beat like a tightly wound toy. "I thought you weren't supposed to get in until late."

"An earlier flight was better for Christopher." His gaze skittered around the room before rejoining hers, giving no hint as to whether he liked or disliked what he saw. "I thought you weren't going to do anything but let the delivery men in."

"I hope you don't mind." She wadded the backing in her hands. "I, uh, couldn't imagine you coming home late, then having to mess with the room. It didn't take much to put it together."

Overwhelmed, Jake hardly knew what to say. "The dinosaurs are great." He nodded at the wall. "Where'd you get them?"

"Back at the store. The walls looked a little bare so I ran into Tulsa after I got finished at the thrift shop." She looked at the dinosaurs. "They're not much, but I thought they'd add a little something."

The strain of trying to cope with Christopher's withdrawn state since their departure from Seattle combined with his lack of knowing how to handle Maggie's going above and beyond the call of duty. He felt his mind jam, trying to sort through it all. "How much do I owe—" Her chin raised and she pinned him with a level look, reminding him of the mistake he'd made with her last time.

Jake ceased his efforts to understand and simply accepted. "Thank you, Maggie. For everything."

She smiled then and began picking up the trash on the floor. "Where's Chris?"

Her question jolted through him. He was no longer a man alone, but a father responsible for a son. He looked around. "He was right behind me. Chris?"

When Jake stepped out of the room, Maggie finished cleaning up. She hadn't wanted to be here when they arrived, and she wouldn't stay. As she knotted the end of the bag, the sound of Jake's voice prompted her to take a steadying breath. "I want you to meet a friend of mine. Her name is Miss Flannagan and she lives next door."

Maggie's heart sank when she saw them together. They'd traveled with comfort in mind. They both wore jeans and sweaters, Jake's black, Chris's red. As they stood side by side, their resemblance was striking, yet the distance between them was miles. The curly-headed boy looked lost, hugging a love-worn rabbit and keeping his eyes downcast. Jake looked unsure.

"Can you say hello to her?"

With the boy's continued silence, Maggie momentarily pushed away her reservations, wanting to put the child at ease. She set the bag on the floor and crossed the room.

"Hi, Chris. Miss Flannagan is quite a mouthful. You can call me Maggie." Lowering herself, she balanced on the balls of her feet. "Hey, that's a nice-looking rabbit you have. I bet you love him a lot."

Though Chris's hold on the stuffed animal tightened, his gaze remained on the floor.

"Can you tell Maggie the rabbit's name?" Jake prompted. "Or how about your room? Can you tell her what you think of it?"

Maggie stood and shook her head. "He's tired, Jake," she said quietly. "Give him a while." She retrieved the trash bag. "I'll just leave the two of you alone to—"

Jake took a step toward her. "You don't have to rush off!"

"I need to, really." Maggie told herself she'd only imagined the edge of desperation in his voice. Her job here was done, and it was time to leave. "I've got to get dinner started."

"Uh, I'll be right back, Chris," Jake said, stepping into the hallway. "Why don't you look around? There's some neat stuff in the toy box."

"Bye, Chris." Maggie fought the need to give the boy a reassuring hug, instead letting her hand linger briefly on his small shoulder. "It was nice to meet you."

Reminding herself their troubles were not her concern, she followed Jake to the front door and fished his key from her pocket. Now would be the perfect time to tell him how impossible it was for her to "consider the possibilities."

"I don't know why he's not talking." Jake stopped at the screen, thoroughly bewildered. "In Seattle I could hardly get a word in edgewise."

"Sometimes change is hard on children. He's had a long trip and a new set of circumstances to deal with, not to mention, he's away from his mother."

Jake glanced outside and massaged his neck. The feasibility of future custody rode on the relationship he would establish with Chris in the next six months. Jake knew how vital beginnings could be. That this one was off to a rough start didn't bode well.

He felt the gentle touch of Maggie's hand on his arm. "Give him time, Jake. Everything will be all right."

Maggie saw the desperate need to believe what she said shining in his eyes and felt the corresponding pull on her emotions. The ground she trod on was all too familiar. With familiarity came a panic of her own. She gave him his house key. "I've got to go."

She brushed past him to the sanctuary of the outdoors. "Thanks again," she heard, but dared not look back.

Jake watched her until she disappeared into Bea's. He'd felt a wave of pleasure upon first entering the house and realizing she was there. Then, just seeing her, he'd ached. Had she thought of him as much as he'd thought of her? Had she made lists of the pros and cons of the two of them being together? He wouldn't doubt it.

He closed the screen and headed for his son's room. Now was not the time for such thoughts; now was the time to remember what she'd said a moment ago. Chris only needed some time. Everything would be all right.

"Chris, what do you say to—" He scanned the empty room. "Chris?" The pounding of his heart grew stronger as he searched the house quickly. Where could the boy have gone? This was definitely no way to begin what amounted to a trial run for custodial visits. Jake entered the boy's room once more, anxiety pushing his breathing. He remembered Claire saying Chris loved to play hide-and-seek. Maybe his son was playing the game now.

Jake searched the closet, then turned and eyed the bed. He went down on his knees and lifted the spread. The sight of two, miniature Nike soles brought a sense of relief. Jake crawled around to the side of the bed, lifted the spread, then lay on his side. "Hi."

Christopher's head was buried in the crook of his arm and Jake tapped his shoulder. "This sure is a good hiding place." He waited for a moment. "Chris, look at me."

A knot formed in Jake's chest when the boy obeyed, silent tears trickling down his face. "Aw, don't cry. Everything's going to be okay. I know this is all new to you, and that you miss your mom and dad and Audrey. But remember, we're going to make videos to send, and your mom will, too, and before you know it . . ."

That had been the wrong tack to take, given the way Chris's lower lip began to quiver. "You can't stay under the bed the whole time," he said, faking a smile. "You can't even see the television from here." Jake reached out, only to have the boy shrink back. Not wanting to forcibly pull him out, Jake dropped his hand.

"Don't you want to look at your new toys? I got some really neat ones." Chris shook his head solemnly.

Jake had seen Mac use bribery on his boys on occasion. Maybe . . . "Uh, did you see my big piano? I'll let you play on it if you come out." He paused. "Not impressed, huh? How about my keyboard? It can really make some weird sounds. . . ."

The tears had slowed, but the blue eyes that watched him showed absolutely no interest. Jake shifted slightly, wishing Chris had picked a more comfortable place to retreat. Now what, Maggie? he thought.

He started to sigh, then stopped. Though it went against his grain to ask for help, perhaps this was one time he should make an exception. Yet he didn't want to leave Chris beneath the bed while he made the call.

Jake smiled inwardly. Though it was Evan whom Chris called "Daddy," Jake had learned that his son had inherited more from him than the color of his eyes and hair.

"I don't know how you feel, but this floor is hard and I'm hungry. I think what I'd like more than anything right now are some homemade, chocolate chip cookies."

Chris sniffed and wiped his nose. "Would you bring me one?" he asked, uttering his first words in hours.

Though the victory was minor, Jake held on to it. "I don't have any... but I know where I can get one."

"Where?"

"Maggie's house." He licked his lips. "Yeah, I bet if I said please, she'd give me one."

"Would she give me one, too?"

"Can you say please?" Chris nodded. "Then I bet she would. Of course, we'll have to go over there. That's where the cookies are."

The boy hesitated only minimally before scooting out from under the bed. Jake sat up, then helped his son to stand. "Of course, we need to wipe the tears off your fa—"

Chris squirmed away and grabbed the bottom of his shirt, then wiped his own face. "Ready," he said, wrapping both arms around the rabbit.

In Seattle, Chris had easily taken Jake's hand, talked nonstop and laughed a lot. He'd allowed Jake to supervise his baths with Claire in attendance and had been tolerant of the shampoo Jake had dripped in his eyes while learning to wash his hair. Chris had even questioned him about what they would do once they got to Oklahoma, and had seemed excited about the idea of staying with his father. But since the tearful farewell at the airport, he'd been quiet and had showed no interest in anything, except his rabbit.

Crossing the yards to Maggie's back porch, Jake clung to the hope that both he and Claire hadn't made a mistake by having the boy come to Broken Arrow.

"This is her house. Maggie," he called, knocking firmly on the screen's wood frame. He looked at Chris. "Normally we'd go to the front, but I figure she's in the kitchen."

The inner door opened and Maggie walked out to the porch. "Is something wrong?"

"Uhh." Jake smiled, feeling suddenly idiotic. "May I please have a chocolate chip cookie?"

"Well . . . sure." Maggie unlocked the door, wondering what he was up to. When she opened it, she saw Chris.

"May I please have a chipolate cookie?"

She grinned. "Yes, won't you come in?" She knew darn well that Jake still had some of the cookies left that she'd made him. Their gazes locked and she raised a brow in question.

"I need to talk to you for a minute," he whispered, passing by her.

Intuition told her his question concerned Chris. She nodded, then walked into the kitchen. "Do you think your rabbit would like a cookie, too?"

"Babbit."

"Your babbit?"

With Christopher's giggle came the second, halfway-easy breath Jake had taken in hours. "Not my babbit, my rabbit. His *name* is Babbit."

"Oh, I see." She bent down and handed him four cookies. "Here's two for each of you."

"Thank you." He held the rabbit to his ear. "Babbit says thank-you, too."

"Would you and Babbit like to go out back and swing?"

Chris looked at Jake, and for a moment Jake didn't know why. "Oh, sure, it's okay with me." When his son started for the door, Jake remembered to add, "Just don't go anywhere else. Okay?"

"Okay."

Jake waited until the screen banged shut before he moved to the porch where he could discreetly watch him. After all, he wouldn't want Chris to think he thought he was a baby. A smile crossed Jake's face as Chris encountered the dilemma of how to climb on the swing while holding his rabbit and cookies. Finally Chris settled for tucking the rabbit under his arm, then leaning across the wood seat on his tummy. Hands free, he ate the cookies while swinging lazily back and forth.

The soft scent of wildflowers with a hint of Oriental mystery told Jake that Maggie was near before she stood beside him. It was a scent that both soothed and aroused. With the slightest turn of his head, he saw her from the corner of his eye. Waning sunlight angled in through the screen, caressing the innocence of her profile and setting the cinnamon in her hair ablaze. Like her scent, her presence filled him with diverse feelings—warm comfortable familiarity and pure heated longing.

Maggie cocked her head to the side. "So, do you really want a cookie, or was it simply a ruse?"

He smiled. "I *always* want a cookie."

"Thought so." She handed him three and waited for him to finish the first one. "I also thought you wanted to talk to me about something."

He focused on Chris, marveling how a small boy could stir such panic. "It all looked so easy in Seattle. He warmed up to me quickly. We talked. We did things. Claire filled me in on everything I needed to know."

"Sounds good."

Jake faced her and she saw that it wasn't. "He hid under the bed, Maggie," he said quietly. "For what seemed like an eternity, I was terrified he'd run away. Then I found him...." He looked back outside. "He'd been crying," he said, his voice growing even softer. "Quietly crying. I didn't know what to do. I couldn't get him interested in anything." He cursed under his breath, then glanced at her. "If it's this hard already, what am I going to do for the next six months?"

Maggie smiled. "You must've done something right. He's here and not under the bed."

His laugh was shaky. "Somehow I don't think chocolate chip cookies are going to be the answer to everything." He raked a hand through his hair. "God, I don't know how to relate to him, what to say, what to do!" He looked at her, the desperation in his eyes no longer hidden. "What do I do, Maggie? What do I say?"

It was two years since she'd heard the same questions, seen the same panic. Two years and fifteen hundred miles, and yet she could almost be reliving the moment verbatim. Maggie steeled herself against vulnerability and watched the boy swing back and forth, dragging the toes of his tennis shoes through the grass. For the umpteenth time she reminded herself she didn't want to get involved in their lives, their problems, their joys. She couldn't let them become important....

But Jake wasn't really asking that, was he? Unlike Brad, who'd literally asked her to come and help, Jake had merely asked questions she could answer, without involvement.

Her own anxiety settled somewhat, and she leaned back against the wall, folding her arms. "First off, relax. Children are very intuitive. They pick up on feelings easily. If you're uptight, they'll be uptight. If you're nervous, they get anxious." She made a face at him, crossing her eyes and sticking out her tongue, trying to break through his intensity.

It worked. A smile wrestled at the corners of his mouth until it won out, dazzling her. She glanced at Chris to find balance, then back at Jake. "The next step is, remember what it was like to be a child."

For a moment, she thought she'd lost the ground she'd gained as something indefinable flickered in his eyes, then disappeared as quickly. "Uh, try and put yourself in Chris's position. He's away from all he's known, so of course he feels scared. All you have to do is reassure him the way you were reassured as a child."

Jake nodded, recalling not the way he'd been reassured, but the way he hadn't. Still, he could remember the way he'd longed for it to be.

"Also remember that you're a lot taller than he is. Size can be intimidating. Remember to stoop down sometimes or squat so he's not always having to look so far up.

"As for Chris's crying," she continued, "accept the fact that he will. Rather than trying to stop his tears, comfort him."

Worry rumpled his brow. "What if I can't think of what to say?"

Maggie held up her index finger. "You're forgetting rule number one. Relax."

"Yeah," he said, still looking unconvinced. "But I don't know how to comfort anyone."

Maggie started to laugh, but saw he was serious. "Trust me, Jake. Take it from someone who's experienced it. You know how."

"That was different," he said, dismissing what he'd done for her that first night.

"No!" She pushed away from the wall and stood straight, hands on her hips. "No it wasn't! You did for me what no one else had been able to." She raised her chin a notch. "You can. You have. You will."

The shine of belief in her eyes affected him more strongly than had the applause of thousands when he'd performed. He took strength from it and smiled, giving her a smart salute. "Yes, ma'am. Anything else?"

Maggie's gaze drifted outside. "Are Claire and her husband affectionate people?"

"Yes."

"Then Chris is used to lots of hugs and touching?"

Jake leaned his shoulder against the doorjamb and watched his son. "I guess so."

"Then don't be afraid to take his hand and—"

"I'm not. It's just that when we left Seattle, he pulled away from me and made it quite clear Babbit was all he needed."

"That doesn't mean forever." She glanced up at him. "Children need affection, Jake. Lots of it. I'm not saying smother him, but don't let him buffalo you, either. He needs to receive your hug as much as you need to give it."

He shifted, then turned her to face him, capping her shoulders in the warmth of his hands. "How'd you get so smart?"

The desire to melt against him had never been stronger. She stood still, barely breathing as she saw herself reflected in the blue of his eyes. She wavered, wondering what it would be like to surrender to his embrace and stay there a while. The ring of the phone delayed her decision.

"Instinct," she finally answered with a saucy grin, then headed for the phone.

"Hello."

"Maggie, this is Brad. I need to talk to you—"

Surprise gave way to the decision she'd made days ago. After a moment's hesitation, Maggie replaced the receiver on the hook. If he'd had to call, at least he'd picked an opportune time. His voice had been as effective as a pail of cold water in bringing her to her senses. She walked back to the porch, her feet once more on firm ground, her head squarely on her shoulders.

"That was quick."

"Wrong number," she muttered. "Now, let's go out and you can help him get situated in the swing properly and push him." She saw the slight frown form between his brows. "Remember step one, and relax. Don't expect instant results, but hang in there and you'll do fine. And don't forget to stoop down a bit when you talk to him."

The Jake that walked to the swing bore little resemblance to the man who'd come into her kitchen. She could still detect a tinge of uncertainty, but resolve far outweighed it.

"How would..." Jake hunkered down in front of the boy, as if recalling her advice. "How would you like to get off your stomach, sit right and let me push you?"

Small blue eyes sparkled with anticipation as Chris scrambled off the swing, then sat on the wooden seat, anchoring his rabbit securely between his thighs. "Ready!"

"Hold on tight to the ropes."

"I will."

Maggie moved behind the swing and watched, both the boy whose dark curls swayed with the movement, and his father whose confidence seemed to go up a notch. She couldn't help but smile when Chris giggled and insisted Jake push him higher. The swing climbed marginally as requested, but it was the muscular arms pushing it that captured her attention. Biceps flexed, forearms tensed, and she felt a forbidden warmth wind through her stomach. Fighting it, she crossed her arms at her waist and trained her gaze, and all her concentration, on Chris.

With each push of the swing, Jake felt a little of the day's strain ebb. After a week of being away, it felt good to be in home territory again. Seattle had still been a mite cold. Here the air smelled of freshly mowed grass, and the faces were familiar.

His gaze touched once more on Maggie's profile—the spunk of her upturned nose, the stubborn chin, the sensuality of her lips, even in repose. He pushed back the thoughts of how easily their touch and taste could turn him inside out, and studied how lovely she looked, how natural. She also looked a bit tired. No wonder, he thought, realizing what a full day she'd put in.

"Maggie, you haven't started your dinner, have you?"

"No," she said, keeping her gaze on his son. "I was trying to decide what to fix."

"How about lobster?"

She gave him a quick grin. "Come on, Jake. The most exotic thing I have in my freezer is a chicken, and I don't—"

"In that case, why don't you come with us? We're going to grab something to eat at—"

"No!" Her posture straightened as if she'd put a steel rod in her back. "Thanks anyway, but I've had a long day and don't have any desire to go get cleaned up."

"Higher, Jake, higher!" the boy begged.

Jake pushed the swing a little harder. "Okay, Maggie. Chris and I will get take-out and bring it back here."

"No thanks. I'm really not in the mood for lobster."

Jake studied the determined set of her mouth. "You're saying no to a lot more than lobster or a dinner, aren't you?" he asked evenly.

"I think it's wise to leave things as they are, don't you?" she asked, finally meeting his gaze. "Really, Jake, be honest. Can't you see how impractical it is for us to start anything?"

Wisdom. Impracticality. She had everything all figured out, and Jake had no doubt that she was right. Even so, he couldn't stop remembering how good her body had felt beneath his, the taste of her mouth, the smell of her skin.

With no small difficulty, he distanced himself from the memories and focused on Chris. "Yeah, I guess you're right. You're going to be quite busy with the house and all, anyway."

"And you're going to be busy, too. Your business, planning the expansion, not to mention what spare time you'll have will be spent getting closer with your son."

Jake smiled grudgingly. "I *am* going to be busy, aren't I?"

"Uh-huh." Maggie recalled the list of pros and cons she'd made, purposely dwelling on the latter to squelch any further discussions. "Besides, even if we had the time, you've admitted that you're not good at commitments. Frankly, I'm a person who needs them, but I'm not looking for one now."

"As long as we're being honest—" he shifted his gaze to Maggie "—there's a bit of déjà vu to the whole situation."

"Yes, quite a bit," she said sadly.

"More than you realize." Surprised he'd said it aloud, Jake shrugged under Maggie's inquisitive gaze. "Claire had been on the rebound when I met her."

"I'm not on any rebound, Jake," she said suddenly. "It's just not—"

"Wise," he finished for her. He pushed back the past and his more recent thoughts of what it would be like with Maggie, and smiled ruefully. "Well then, I guess we've pretty well said everything there is to—"

"Stop, Jake, stop!" Chris cried.

Jake brought the swing to a halt and rushed around to the front. "What's the matter?"

Chris leaned forward and whispered in his father's ear. She sensed the smile Jake was hiding as he picked the boy up and started backing away. "Uh, we've got a slight emergency and need to get home."

"Thank you for the cookies," Chris said, a pained look on his face.

Maggie bit her lip to keep from grinning and hooked her arm around one of the swing's ropes. "You're welcome."

"Thanks, too, for the help," Jake said, walking faster at Chris's obvious urging.

"You'll do great," she called out. "Remember, relax."

"Right!"

Maggie laughed softly as Jake ran the rest of the way. Though he'd doubted his fathering abilities, she didn't see how he could be anything but wonderful. That he so obviously cared and wanted to be good was half the battle.

She sighed heavily, then started for the house. Jake and Chris would be fine, and so would she. Maggie was glad they'd had the opportunity to talk and get everything out in the open and settled. Now she could get on with her work on the house without interruption and—as he'd said—there *was* nothing to worry about. She climbed the steps to the back door and opened it, her gaze settling on Jake's house as she frowned.

So why didn't she feel relieved instead of empty?

Chapter Six

Men, Maggie. I'm talking men." Maggie rolled her eyes, glad Pam couldn't see her through the phone line, as Pam repeated, "Aren't there any interesting *men* in Oklahoma?"

Unwanted, an image of Jake formed in Maggie's mind, a man of whom—no doubt—both Pam and Kathie would heartily approve. She dropped a towel on the kitchen counter and pushed both his image and the accompanying longing from her mind.

"What is it with you two?" she said with a chuckle. "You don't bat an eyelash about my work taking longer than I'd anticipated, but you get up in arms about my social life, of all things."

"Oh come on, Maggie. A few dinners with old people and working at a thrift shop hardly constitute a social life!"

"Pam!" Maggie protested.

"I agree with her," Kathie chimed in. "I think you've been breathing too much paint stripper and it's affected your brain. Forget wallpapering for an evening, forget painting—"

"And for heaven's sake," Pam added. "Stay away from bathroom grout!"

"I told you, I finished grouting yesterday."

"Good," Pam said. "Reward yourself by going out and having some fun! Surely Marilee what's-her-name—"

"You mean Marilyn?" Maggie asked dryly.

"Whoever, she must know some man she could fix you up with."

Maggie gasped with amused outrage. "You both are incorrigible! You're also obsessed. I'm here to work on the house. What do I need a man for?"

"If you have to ask, I think it's too late," Pam said gravely.

"Try companionship," Kathie added. "A simple night out. A little fun."

Maggie leaned against the kitchen counter and exhaled in defeat. "Okay, I get the point."

"It's a good thing," Pam said, "because we need to get back to work ourselves. Your advertising ideas have worked and we have a full house. Not only that, but we have bookings as far in advance as August!"

Maggie winced, once more feeling the pangs of guilt for not being there to help.

"Take the time you need to get the house in shape, but don't kill yourself doing it, and we'll see you whenever. In the meantime, quit feeling guilty," Kathie instructed. "Promise?"

"Promise," Maggie agreed, knowing it was something easier said than done. "Do keep writing, though, and keep me up-to-date."

"Will do, and take it easy."

"Don't forget the part about a man," Pam added.

"I won't forget. Bye now." As she hung up, Maggie found her thoughts weren't on just any man, but Jake Wilder.

She retied the ends of her shirt, knotting it firmly at her midriff. It was nine days since Jake had come over with Chris. Nine days since they'd shared anything more involved than a wave in passing or a called-out hello. Nine days since she'd last felt compelled to make comparisons between Jake and Brad.

She pushed away from the counter and stood in front of the kitchen window, relishing the May breeze. In that time it had become apparent that beyond the obvious comparisons of the situation, Jake didn't seem to have much in common with Brad. Brad had relied on *her* to develop a close relationship with his children. Jake had only asked for advice, then had taken the responsibility for its success on himself.

Brad had needed her. Jake had needed only a little affirmation. That he'd come to her for it didn't mean anything other than she'd been close at hand, therefore a logical choice. Her heart skipped a beat, a reminder that beyond their friendship was a passion that flared all too easily.

Maggie took a sip of lemonade, its tart-sweet taste as ambiguous as her feelings toward Jake. It made no sense. Like the fabled tortoise, she was the slow and steady sort where men were concerned. Yet from that first night there'd been an immediate and intimate bonding, she admitted. A bonding more powerful than if the attraction had been purely physical. His humor when facing the broken refrigerator had been endearing, his strength later that night comforting, his vulnerability when asking for advice touching. Beneath it all was a smoldering fire, ever threatening to burst through the boundaries of all her previous conventions.

He was getting to her, Maggie realized, looking down at her white-knuckled grip on the glass. The man hadn't even been around, and still he was getting to her. She set down the glass defiantly. "*Everything's* getting to me. The heat, the house..."

She strode into the living room to start masking the woodwork, her mind gladly seizing the new train of thought as she reflected on all she'd accomplished. Two of the bedrooms had been rejuvenated with paint; the bathroom shone with the warmth of restored wood, fresh grout and softly flowered wallpaper—

Her gaze fell to the coffee table covered with newspaper. The two cans of paint were there, as were the roller and tray, two paintbrushes, a clean rag...but no masking tape. Maggie closed her eyes, visualizing the moment she'd laid the tape atop one of the paint cans. Eyes open, she did a quick survey of the room.

"Dammit! I don't believe in ghosts and things that go bump in the night! I don't!" She went down on her hands and knees and began looking under furniture. Even if she did believe, it wouldn't make any sense. Why would Gran want to delay the projects they'd planned together so enthusiastically?

"Yoo-hoo, Maggie."

The knock on the screen door and Mrs. Lacey's voice brought Maggie to a standing position. She pushed her frustration aside and walked to the door. Elvira Lacey wasn't the type of widow who had given up on life. She played a mean game of tennis and looked years younger than her early seventies, thanks to the stylish coif of her silvery hair, trim figure and sparkling dark eyes. Though she was a trifle gabby, she was good-hearted and Maggie liked her.

"Don't you look fetching this evening," Maggie said, opening the door.

"It's new." The older woman did a slow twirl, showing off her gaily striped dress. A sweater was folded over her arm.

"Won't you come in?"

"No, thank you, I won't be here but a moment. I've got a date." Her gaze turned wistful as it took in Maggie's white knotted blouse and red shorts worthy of the name. "You look pretty fetching yourself."

Maggie tugged on the hem of her shorts. "I just finished redoing the woodwork in the bathroom a bit ago."

"Believe me, sweetie, if I looked like you in those clothes, I wouldn't confine it to bathrooms."

Maggie smiled as she joined Mrs. Lacey on the porch. With the setting of the sun, the warmth of the day was cooling. Glad to be outside, if only for a moment, Maggie noticed cars were parked on both sides of the street as far as she could see. Music drifted to her on a breeze and she turned to Mrs. Lacey. "What's going on?"

"It's one of the reasons I came by, but first let me thank you for taking the time yesterday to write down those instructions for the VCR. I programmed it to tape a Cary Grant movie this morning while I was at the dentist, and it worked! As to the cars, it's Rooster Day weekend."

"Oh yeah, I've seen the posters around town." Maggie leaned against the weathered white railing. "It's like a carnival, isn't it?"

"More or less. Both tonight and tomorrow Main Street will be barricaded off for several blocks and filled with rides, concessions, midway games and arts and crafts."

"No roosters?"

A green sedan pulled into Mrs. Lacey's driveway and she smiled. "Oops, gotta go. Mr. Shipley's taking me to the festivities." She started down the steps, then looked back at Maggie. "You're going to go, aren't you?"

"I don't think so. I've got so much to do and—"

"Piffle! You're only three blocks away. Surely you can spare a few minutes to at least walk up there and look around. Besides, you need to get out of the house and have some fun. You might even find something to buy. Be sure to take a sweater or jacket, though. It gets pretty chilly in the evenings."

"Thanks for the advice. You have a good time."

"We will," Mrs. Lacey said as she headed toward Mr. Shipley.

Amused, Maggie ran a hand through her bangs. Her having fun seemed to be the topic *du jour*. She paused a moment, listening to the music. It had been years since she'd had cotton candy... She opened the screen door and started back inside. Maybe she would walk up there for a few minutes tonight or tomorrow.

Then again maybe she wouldn't, she thought, eyeing the walls. They suddenly looked dingy, as if they were begging for attention. And she *had* planned on masking the woodwork and getting a first coat on them tonight before she went to bed.

With a frustrated growl, she renewed her search for the tape. After five minutes, she began muttering to herself. "This is ridiculous! Things can't disappear into thin air!" She stalked through the dining room and into the kitchen, her gaze skimming over the countertop.

"Dammit, Gran, if you can hear me and you have anything to do with this, I want you to quit—" Maggie yanked the rumpled kitchen towel from the counter to hang it up, and the roll of tape hit the floor with a thump.

She didn't move; she didn't breathe. Goose bumps rose on her skin from the chill that skittered up her spine. Hesitant, Maggie allowed her gaze to travel in a semicircle around her, half expecting to see a misty human outline. Necessity forced a slow breath, and though she saw nothing, a trace of lavender scent hung in the air.

"Gran?"

Silence roared in her ears and she took a deeper breath, only this time all she smelled was the aroma of wood stain from the rags she'd brought downstairs. She broke the silence with a nervous laugh. "I'm letting my imagination get away with me," she murmured, staring at the tape.

Imagination, however, hadn't brought the tape into the kitchen. Could she have carried it in with her when she made the call to California? She could swear she hadn't, yet there it was. "Maybe I *have* smelled too much paint stripper," she said, hanging the towel on the rack. "Or maybe I'm simply going crazy!"

Maggie bent to pick up the tape, then yelped and straightened when a bell rang. Her heart was thudding wildly when the bell rang again, and she realized it was the front door. "Get a hold of yourself, Flannagan," she grated, snatching up the tape. "Ghosts don't ring doorbells...."

Or did they? She stood still once again, thinking how the doorbell *had* rung several times lately, and how she'd had to stop what she was doing to answer it, only to find no one there. And now that she thought of it, similar episodes had happened with the phone.

Maggie strode from the kitchen, half expecting nobody to be there. Her gaze on the screen door, her steps slowed as pleasure stole over her and her lips lifted in a smile she couldn't prevent. Jake was in profile, crouched before Christopher, doing something with the boy's shoe. They wore jeans and matching windbreakers. She stopped a foot away from the door, enjoying the chance to watch them unobserved.

"There," Jake said, smoothing the strap against the Velcro catch. "How does your sock feel now?"

Chris walked in a circle. "Perfect." He came to a stop in front of the door, then looked up. "Hi, Maggie."

"Hi there." Maggie opened the door and stepped outside. "Hello, Jake," she said a little more softly.

Jake stood slowly, taking in beautiful, long, stain-spattered legs and a flat, creamy midriff. He swallowed, hard, forcing his gaze upward, past the temptation of her breasts. Blue eyes met green and time hung suspended, allowing him the simple luxury of sight.

He hadn't intended to stop by, hadn't intended on ever exchanging more than simple pleasantries with her again. Yet he'd felt irresistibly drawn here, and with each step he'd taken up the walkway, he'd wondered how he'd managed to stay away so long.

He swallowed again to diminish the dryness in his throat, then smiled. "Hi."

Her dimple twinkled into play, highlighting a smudge of brown on her cheek. More than ever he felt the need to push for something beyond a platonic relationship; more than ever he knew he must hide that need.

Chris tugged on his hand. "Hurry, Jake. Ask her."

Maggie's brows lifted in question, and every clever, convincing way he'd come up with in the past two minutes flew from Jake's mind. "Well, we were on our way to Rooster Day and thought we'd stop and see if you'd like to go with us."

She wanted to accept. He saw it in her eyes and on her lips before she looked down at the masking tape she held.

"It's very nice of you to ask, but I'd better not. I was just getting ready to paint the living room."

"The living room will be there tomorrow. Rooster Day is only once a year. You can't miss it. Why, that'd be un-American!"

"Why do they call it Rooster Day?"

"It started back in the early thirties, and I think it had something to do with auctioning off the little fellows to keep them from fertilizing the eggs. To get people to come, they turned it into an all-day event, complete with horse-shoe-pitching contests and greased-pig catching."

Maggie grimaced. "Do they still auction off roosters?"

"No, and I've never seen a greased pig around, either," he said, waggling his brows. Hearing her laughter made him realize how much he'd missed her. "So, you'll come?"

"Thanks, but I really can't."

He'd seen the regret in her eyes before she said a word. Because of it, he decided to press a bit longer. "You know what they say, all work and no play makes Maggie a drone."

"But—"

"Please hurry and say yes," Chris pleaded. "We're gonna miss it."

"No complications, Maggie," Jake said earnestly. "Just pure fun." He grinned then and added, "A little cotton candy, a few rides . . . it's the social event of the season!"

Maggie bit her lower lip, looked down at Chris, then back at Jake. No complications and pure fun. For the past hour all she'd heard was how she needed to get out of the house and have a little fun, and now opportunity had literally rung her doorbell.

She had been working hard. Maybe *too* hard, considering what had just happened in the kitchen.

"Look, I'll even help you paint tomorrow. What do you say? A night on the town and free labor. What more could a woman ask for?"

Jake held his breath as her gaze once more took a path between him and his son. The fact that she hadn't said no immediately gave him hope. She looked over her shoulder into the house, fiddling with the knot in her shirt. When she faced him, a smile was on her lips.

"Fifteen minutes to clean up and change clothes?"

"You got it."

"Come on, can't I get anyone interested?"

Maggie stood unconvinced, her hand on Christopher's shoulder, their disdain plainly written on their faces.

Jake gestured toward the garish sign. "Really now, how many chances are you going to have to see giant Russian rats, three feet long and weighing fifteen pounds?"

Maggie shivered. "Hopefully none."

"Gross," Chris said with a grimace, then his brows lifted. "Can we go on the Ferris wheel now?"

Outvoted, Jake sauntered toward them. "I thought we were going to save that for when we left."

"Oh, yeah."

"Now what?" Jake asked, picking the boy up and settling him on his hip.

Chris locked his legs around his father's waist. "The airplanes," he said, pointing toward the opposite end of the midway where a side street was filled with children's rides. "No, the motorcycles."

"Again?" Jake shook his head at Christopher's enthusiastic nod. "We've been here an hour and you've already ridden them three times." Chris's giggle had Jake sighing in defeat. He gave Maggie a resigned look before linking his free arm through hers. "Onward, through the masses."

The cool evening breeze that ruffled Maggie's bangs made her glad she'd worn her light jacket as together they forged into the sea of people. Night ruled the sky, providing the perfect backdrop for the strings of yellow, red and green lights hung along Main Street. The noise surrounding them was jubilant, each few steps bringing a new assault of buzzes and bells, barkers' cries and joyful screams, loud music, both rock and country. The air smelled of mustard, cotton candy and popcorn. It was the perfect night for no complications and pure fun, Maggie thought. And it was wonderful.

Maggie pressed closer to Jake, avoiding a woman who pushed a stroller. She was glad for the talk they'd had so many days ago and that they'd reached an understanding. With understanding came the freedom to relax.

"Are you going to eat that all by yourself and not even offer me a bite?" Jake asked.

Maggie gave him a sidelong glance as she plucked a piece of the sky-blue confection and put it into her mouth. "After all the disparaging remarks you made about blue-tongue disease?"

His shrug was apologetic. "What can I say? The color intrigues me."

Maggie plucked another piece of cotton candy and reached up to give it to him. She took pleasure in teasing him a bit with it, leading him on a few steps before allowing him to snatch it away from her with his mouth. His eyes met hers, victorious in the capture, as his tongue worked to get it all inside.

Attraction shimmered between them, disrespectful of their understanding. At times like this she almost regretted her decision. There was something between them, something special. Yet Maggie knew it was best for all concerned to leave it as it was. Friends, neighbors and nothing more.

Chris's feet nudged her arm as he leaned around his father's body, getting her attention. "So can I?"

Happy for the distraction, she asked, "Can you what, sweetheart?"

"Can I have some, too?"

"Oh, sure." Maggie gave him a piece.

Chris savored it as if he were a connoisseur and licked his fingers. "Can I have another?"

Maggie had just handed it to him as they approached the fringe of the crowd around the bandstand. As the final chords of a country and western tune sounded, applause broke out. Her gaze rose to the red-white-and-blue-decorated stage where a seven-man band took their bows. She smiled, thinking how in every letter Pam and Kathie wrote, they asked if she'd seen any cowboys. Though they weren't exactly cowboys, she had a feeling the men in Western dress would be as close as she would come to seeing any.

Still walking, Jake added a shrill whistle and a hoot of appreciation. "Burn up those strings, Billy!" he hollered, and the man at the mike waved back at him.

"Hey folks, I see in the audience one of Broken Arrow's own celebrities, Jake Wilder." Maggie heard Jake's murmured curse behind his polite smile and noticed his increased pace. "As most of you know, Jake was once in a little band of his own that made a record or two," the announcer said, tongue in cheek. "So let's give him a down-home hand and see if we can get him up here."

People were looking at the three of them now, and Jake had no choice but to stop. He shook his head, but the applause continued. "Thanks," he called out as the clapping slowed. "But as you can see I've got my hands full."

"What do you think, folks? Jake's got that store full of guitars, maybe he's forgotten how to play one."

The applause started again, this time with people yelling out encouragement for Jake to go up and prove the man wrong.

"Did you forget?" Christopher asked.

Maggie felt Jake's sigh rather than heard it. He smiled at his son. "No, I didn't forget. I thought you wanted to ride the motorcycles."

"I want to see you up there," Chris said, pointing to the stage. "Then I ride motorcycles."

Jake glanced at Maggie. "Do you mind?"

"No, not at all."

He set Chris on the ground, then crouched in front of him. "Don't run off, and don't give Maggie any trouble."

"I won't."

Jake stood and gave Maggie his jacket. "Keep this for me, will you? And pray."

"Why pray?"

His eyes closed a moment, and when they opened again, his expression had changed. There was a light in his eyes that went along with his seductive smile. "Because it's show time, darlin'." He gave her a wink and a quick kiss. "For luck," he explained, then took off for the bandstand. Halfway there, he stopped and borrowed a bandanna that a girl wore around her neck, then tied it around his own.

Show time it was, Maggie thought, as he mounted the stage. The change in his expression, she realized, was part of his stage presence. She knelt down and had Chris climb atop her shoulders so he could better see his father, then stood again. The thrill of anticipation that murmured through the crowd added to her own excitement.

For all his reticence, Jake looked at home on the stage as he took a guitar and slipped the strap over his head. After a quick conference with the other musicians, he whirled with a flourish and started off a foot-stomping, hand-clapping piece she'd never heard before. Her heart warmed, sure that the man who'd performed at Carnegie Hall was playing with no less enthusiasm now.

Music, no matter the form, was the stuff that kept Jake's blood pumping. He gave himself over to it. He ignored the pain in his hands; fingertips more accustomed to nylon strings traced the melody over the fret board of the steel-stringed guitar. His gaze moved over the crowd, then settled in one place. Pride welled inside him. In the past when he'd played, he'd done so for himself and the sheer love of the music. Tonight was different. Tonight he played for his son ... for Maggie.

By the end of the second song the crowd had nearly doubled. Jake thanked the audience and the band, then left the stage over their objections. After a stop to return the bandanna to its owner, along with a kiss on the cheek, he headed toward Maggie.

People crowded around him, patting his back and shaking his hand. He smiled and hoped he was saying the right things, for though he loved the playing, he'd never felt comfortable with the aftermath. He was grateful when the band started to play again, diverting people's attention.

"You really are good," Maggie said as he approached. "It made me wish I'd seen you in concert."

"Thanks."

"Are you gonna teach me how to play?" Chris asked, his arms outstretched.

Jake took the boy from Maggie's shoulders and held him in midair. "What about the piano? Are you ready to quit your lessons so soon?"

"No. I just want to play both of them. Like you."

He hugged the boy to his chest, knowing he couldn't have stopped grinning if he'd wanted to. He set him down, but kept hold of his hand. "Sure, I'll teach you." He glanced at Maggie and held out his other hand, smiling when she took it. "To the motorcycles, at last!"

Jake guided them out of the crowd and started down the midway when a familiar cry stopped him. "Hey, Wild-man!"

There was only one person who'd ever gotten away with calling him that. Jake searched the crowd, then spotted Mac and his family on the corner. "You son of a—" He stopped himself, remembering his son and the surroundings, then changed direction.

Maggie was confused until she saw Mac. Beside him stood a tall brunette with long, wavy hair. Her hand rested on the head of a boy a little bigger than Chris, while a smaller one tugged at her red sweatshirt.

"Where were you fifteen minutes ago?" Jake asked.

"Sitting over there eating a hot dog and watching the entertainment," Mac replied without a note of remorse. He looked at Maggie and smiled. "Hello, again. This is my wife Brenda. Brenda, you remember me mentioning Jake's neighbor, Maggie Flannagan, don't you?"

"Hi. I only met your grandmother twice, but she was a lovely woman." Brenda lifted the younger boy with a groan. "This little ton of bricks is Mitch." She deposited him in her husband's arms. "And that one—" she nodded to the boy showing Chris his pinwheel "—is Jeff."

Maggie smiled. "It's nice to meet all of you."

Jake glared at Mac. "It would've been even nicer if certain friends hadn't sat around while other friends had to go up on stage!" He looked down at his son, who was tapping him on the hand. "Why don't you and Jeff sit on the curb a minute while we talk?"

"But when are we going on the motorcycles?" Chris asked.

"In a minute." Jake turned back to his friend, continuing his complaint. "I would've come forward for *you*."

Mac laughed. "In a pig's eye."

Brenda shook her head and moved to Maggie's side. "They could quibble over this for hours. Have you been here long?"

"Oh, about an hour and a half, I guess."

"Have you been to the arts-and-crafts square yet?"

"No," Maggie replied. "Do they have any quilts?"

"They always have in the past." Brenda glanced at the men who were deep in conversation. "Look, Mac just hates it when I drag him down there and—"

"Want to go together?"

"Do you mind? I mean, I hate interrupting a date—"

"We're not on a date," Maggie said quickly. "We're just neighbors, like Mac said." She followed Brenda's gaze to the subtle, yet proprietary hold Jake had on her hand. Feeling heat rise in her cheeks, Maggie slipped from Jake's grip. "Really, we *are* just neighbors. You see, Jake and Chris were on their way here, and on the spur of the moment decided it was their duty to get me out of the house. I'm about to put my grandmother's home on the market and I've been getting it fixed up."

"Yes, so I heard." Brenda stepped between her husband and Jake, a smile on her lips. "Gentlemen, and I use the term loosely, Maggie and I are going to the arts-and-crafts square." She patted her husband's cheek. "I know you're distressed, darling, but you'll get over it." Mac looked over his wife's head and mouthed a heartfelt thank-you to Maggie.

Brenda turned her attention to Jake, her expression telling him she detected the glimmer of disappointment in his eyes. "You don't mind if I steal your *neighbor* away for thirty minutes or so, do you?"

Jake smiled politely, before settling his gaze on Maggie. "No, of course not."

Brenda gave her husband a quick peck on the cheek. "Where shall we meet you?"

"I'd say the kiddie rides would be a good choice. How about you, Jake?"

"Sounds good."

While Brenda gave last-minute kisses and admonishments to her children, Maggie's gaze was drawn to Jake. His eyes met hers in a way that wasn't neighborly at all, and her stomach turned somersaults, rivaling those achieved by any ride.

"Okay, let's go," Brenda said, breaking the spell.

"Don't let Brenda talk you into any chain saw sculptures," Jake advised.

"Chain saw sculptures? As if I would." Brenda grinned. "On second thought, Wilder, maybe we'll buy one and have it delivered . . . to your front yard!"

"Really, Maggie," Mac said. "Don't be a stranger. Come over to the house sometime."

"Thanks, I may do that."

"Hey, I've got a great idea," Brenda said, pushing aside Jeff's balloon, which kept bobbing in her face. "Next week there's a three-day weekend because of Memorial Day. You were saying that you really missed being around the ocean, Maggie. Well, we don't have an ocean, but we've got a condo on Grand Lake and we'll be going up there. Why don't you join us?''

The thought was more than a little tempting, until she thought of the work waiting to be finished. ''Thanks, but—''

''No buts.'' Brenda put her hands on her hips. ''Quite frankly, I get tired of being the only female. What do you say?'' She took a step forward, lowering her voice and making a sweeping gesture with her hand. ''Imagine being able to swim, ski or laze around in the sun. You can even fish, if you're so inclined. Warm days, cool nights...''

''It does sound wonderful.''

''It is!'' Brenda smiled. ''Besides, if you're rested, think how much faster you can work when you get back.''

''Okay. You talked me into it.''

''Great! It's set. A weekend of fun in the sun.'' She looked at Mac and Jake. ''And that means fun, you two, not a weekend of talk about business. You got it?''

Jake was going too? Maggie could have kicked herself for having agreed so quickly. Now what was she going to do?

''Yeah, Bren. We got it. Now let's head for the car. I don't know how Jake's arm is holding up, but Mitch is about to break mine.''

After the goodbyes were said, Maggie and Jake headed for home. Chris had fallen asleep and lay slumped against his father's shoulder. Her gaze downcast, Maggie walked along silently. Blown by the wind, red-and-white cola cups tumbled along the street, much like her thoughts. As much as she hated to cancel the weekend, by the time they'd left the midway and were going down a side street, that was what she'd decided to do.

''Well, did you have fun tonight?'' Jake asked, breaking the silence.

"Yes, thanks for insisting I come." She shifted the load in her arms. "I love the quilt I bought."

"What about Cuddles Malone?"

Maggie glanced down at the bear Jake had won for her. "Yeah, he's pretty cute, too. Thanks."

The hum of the machinery that gave the rides life grew louder, then receded, as they passed. It was quieter now, and the sounds of crickets emerged.

"You're upset."

She looked up at Jake. Even in the darkness of night, she could see the intensity in his gaze. "Pardon?"

"About next weekend, that Chris and I will be there."

Maggie opened her mouth to lie, then focused her gaze on the sidewalk. "I don't think it's a good idea."

"I'll be with Mac most of the time and Chris will be playing with the kids. There's nothing to worry about." The moment he'd said that, he regretted his words. He'd told her that once before, then proved himself a liar. He sighed heavily. "I'll make an excuse at the last minute and—"

"No!" She stopped abruptly. "Don't be ridiculous. If anyone's going to make up an excuse, it'll be me."

He looked down into her face, into her eyes so bright with conviction, and wanted her desperately. She would always be the kind of person who went the extra mile, the kind of person you would want on your side in a fight, the kind of woman a man could never forget.

"Don't argue with me," he said softly. "Brenda wasn't kidding when she said she was tired of being the only female. I know she's looking forward to your going."

Jake started walking again, knowing he'd given her a dilemma. She wouldn't want to disappoint Brenda, so she would have to accept his solution.

"Was tonight so bad?" he asked when she caught up with him. "I mean, I thought we did real well. No complications, just pure fun."

"Tonight was fine. Finding out you were going to the lake surprised me, that's all."

"I know, but it's settled."

She stepped in front of him again, looked away, then up at him. "No, it's not."

"Maggie—"

"Tonight was fine, and I'm sure everything will be next weekend, too. Please, don't cancel on my account, and I won't on yours. Deal?"

How could anyone resist her? he wondered. "Deal."

On their way again, Maggie felt better. She'd done the right thing, she decided. It had been silly to panic in the first place. What could happen with five other people around anyway?

Chapter Seven

I really appreciate you coming in early today." Marilyn deposited a box of children's clothes at Maggie's feet. "Especially since it's the perfect day to sleep in."

"Isn't it?" Maggie glanced longingly out the front window of the thrift shop. "I love this kind of weather." The day was beautifully gray, the rain gentle, the occasional rumble of thunder a comforting roll. When she'd gotten out of bed, she'd thought how wonderful it would have been to do nothing but sit on the window seat in her room with a good book and a cup of hot chocolate.

"How's work going on the house?"

"Slow, but sure." Maggie combined two partial stacks of shorts to make more room on the table. "I finally picked out a wallpaper for the dining room and kitchen, but there's a holdup. The kitchen paper won't be in for a couple of weeks."

"Saw you at Rooster Day," Marilyn said, sitting on the table's edge.

"Really?" Maggie pushed a pile of size-four shirts to the back. "I didn't see you." She scanned the table, searching for what else she might double up to make space.

"I know," Marilyn said cryptically, gaining Maggie's attention. The woman's smile was positively smug and her eyes sparkled with secret knowledge. "Why didn't you tell me you were seeing Jake Wilder?"

Maggie felt a flustered blush rise to her cheeks. "Because I'm not."

"It sure looked like it to me. Walking around holding hands and—"

"He's my neighbor. We're friends. Period. And we weren't holding hands." When Marilyn arched a disbelieving brow, Maggie rushed on impatiently. "Not like that, we weren't. It was crowded, and he…" Maggie shook her head and grabbed a bunch of clothes from the box. "His son was with us," she declared haughtily, as if that should dispel all misconceptions.

"I saw." Marilyn folded her hands loosely. "It looked," she said, her voice deepening, "very domestic."

"It wasn't!" Maggie dropped the clothes on the table. "He and Chris stopped by my house on their way there. I haven't been getting out much, and he thought I should take the chance to soak up a little local color. Really." She pushed up the sleeves of her pink sweatshirt, wondering if she should take out an ad in the *Broken Arrow Ledger* to that effect!

"Okay." Marilyn moved to the counter and opened the cash register to prepare for the day's business. "But if you ever want to talk about it, I'm all ears."

Maggie bit her tongue. "There's nothing to talk about," she said evenly.

There wasn't, Maggie assured herself, straightening the mess she'd made. What was, or rather what might have been between her and Jake, was settled. Of course she had wondered if there might be a difficult moment when he'd insisted on walking her to the door. But there hadn't been. He'd acted like a good friend and nothing more, which was the same behavior he exhibited the next day.

Smiling at the memory, she started arranging clothing into neat piles. She'd told him he didn't really have to help her paint the room. He'd shown up anyway, after taking Chris over to Mac and Brenda's to play. They'd talked a little, sung along to the radio, laughed a lot and painted. Though she'd missed him when he left, it was simply because she'd enjoyed the camaraderie of someone helping her. Why, she would've missed anybody—

Maggie bumped into the box and groaned, seeing there was clothing yet to be displayed. She counted to ten and began once more to condense stacks.

The morning moved quickly after that. Customers, as always, seemed to come in groups. There were times she and Marilyn wished for at least two extra volunteers. Other times, there hardly seemed a need for the door to be open. Maggie yawned, praying the day would stay true to form and provide a lull.

"I'm going in back to get a soda. Want me to bring you one?" Maggie asked.

Marilyn looked around from the aisle she was crouched behind. "I'd love one."

No sooner had Maggie stooped to open the cooler than she heard the buzzer on the front door. "Darn!" She stuck her hand into the ice and retrieved two cans.

"Maggie, someone's here to see you," Marilyn called.

"Be right out." Maggie opened a can, took a quick sip, then stood, realizing it was probably Mrs. O'Dell coming by to pick up the pair of cowboy boots for her son. Shoving the drinks on a shelf, she rounded the corner before coming to an abrupt halt.

Jake stood at the front of the store, looking indecently handsome in a pair of slacks, a pale plaid shirt and the ever-present suspenders. Maggie justified the small sigh that escaped her as typical feminine appreciation. Marilyn certainly looked no less affected as she stood there, gazing up at him while they talked as if she weren't happily married and had two kids.

His timing couldn't have been worse, Maggie thought. Why did he have to pick today of all days to come to the store? Marilyn would never believe her now.

Maggie fluffed her bangs, then walked forward, doing her best to look casual. No mean feat, considering the smile he gave her when he saw her approach, the appealing way raindrops glistened in his hair like stars on a dark night, the way her body warmed as if someone had just turned up the heat.

"Drop them off anytime," Marilyn said, regaining his attention. "Good men's shoes are really hard to come by."

He nodded. "I'll try to remember to bring them tomorrow."

"If not, you can always give them to Maggie and she can bring them next Wednesday." Marilyn moved down the side aisle to a rack of ties a child had knotted together. "It was nice talking to you."

"Same here, and tell Dan I said hello."

Maggie stopped in front of a display table and leaned back against it, slipping her fingertips into her pockets. "Better not stick around too long, Jake, or Marilyn will have you working here." This time when he smiled, she wasn't off guard. The change in her pulse was minimal.

He brushed a hand over his damp hair. "Did I catch you at a bad time?"

"No, not at all," she said lightly, very much aware that Marilyn could hear every word spoken. "What's up?"

"Mac bought a sandbox to take up to the lake for the kids, and it's going to make the van a little crowded. He was wondering if you'd mind riding with me."

"Oh. Well, sure." Maggie sincerely wished a hole would open up beneath her so she could drop out of sight and be spared Marilyn's questions when he left. "Whatever."

"That's not all. I've got a delivery to make in Pryor on Friday and—"

"Pryor?"

"A town that's on the way to the lake," he said, dipping his hands into his pockets. "Will it pose a problem for you to leave, say at three, instead of five-thirty?"

Maggie shrugged. "No, three's okay."

"Great. I'll see you then."

She nodded. "Fine."

Instead of heading for the door, he moved toward her, his eyes dark and intense. Maggie froze. He was going to kiss her, she thought wildly. Right here, right now, in front of God and Marilyn, he was going to kiss her... and she couldn't even move!

Locked in his gaze, she felt herself tremble as he lowered his head. Involuntarily, her eyes closed and her lips parted, waiting for the inevitable. She felt the brush of his fingertips against her cheek. Once. Twice...

"Dust," he said quietly, and she opened her eyes. "You had a smudge of dust on your cheek." He straightened and slipped his hand back into his pocket.

Giddiness tinged with disappointment flooded through her. "Dust?" she asked loudly, afraid he'd spoken so softly that Marilyn hadn't heard. "You say I had *dust* on my cheek and you were only wiping it off?"

He gave her an odd frown. "Yeah."

"Well, thank you, Jake."

"Uh-huh." He looked around her. "Bye, Marilyn."

"So long."

"And I'll see you on Friday," he said, glancing back at Maggie.

"At three." She wiggled her fingers in a wave as he left the store, then headed quickly to the back to retrieve their sodas and prepare for the inquisition. A roll of thunder sounded and the lights flickered. Not wanting to be caught in the storeroom if the electricity failed, she grabbed the two drinks quickly and turned, then almost dropped them. Marilyn was right behind her, wearing a so-you're-just-friends? smile.

Maggie took a deep breath to calm her startled heart and thrust the soda at her friend. "I don't want to hear it!"

"I didn't say a word," Marilyn said innocently, then sighed as she pulled back the tab on the can. "There's nothing like a quiet, mysterious, remote man to get a woman intrigued, is there?" She eyed Maggie while taking a sip.

Jake, quiet? Sometimes. Mysterious? Yes, he was private. But remote? Remote sounded too cold and unfeeling, and if there was one thing Maggie knew about Jake, he was neither. She took a drink, deciding to ignore the obvious baiting and subtly redirect the conversation. "I didn't know you knew him, Marilyn."

"I don't, really. Bea brought him to a fund-raiser once." She shook her head. "He's a hard one to figure. I mean, he's certainly generated more than a fair share of interest in the female population around here, yet he hasn't gone out much."

"How would you know?"

"It's one of the advantages or disadvantages of living in a small town, my dear. People notice things, like he's never been seen with the same woman more than twice. There's something else, too, that I've noticed," she added confidentially, leaning forward.

Maggie couldn't help but be hooked. "What?"

"Besides his looks and mystique, he's a very nice man." Marilyn stood straight and gave Maggie an honest smile. "So why haven't you taken him up on the interest he's showing?"

Maggie paced the back room, the frustration of the past few weeks prodding her steps. She needed to talk about it with someone. She'd even tried to call her sister Kelly a couple of times, but kept getting the answering machine, which she refused to talk to. And Colleen naturally had picked this time to be in Europe.

"Surely you can see the timing's not right," Maggie said finally.

Her friend chuckled. "Men are only supposed to come along at right times?"

"It would help." She stopped and raked a shaky hand through her bangs. "Oh hell, Marilyn. Neither of us want to get involved. We even had a conversation about it. You should've heard us. I was pointing out the reasons he shouldn't, and he was pointing out reasons I shouldn't. So we agreed not to pursue it, and not to see each other."

"You went with him to Rooster Day."

"As neighbors, that's all. It was a spontaneous gesture, and an innocent evening."

"And the lake?"

Maggie started pacing again. "I'm not really going with *him*. Do you know Brenda McKinley?"

"I know of her."

"Well, I met her at Rooster Day, and she and her family spent most of the evening with us. I'd talked about California and the ocean, and before we went home she invited me up to the lake with them for the holiday weekend." Maggie stopped and plucked at her braid. "I didn't even know he'd be going until after I'd accepted." She cursed under her breath and stuck her hands into her back pockets. "On the walk home we discussed me not going and him not going, then I decided we were being silly. So now we're both going, but I don't know... Normally I'm not an ambiguous person, but this has me going in circles."

Marilyn walked over to her and placed her hands calmly on Maggie's shoulders. "It seems to me that you need to ask yourself a question. Do you enjoy being around him? If the answer is yes, then enjoy. Relax. Don't make it more complicated than it has to be. It's kind of a matter of perspective. He's nice, you're nice. Can't it just be two nice people enjoying each other's company?"

The buzzer sounded and Marilyn smiled, giving Maggie's shoulders a squeeze. "Finish your drink and...lighten up." She headed for the doorway. "I'll take care of whoever's out front."

Lighten up, Maggie mused. Hadn't she told herself that same thing before coming to Oklahoma, and about men in particular? She finished off the soda and dropped the can into the trash, thinking of the upcoming weekend. Chances were that once they got there and were joined by the McKinleys, they wouldn't even be around each other all that much, as Jake had said. And when they were, two nice people enjoying each other's company didn't sound all that complicating.

Maggie was still holding on to her new perspective two days later when Jake came to pick her up. Chris had spent the night with the McKinleys and would be traveling with them. Though it had given her a moment's discomfort, even that hadn't been necessary. They made a stop in Pryor for Jake to deliver the guitar, then picked up hamburgers and fries and ate them in transit. Throughout the drive, whether they were talking or silent, the rapport between them was relaxed.

From the time they crossed the first bridge spanning a part of the lake, Maggie's anticipation grew. She hadn't been exaggerating to Brenda when she'd said how much she missed being around the water. Once they were in the condominium and Jake was opening the drapes, her eagerness could hardly be contained.

"Oh, Jake, it's lovely." She opened the sliding glass door and walked onto a balcony that ran across the back of the home. "What a view!"

Maggie moved to the railing, her restless gaze going from the trees that seemed to be everywhere to the bottom of the hill where dock slips held both motor and sailboats. Sun danced on the blue water that reached far and wide in all directions. Trees were scattered along the opposite shoreline and up the hills, dense, green and beautiful. She breathed the fresh, lake-scented air and allowed the serenity she felt around water to fill her.

Jake drew up beside her. "It's not the Pacific."

Maggie closed her eyes and for a moment could see her ocean in all its magnificence and grandeur. She felt a twinge of homesickness, then opened her eyes and found contentment. "No, it's not the Pacific, but it's beautiful, nonetheless. Too beautiful to enjoy from a distance." She glanced up at him. "What do you say we go down to the dock for a bit and walk around?"

He turned his back to the view and leaned against the railing, hooking his thumbs in the belt loops of his shorts. "Well, we do need to unpack and open the rest of the house."

"Oh come on, we can do that in a bit." Impatient, Maggie grabbed one of his hands with both of hers and gave it a tug.

Jake stifled a smile, watching her trying to budge him. Her white shorts and red shirt somehow emphasized how small she really was. Still, he hesitated, not because he was against going down to the dock, but because he enjoyed being coerced. Her hands were delicate but strong, and held within them the power to make him do anything. Looking at his reflection in her eyes, he was amazed she couldn't see it.

He glanced at the house. "I don't know. We need to get it done before Mac and—"

"Ja-ake," she drawled. She was tugging harder now, her brows lowered and her lips pursed. Sunlight dappled onto her cheeks through the leaves overhead as her dimple played a game of hide-and-seek. "You yourself said not ten minutes ago that they'd just be leaving around now. We've got plenty of time."

"All right," he said slowly, letting her pull him away from the railing. They were standing close, so close that their bodies almost touched, and it took every bit of his willpower to keep from lowering his mouth to hers and tasting again that which he wanted. He angled away from her and headed for the stairway leading to the ground floor, casually keeping hold of one of her hands. "I don't want you pouting all evening."

"I don't pout. I may be quiet on occasion, reflective, perhaps, but I don't pout."

At the bottom of the stairs, Maggie stopped. "I didn't realize it was a trilevel."

"Yeah, you enter on the second level where the kitchen, dining room and living area are. Then upstairs—" he took a few more steps away from the house and pointed "—are the bedrooms."

She shaded her eyes with a hand and saw the top level had a balcony as well. "That's really lovely," she said, lowering her gaze. "So is this level for storage?"

"No, it's a game room, and there's a laundry room hidden behind a set of double doors."

"What a setup." They started down a curving set of railroad-tie stairs. "Do they come here a lot?"

"As much as possible. Sometimes Brenda will pack up the boys and come here during the week."

"What I would've given for a place like this when I was a kid." She tilted her head up at him, her smile tripping longings inside of him that he had no right to experience. "When I was little I was sure at one point that I had once been a dolphin."

"You believed in reincarnation?" he asked with amazement.

"Back then it seemed logical." She turned her gaze to the lake. "I've always loved water, felt drawn to it. I hated wading pools when I was small. I wanted to be in the big people's pool where I could lose myself in the depths." She paused on the landing and gave him a dry look. "Having to come up for air was a very frustrating limitation."

He laughed, easily able to imagine her then, recalling a picture Bea had of her when she'd been a little bigger than Chris. She'd been standing next to a pool, wet hair plastered to her head, her tummy childishly round, and on her face a front-toothless smile that showed the love of water she spoke of.

Jake led her onto the bobbing dock and they headed for the boat slips. "Do you snorkel or scuba dive?"

"No, just ski."

"There's Mac's," he said, pointing to a sleek, metallic-blue power boat. "Perhaps if you ask nicely, he'll take you skiing."

"I'm in no hurry," she murmured. "I've always wanted to do some diving, though. Unfortunately I was eighteen and ready to start college when we moved to Los Angeles, after my dad retired from the Air Force. When I wasn't studying, I was working, and there was no time for any little side trips. Oh," she said, passing a large, camel and dark brown sailboat. "I wouldn't mind having that."

"Have you done much sailing?"

"No, only twice. I enjoyed it, though."

As they came to the end of the dock, Maggie's imagination took flight as Jake stood looking out over the water, both hands clasped behind his back. With his dark good looks and the wind ruffling his hair, she pictured him as a pirate. Maggie mentally traded the white polo shirt for one with billowing sleeves that was open to the waist, then traded the navy shorts for a pair of tight black pants and a red cummerbund. He would have a saber, of course. She, of course, would be dressed appropriately in a low-cut gown and have a lot more up top than she had now. He would be captivated by her instantly and sweep her off her feet, taking her away on his ship—

Dark blue eyes locked with hers. "Ready to go?"

Maggie sighed dreamily, then realized Jake was back in the twentieth century. She covered her mouth to keep him from seeing her smile as she realized whichever century he was in, he had gorgeous legs and a marvelous backside. Be still, my beating heart, she thought. New perspective or not, she would be blind not to notice.

"Let's get our feet wet," she said. She undid her sandals and sat down, dangling her feet over the side of the dock and barely skimming the top of the chilled water. "What about you?" she asked as he sat beside her. "I loved to swim as a kid. What did you like?"

"Music."

"No, I mean . . ." She paused to watch a soaring hawk, then looked back at Jake. "I mean when you were little."

"Music." His laugh was as warm as the sun as he leaned back, his hands behind him. "One of my first memories is sitting in the playroom, coloring to music. I started piano lessons when I was three."

Maggie didn't bother to mask her astonishment. "You're kidding."

"Nope."

She turned toward him, bringing one foot out of the water. "You didn't whine about having to practice instead of getting to play with kids?"

"There weren't any. I was an only child."

"But surely there were kids in the neighborhood."

His smile was easy. "We lived on an estate."

She leaned forward, her eyes wide. "As in gates and stables and all that?"

"Uh-huh. Pools, too, inside and out, and of course the obligatory tennis court."

Maggie's mind boggled. "Then you must know how to ride and everything!"

"Everything," he said with a groan. "Each day of the week, except Sundays, someone was coming out to teach me something. My parents thought it was important that I be accomplished in all areas . . . as befitted a child of my station," he drawled snobbishly.

Maggie grinned, relieved he'd turned out the way he had despite his privileged upbringing. "I knew an only child once. They didn't live on an estate, but her house was much bigger than ours, and she didn't have to share her things," she said wistfully. "Not that I didn't love my sisters, mind you, but I was a bit in awe of them. Even as children they were talented and beautiful. Whenever we put on a neighborhood show, Colleen would dance because she took ballet, and Kelly would double as a singer and the emcee."

He lifted his hand and caught her chin on his fingertips. "What about you? What did Maggie do?" He looked at her with such interest, all she could think of was where had he been when she'd felt so painfully plain back then.

"What do you think?" she said, rolling her eyes. "I was the organizer. Colleen called me the director to make me feel important, but I was also the one who took admissions, and hammered all the little posters onto trees for publicity."

"Then I doubt I would ever have seen the show. I would've been too busy hanging around the ticket taker." He touched her nose before putting his hand back on the dock. "Were they big money-makers?"

"Hardly. We did it as a way to meet kids. With Dad being in the service, we moved a lot. Putting on a show was a great icebreaker. We'd con other kids into joining us, and get to know them in the process." She sighed, remembering how hard the moves had been, and not always fun.

"I'll tell you a secret," she whispered. Jake moved closer, his brows lifting. "I used to wish I could be an only child, have anything I wanted, and live in a big house...the same one without ever having to move."

"Believe me, Maggie, it's not necessarily what it's cracked up to be." She saw the sadness in his smile. "Since you told me a secret, I'll tell you one." He sat up straight, planting his hands on the edge of the dock and looking out over the water. "When I was young, my fantasy was to live in a regular house and have friends over whenever I wanted."

"Didn't you ever bring friends home from school?"

"I was born to my parents late in life. They didn't know what to do with me, much less an extra kid. Besides, it wasn't really feasible. From the time I was in first grade, I attended boarding schools. I only came home for Christmas, Easter and part of the summer."

Maggie was horrified. She'd heard the expression "poor little rich kid," but had never really stopped to think what it meant. Scars. How many did he have? How deep did they run? Suddenly she began to have a real understanding of why he'd chosen to live where he did. Still, she had trouble imagining the man she saw now existing within such a sterile, structured life.

"Did you ever rebel against anything?"

He glanced over at her, then shrugged. "Once."

"What'd you do?" she asked, pulling her other foot from the water to sit cross-legged.

"It was after high school graduation. My father had my life all planned. I was to go to Harvard, get a law degree, then join his firm. In time, he said, I would take it over. I told him, 'no thank you,' and brought up the subject of going to Juilliard to carry on with my music. He made it very plain that there was no alternative offered. Then he laughed and said, unless I wanted to join the service, as he had."

"Then what?"

"I left during the middle of the night, taking nothing but the clothes on my back. I told Sheffield—"

Maggie shook her head, puzzled. "Sheffield?"

"The chauffeur," he explained wryly. "I told him that a friend of mine had been in an accident and that I was too upset to drive. That got me into town. I stayed in a hospital waiting room that night, thinking. I'd refused to take any money, and I had no place to go...." He laughed, then grimaced. "This is getting very Charles Dickens-like, isn't it?"

Maggie hit his shoulder. "No, it's not! It's very interesting, and if you don't finish I'll push you in the lake."

Jake set his focus on the opposite shoreline. "Perhaps it was the way my father had laughed that set my mind on the service. It certainly wasn't the popular thing to do, nor had he really wanted me to, which is probably why I did it. The next day I enlisted, with plans to save my money to go to Juilliard when I got out. Life in the service wasn't really all that different from the prep school I'd been at...except for basic training."

Maggie brought her knees up and wrapped her arms around her legs. "What did your parents say when they found out?"

"I have no idea. I'd left them a note, of course, and I sent them a Christmas card the first year. Not getting a reply, I never tried to get in touch again. However, when I got married several years later, it made the paper, and I got a call from them. Thanks to Claire, we got together and sort of agreed to disagree on things, which was quite a compromise if you'd known my parents. We saw them a few times after that, and of course, when Chris was born. They were killed in a wreck a few weeks later, so I was always glad we'd gotten back together—more or less."

When Jake pulled his feet out of the water, Maggie handed him his shoes. "Did you ever make it to Juilliard?"

"No. I met Mac while we were in an Army stage band. Our terms were up within a month of each other, so he waited around for me and we struck out for California."

Jake stood, somewhat stunned by the realization of all he'd told her. Never, not to Claire or even Bea, had he revealed so much. He helped Maggie to her feet, knowing she'd slipped past a lifetime's worth of reserve and guarded privacy. What he found even stranger was that he didn't feel odd about it.

"Enough ancient history," he said, when she'd slipped on her sandals. "It's time to be good little campers and do our chores."

She clasped her hands together and raised soulful eyes to his. "Gee, Ranger Bob, after we get them done, do we get to come back outside?"

He grabbed her hand before thinking better of it, and started up the dock. "Maybe."

"So," she said casually, "how're things going with your son?"

His son, he thought with pleasure. "Pretty well, actually. Mrs. Stephenson down the street keeps him during the day. She has two kids of her own and keeps three other children, too, so Christopher has made plenty of friends. He still misses Claire and Evan, and his little sister, Audrey, of course, but the videos we've been exchanging really help, and he loves hamming it up for the camera. Plus Claire calls each weekend, and we call every Wednesday."

"Sounds like it's going well."

Jake realized how it might easily have turned out differently. "You know, I had my doubts in the beginning about whether Claire and I had made a mistake. But I did as you said, kept putting myself in his place, and surprisingly, I kind of figured how to handle some of the roughest moments. He's figuring me out, too." He laughed and pushed his hand through his hair. "You know, children really are smart. I came home one night last week in a really bad mood, but I was trying to hide it, and thought I had. Then he came in the kitchen when I was fixing dinner and gave me Babbit and a big hug, telling me everything would be better, real soon."

"He's a sweet boy, Jake," she said, resting her head against his arm as they walked.

Desire shot through him, making him long to pull her against him and forget everything for the moment but the two of them. He acknowledged the feeling, then controlled it, very much aware it was better to have at least this small part of her than nothing at all.

"Thanks, Maggie."

"For what?"

"For being there when I was on the brink of total panic the day I brought Chris home. It helped."

Maggie lifted her head. "I only told you what anyone would have."

"It wasn't just what you said. It was the way you looked at me, with absolute faith, and said you knew I'd do just fine." His grip tightened on her hand and his eyes were darkly serious. "It meant a lot to me."

"In that case, you're welcome. Just don't sell yourself short. You've done all the work." As they stepped up onto the landing, Maggie knew she wanted to share with him the way he had with her. She stopped. "You've helped me, too."

"I have?"

"Uh-huh." She grinned. "Now don't get the wrong idea and think that I go around dwelling on the past, because I don't. But you know how something can start you thinking and pretty soon you're wondering where you went wrong? Well, the few times I've started wondering if I'd done this or that differently, maybe Brad wouldn't have been so eager to get rid of me, I've stopped myself. Know why? Because I'd remember the way you said, 'The man was a jackass, Maggie,'" she said, imitating his deep voice. "And I'd think, yeah, he really was, and then I'd laugh."

She loved the way his eyes sparkled when he smiled. "He was, you know."

Maggie nodded in agreement, then reached up and caressed his face with her hand, wanting him to understand how much he truly *had* helped. "At a time in my life when I didn't feel special, you made me feel that I was."

He covered her hand with his own, holding it in place. "You are," he said softly.

All that was forbidden filled the air between them. Yet Maggie stood there, savoring the moment, wishing it could be different while knowing it couldn't. On an inward sigh, she withdrew her hand, then flashed him a grin. "Well, enough of this mutual admiration society, Ranger Bob. We've got work to do." She ducked around him and started running up the stairs. "Last one there's a rotten egg."

"You cheat!" he called, running after her.

"I know. I like to win!"

Maggie happily busied herself with unpacking the groceries while Jake unloaded the car. Searching for a place to put the cocoa, she opened a cabinet as the phone rang. "Hello," she said, cradling the receiver between her ear and shoulder.

"We've got a problem."

The familiar voice triggered a wave of uneasiness. "Brenda?" she asked, setting the can on the counter.

"Yeah, it's me, and we're home and we're going to stay home. Mitch woke up from his nap dotted with chicken pox."

"Oh no! How's he feeling?"

"Miserable and itchy."

Maggie twisted the phone cord around her finger. "Poor thing. Well, we'll get right back and—"

"No, please, feel free to stay. I know how much you were looking forward to being there, and Jake so rarely takes any time off, and he really needs to. Besides, Chris says he's had chicken pox already and he's being an absolute godsend as far as keeping Jeff happy and occupied."

Stunned, Maggie didn't know what to say. "Well..."

Jake came in the door, carrying the suitcases. Seeing her expression, he set them down and whispered, "Who is it?"

"Wait just a second. Jake walked in." Maggie covered the mouthpiece. "It's Brenda. There's been a slight hitch in the plans." She handed him the receiver, then walked into the living room.

Jake listened to Brenda but studied Maggie. She stood in front of the sliding glass door, arms wrapped around her waist, bouncing slightly on her heels. He'd seen her like this once before. He hadn't known what to say to her then, and he sure as hell didn't know what to say now.

"So?" Brenda asked. "Are you going to stay?"

"What did Maggie think?"

"I don't know. You walked in and she handed you the phone. If you ask my opinion, you both need to stay and relax. You work too hard, and she apparently has been equally as bad where her grandmother's house is concerned."

"Hold on a minute." Jake put the phone down and walked into the living room. "Well, Maggie, what do you think?"

The bouncing stopped and she turned to face him. "I'm game if you are."

Jake saw the worry in her eyes, but remembered her enthusiasm when they'd pulled up—the way she'd run outside, the way she'd been so happy to finally be here. "Then I'll go tell Brenda we're staying?"

"Great."

In the moment before he turned, Jake vowed to himself that he wouldn't touch her. So help him God, he swore he wouldn't!

Chapter Eight

He couldn't keep his eyes off of her.

Jake forced his gaze back to the fragmented pieces of teddy bears scattered on the card table before him. Maggie had been delighted when she found the jigsaw puzzle in the closet, and he'd thought it would be the perfect diversion to keep his mind off the fact that they were alone. After all, whenever he'd worked a puzzle at Bea's, not only had he forgotten all else, but time had flown. Tonight, however, time was taking a leisurely stroll.

He glanced up at Maggie. Her eyes still roving over the puzzle pieces, she picked up a chocolate marshmallow cookie and took a bite. An errant piece of chocolate lingered on her lower lip. Jake watched in growing fascination as the tip of her pink tongue sneaked out and retrieved the sweet sliver. The innocence of her action made it no less provocative, and for the umpteenth time, Jake shifted in his chair and redirected his gaze.

Stroll, hell! Time moved at a protracted crawl, each slow, torturous second fashioned as a test of his vow.

"All right!" She fit another piece along the outside. "Now, all we have to do is find the last two pieces and we'll have this baby framed and can start on the inside!" She walked around to the side of the table and, leaning over, scanned the parts. Jake's gaze traveled up the appealing line of her bare legs to the curve of her bottom. Muscles in his stomach tightened in response.

"I hate this," she muttered. "I'm always afraid that somehow the pieces I'm looking for have been lost and I'll go crazy trying to find them." She cocked her head toward him. "How about you?"

The last word still hovered on her lips, forming an evocative pout. Mere inches separated them, and with the slightest movement forward, he could—

"You fink!" she said. Startled, Jake jerked his gaze from her lips to her eyes as she stood straight and put her hands on her hips. "You've been holding out on me!"

"I have?"

Her eyes narrowed. "Why didn't you warn me that you were a . . . a piece hoarder?" She gestured to his hand.

"You want these?" he asked, lifting his palm.

"No." She gave him a long-suffering look, then bent over the table again. "*You* have them," she said, sounding like a much put-upon martyr. "*You* put them in." She scowled dramatically. "Just be quick about it!"

"Yes, ma'am." Jake surveyed the frame and found a hole, a grin plastering his lips as he started to fill it.

"Not that one, you goose!" She exhaled pointedly, gripping his wrist and trying to take his pieces away from him. Jake closed his hand. "Open it, Wilder," she warned.

"No. I gave you your chance and you didn't take it. It's mine and I want to . . . savor it." Their tug-of-war brought Maggie around to his side of the table.

"They aren't chocolate, for pity's sake, they're damn puzzle pieces . . . and you're supposed to play them!"

God, but he was crazy about her. Her eyes fairly gleamed with the heat of battle and her cheeks grew pink with the struggle. She was strong, he discovered. Much stronger than he would have thought. He pulled in earnest, drawing her close to his chair.

She turned her back to him, tucking his hand against her waist. "Give it up, Wilder. You're a beaten man," she said, succeeding in prying one of his fingers open.

"I am, am I?"

"Yes, you am, am you."

Maggie yelped when he pulled her off balance. She fell across his lap, momentum carrying her backward. Jake caught her with his free arm a moment before she would have bent back far enough to hit the floor. Maggie clutched at his hand, trying hard to pull herself up. She was at a distinct disadvantage, and he couldn't keep the triumph from his lips as he bent over her. "You were saying?"

He wouldn't have guessed haughtiness was an expression she could pull off, given her position. She raised a single brow eloquently. "Gloating isn't considered polite, you know."

"Politeness has never been one of my virtues."

He found her snarl amusing as she tried again to pull up, then stopped abruptly. Awareness sprang between them. His hand that she'd held at her waist had shifted with the tumble, and was now held in place over her heart, cushioned by her breast. Demand tightened the back of his neck and heated his blood. He didn't move, didn't utter a sound. He wanted to open his hand, feel the softness beneath it. He wanted to discover for himself if her skin burned as hotly as his own. He wanted...he wanted everything he'd vowed against.

Realizing how close he was to violating that vow, Jake carefully slipped his hand from her grasp and raised her to a sitting position. He opened his fingers, displaying the bits of puzzle. He even managed a smile. "I may not be polite, but I do share. Pick one."

Maggie stared, not at the puzzle pieces, but at the hand that held them. His palm was large, his fingers exquisitely long. Heaven help her, but for that moment when they'd both realized how compromising her position was, she'd longed to feel his hand claim her. Even now her skin burned with the promise.

"Thanks," she said a little too brightly, then stood. Not chancing a look at him, she plucked the piece from his hand, put it in place and returned to her chair. As she watched him belatedly complete the frame, she was struck by irony. Despite the fact that he could make her pulse race with a mere look, despite the fact that her desire for him simmered barely under the surface, she was comfortable being in his company. It made no sense; it was simply true.

When he sat back in his chair, Maggie focused on the puzzle. "Well now, we can really get started."

"Not me, I'm afraid. Not tonight." Jake made a big production of yawning and stretching as he stood, and looked at his watch. It was early yet, only ten. But he knew his limitations; tonight he'd all but exceeded them. "There's something about being here that makes me sleepy."

"Me, too. I think I'll join you." To her chagrin, it wasn't until Jake did a mild double take that she realized what she'd said. "I mean, I think I'll go to bed, too...in my bed."

Not wanting a repeat of such idiocy, Maggie kept silent as they turned off the lights and locked up. She followed him upstairs, her gaze anywhere but on him.

Jake stopped at the end of the hall. "Are you sure you wouldn't rather sleep in Mac and Brenda's room?"

"That makes no sense. As tall as you are, you need the king-size bed. Your feet would hang over that one," she said, motioning to the room she was using.

When he didn't move, she had no choice but to look up at him. Why couldn't he have cool blue eyes instead of a shade so dark, so disturbing that she felt as if she could melt?

He shrugged. "I guess this is good-night. Remember, you're here to relax, so sleep late if you like."

"Yeah, I will. Sleep easy."

It was midnight when Jake stood in the glow of the bedside lamp, scowling at the clock. He'd tried to sleep, but couldn't. He'd taken a cold shower to quell his desire, then a hot one to relax his muscles. Neither had worked.

"Sleep easy," he muttered, looking at the rumpled bed. "Ha!" At the rate he was going he would be surprised if he got any sleep at all!

Jake tightened the towel around his hips and stalked out to the balcony. Cool air closed his pores with a tingling sensation; the night smelled of earth and the coming rain. Lightning flashed in the distance, thunder grumbled, leaves whispered on the trees. It wouldn't be long, he thought, before the storm was upon them.

Was the barometric pressure responsible for the edginess that plagued him? He paced the length of the deck, his feet slapping against the wood. Passing Maggie's door, he knew his edginess had nothing to do with the weather.

He wanted her. He strode to the railing and gazed out at the dark water. Maggie was more than just a body to caress, a mouth to kiss, a woman to fulfill a physical need. He wanted to know what she thought, what she felt. He wanted to wake up beside her in the mornings and snuggle with her at night. He wanted her smiles, her touches, her laughter...even her tears so he could be there to dry them. He wanted—

It didn't matter what he wanted, he reminded himself sharply. Maggie was off limits. Not only would she be leaving soon, the last thing she needed now was an involvement with another man.

Lightning blazed across the sky, and Jake took his fill of the night air. Perhaps with the breaking of the storm and the dawn of tomorrow he would acquire not only the strength to face her again, but the strength to honor his vow.

The quiet shoosh of a sliding glass door as it opened had him gripping the rail. Tomorrow had come too soon.

She shouldn't have come to bed. She should have stayed in the living room and worked on the puzzle. No, she should have insisted they leave when she'd found out the McKinleys weren't coming. Best yet, she never should have accepted Brenda's invitation!

Maggie rolled to her back, uttering a curse. Marilyn had been wrong, and so had she. There could be no such thing as two nice people simply enjoying each other's company. At least, not with her, not with Jake. They were learning too much about each other. And that incident around the puzzle... Her body heated with longing and she flopped on her stomach, covering her head with the pillow.

The whole thing was dangerous. Damn dangerous. Come tomorrow, she would fabricate an excuse to leave. It wouldn't matter that he would probably see right through it. He understood, didn't he? They'd talked about no complications, then resolved them by eliminating the source. Their only mistake had been to stretch the boundaries again. Tomorrow they would go back to the old way, and the problem would once again be solved.

Maggie tossed the pillow aside and rolled on her back, then reached beneath the sheet and straightened her white, silk nightgown. Expensive nightwear had always been her weakness. After a long day, the small luxury always made her feel better. Tonight, however, she didn't think an entire closetful would help.

The sound of thunder brought a smile to her face and enticed her from bed. Her first memories of a spectacular storm dated back to a visit at Gran's. She donned the robe matching her gown and headed quickly for the sliding glass door. Opening the drapes, she stopped at the sight of Jake.

For the first time Maggie allowed herself to admit she'd dreamed of him. Not once, not twice, but several times. She'd hoped by denying it that the dreams would stop. They hadn't. And now, stripped but for a towel and looking at one with the night, he stood there...alone. From what she'd learned today, she realized he'd already spent too much of his life like that. She sighed deeply, no longer able to deny what she felt.

She loved him. It was as simple and complex as that. There were no violins playing in the background, not even a full moon to set the mood. In fact, from the beginning there'd been everything against her feeling like this. Maggie rested her head against the doorjamb. Perhaps the song was right. Perhaps there *was* more room in a broken heart. For as surely as Brad had split it in two, Jake had filled it beyond its previous capacity.

"So what are you going to do about it, Flannagan?" she murmured. Wisdom reminded her of the circumstances—

he wasn't one to make a commitment; she was leaving; he had a child waiting at home.

A flash of lightning illuminated his solitary figure. There was so much more to him than a handsome face and raw sexuality. She thought of the tenderness he'd showed her, the understanding, the support, and suddenly knew that none of the circumstances mattered. That for now, until she left, she wanted the chance not only to be made love to, but the opportunity to give her love to him.

Maggie opened the door without hesitation, then closed it behind her. Oddly, though her heart beat a mile a minute, she didn't feel nervous. Wind whipped at her unbound hair and tugged at her gown and robe, still her steps remained steady. She'd made her decision, the rest was up to him.

"I've always been fascinated by lightning and thunder. They have such power and primal energy. I appreciate and enjoy good weather, but storms ... they're magnificent."

If it had been possible for a person to petrify like a tree, Jake was sure he would have. From the moment she opened the door he felt it imperative not to move, not to look at her, and if it were possible not to breathe, he wouldn't have done that, either. But he had, and because of it, he took in her seductive scent. Something white caught his eye, increasing his discomfort ... she wasn't wearing what she had been earlier. She leaned against the rail, and like the melody that had haunted the edge of his mind, so did her image.

"I've only been frightened by one storm, and that was when I was twelve. Even then, I was in awe."

She laughed then, softly. He hadn't realized a sound could rip at him so.

"Gran had to pull me inside. It was the only time she ever raised her voice at me. Tornadoes had been reported dipping out of the clouds and they were all around the area. I couldn't understand her concern. After all, I only wanted to look at them. She told me, quite crisply if I remember, to settle for watching them on the news.''

The nerves Maggie had eluded found her full force. Sculpted by shadows and light, his face was fierce in line and form. Perhaps she'd been wrong. Perhaps he didn't want her. Though her head opted for a strategic retreat, her heart demanded full steam ahead. Whatever the outcome, she'd know where he stood before going back inside.

"Jake, look at me." She reached up to touch his shoulder, but he jerked away sharply.

"Don't touch me," he said through gritted teeth. "Please. Go back inside."

"I don't want to."

"For God's sake, Maggie—" He made the mistake of turning toward her. Swept by the wind, her hair danced about her head in wild abandon and her robe billowed behind her like fluttering wings. The gown revealed beneath was low-cut. Molded to her body by the breeze, it accentuated the swell of her breasts, the small span of her waist, the length of her legs. He swallowed hard and curled his fingers into his palm. She looked like an angel... and he was tempted as hell.

When his eyes returned to hers, he was reminded what kind of person she was. Loving, giving, caring... always putting the needs of others before herself, while he'd virtually led a singular existence. He folded his arms to keep from reaching for her.

"Don't you see, Maggie?" he asked hoarsely. "I'm a very selfish man, and you're not nearly selfish enough."

Maggie's mouth opened in disbelief and she rested her hands on her hips. The man was actually protecting her—

and from himself yet! The love in her heart grew impossibly stronger. She shook her head slowly, her lips curving. "Jake Wilder, that's the *dumbest* thing I ever heard."

"What's that supposed to..." His mouth went dry as his gaze dipped below her throat. Pulled by her hands, the low neckline had gone lower, and tighter. He jerked his eyes back to hers with a frown. "Quit standing like that!"

"What?" Maggie glanced down at herself, then realized why he'd all but yelled. Her body, what little there was of it, had never been the sort to drive men mad. The thought that it could cause him a problem made her feel deliciously sexy for the first time in her life. She clasped her hands demurely in front of her. "Better?" she asked innocently.

"No! Now go to bed."

"I can't sleep."

The world around them brightened momentarily before a crackle of thunder rent the air. With a return of the darkness came an increase of the wind. Maggie felt the first drops of rain hit her face, saw the second hit his shoulder. Spellbound, she watched it meander down his skin and get lost in the dark thatch of hair on his chest.

A loud hissing sound warned that a curtain of rain sped their way. Jake murmured an unintelligible curse and grabbed her hand, heading for his door. Two steps away from safety, they were covered by mist. The rain hit in earnest as they crossed the threshold. Maggie stayed at the doorway, skirting the line between protection and sogginess, and watched the deluge until Jake closed the door and retrieved a towel from the dresser.

"Here," he said, thrusting it at her, then moving away. "You can dry off before you go to your room."

Maggie slipped out of the dampened robe and laid it over a chair. Patting her face with the towel, she turned toward him. Jake sat on the bed, his feet firmly planted on the floor a foot apart. The towel hit above his knees, draping discreetly between his legs. The side split exposed the long muscled length of one thigh, dusted by dark hair. He looked irrefutably virile as he focused on the clock, his expression thunderous.

He wanted her. She'd felt it in the few kisses they'd shared; she'd seen it in his eyes when he'd finally looked at her outside. But now his jaw was clenched with determination, and she wondered if she could break through it. She smiled. "You know, if you try a little harder you might be able to make me feel unwanted."

"It's not that, and you damn well know it!" Their eyes met for the first time since they'd come inside. "What about the complications you didn't want?"

The darkness of his gaze told of a passion barely leashed. She lifted her chin. "No strings, Jake." Even as she said it, she knew a part of her would always feel bound to him. "No regrets."

In the past such a promise would have been all he was waiting for. So why was he holding back? "Don't lie to yourself, Maggie. There're always regrets."

"If there are, I'll cope with them. I trust you'll do the same."

He thought of his mistakes with Claire, of what Maggie had gone through with Brad. A peal of thunder sounded; the room turned pitch-black. Jake cursed, bending as he groped for the bedside table, then fumbled in the drawer for matches. Seizing them, he scraped one against the box and touched the flame to a candle on the table.

Jake sat straight and found Maggie standing but a foot away. She extended her hand, palm up. "Meet me halfway. Mutual give, and mutual take."

Desire clawed at him and needs that had been building from the first time he saw her, or maybe even from the first time he'd heard about her, pushed his hand to hers. "You're chilled."

With her step forward, the gown teased the inside of his knees. "Not for long, I trust."

Her skin, as creamy as the silk she wore, beckoned him. Jake slid his hands up her arms, luxuriating in the feel of her. "I've thought of you...of this...for weeks." The straps at her shoulders were as insubstantial as moonlight. It took no more than a single finger to nudge the first aside, then the second. "I've never wanted to—" The silk slithered to a stop at the peaks of her breasts. It shimmered, luring him with each breath she took while reality bade him wait.

Jake took a deep breath and dragged his gaze to hers. "I've never wanted to touch anyone so badly in my life, but I didn't come prepared for anything like this to happen. Are you protected?"

She trailed a fingertip down his cheek as she nodded. "So touch me," she whispered.

He followed the curve of her back with his hands and slowly pulled her close. Savoring the moment, he teased the silk at her breast with his tongue, dampening the cloth before adroitly pushing it away. Her skin was cool to the touch. Much smoother, much softer than the fabric that had adorned it, her flesh warmed quickly beneath his attention. "So sweet," he murmured. "You can't imagine how sweet."

"Jake...Jake..." Her raspy moan echoed inside him, flaming his ardor. Her eyes were closed, her hands impatient as she kneaded his shoulders. He felt too much, wanted too much. He laid his cheek against the silk still at her midriff, fighting hard for the control he felt was paramount. The stroke of her hand against his cheek was infinitely gentle and reassuring.

Jake lifted his gaze to hers, fully aware that the only thing that kept her gown in place was the delicate, string bow beneath her breasts. His eyes steady on hers, he took a trailing end of the bow between his teeth and pulled. His gaze lowered as the gown pooled at her feet. Candlelight bathed her body in adoration, making her look as ethereal as the angel he'd compared her to earlier.

"You're beautiful, Maggie," he whispered, claiming her mouth as his own. Needs and wants entangled as one and he lowered himself back on the bed, taking her with him.

She'd dreamed of this—holding, being held, by him. Bodies entwined, they rolled over while her mind swam with the clarity of sensation. His body was damp and corded with muscle, his kiss hungry, his touch rapture as it played over her body with consummate skill. Drowning in sensuality, her head lolled back to accept his heated repetitions of her name as he moved to the base of her throat, lingering where her pulse beat a frantic rhythm.

Need. Had she ever truly ached so before? Want. Had it ever been so acute? She felt the warmth of his breath at her breast, the coolness left by a teasing retreat, the fulfilling heat as he at last took it in his mouth. She arched toward him, suddenly impatient, demand in her hands as she followed, muscle by muscle, the tension up his back. Still he tarried with flicking tongue and nibbling teeth, lavishing devotion over her breasts while he stroked her inner thighs with his hand.

How could he have thought himself selfish? Maggie wondered. The thought was stripped away by longing as she pulled him back to her and kissed him with all the love spilling freely from her heart.

Outside the storm raged. Inside Jake fought for control. He'd known desire before, easily quenched and forgotten. Maggie was different. Without even trying, she'd pushed her way into his mind and filled it until he could think of nothing but her. She smelled and tasted of rain and innocence, yet there was something about her that threatened to demand more than he'd ever given before.

His mind swam, trying hard to hold on. Yet her hands slipped lower and lower down his back, enticing, compelling as she arched wantonly beneath him. Madness was her taste, her scent, her touch. Poised above her, Jake searched her eyes for an answer to a question he did not know.

"Now, Jake. Make love to me now."

"With you, Maggie," he whispered, losing himself inside her. "Always *with* you."

Mouth to mouth, body to body, heart to heart, they moved as one. Control forgotten, they drove each other over the brink, then beyond....

When his mind cleared, Jake rolled to his back, taking her with him, not wanting her to bear his weight. She sighed contentedly and nestled her head in the curve of his neck. Stroking her back, he tried to sort through the emotions hovering just out of comprehension. What he'd just experienced—was experiencing now—was new to him. He wanted to say something, but didn't know what it was.

Jake felt as well as heard the hungry growl of Maggie's stomach, followed quickly by her laughter. She raised her head sheepishly.

"How could you be hungry after that sandwich you ate?" he asked, grazing his thumb over her dimple.

"Truth is, I didn't eat it."

"You did, too. I saw you!"

Her laugh was silky soft. "You also made three trips to the kitchen. First for salt—" she kissed his cheek "—second for napkins—'' then his other cheek ''—and third for a refill on your drink,'' she said, pecking his chin.

''You sneak!'' Her hair cascaded around his face and he tunneled his fingers through it. ''What'd you do with it?''

''I was too nervous to eat, so I kept throwing it out the window. I figured some little creature would be thankful.''

Another rumble sounded, this time louder. ''Let's go get you something to eat now that you're more . . . relaxed.''

Her pout was beautiful. ''I don't want to move.'' She snuggled against him provocatively, making him catch his breath. ''I'm comfortably exhausted and—''

''There's chocolate toffee ice cream in the freezer.''

''Then again,'' she said, smiling brightly, ''I guess there's something to be said for keeping my strength up.''

He kissed her then, when he hadn't intended to. Short, simple and sweet. It shouldn't have had him wanting her again so soon, but it did. He released his hold to prove to himself he could let her go, and pushed back the longing as she climbed out of bed. When she chose to wear his shirt rather than her gown, it pleased him immensely.

Maggie fastened three of the buttons, then faced him as she pulled her hair from the collar. The look in his eyes made her pulse skip and she cautioned herself against reading too much into it. ''Want me to bring you some?''

''No,'' he said, sitting up. ''I'll come with you.'' He pulled on his jeans, grabbed the candle and her hand, then led the way downstairs to the kitchen.

''What do you think you're doing?'' he asked as she opened the freezer.

''Getting the ice cream.''

He moved in front of her, closing the door. ''I'll make you a sandwich first, then you can have dessert.'' She made a delightful picture when she put her hands on her hips and lifted her chin. Her waist looked nonexistent and the shirt gaped seductively, revealing a hint of breast.

"Now that you've had your way with me, do you think it gives you the right to get pushy?"

Desire flamed white-hot inside him and he stepped forward, sliding a hand over her hip and under the shirt. His palm against her bare buttock, he pulled her to him and ravished her mouth thoroughly. Releasing her, he stepped back.

She stood as breathless as he and a beguiling smile slowly curved her lips. "Only half a sandwich, please."

Jake laughed, then pressed a kiss to her forehead. "You know what I like about you, Maggie?" Her eyebrow rose. "I mean, besides the obvious everything."

"What?"

"You're fun." He handed her the candle, then opened the refrigerator. "Now, if you'll just hold that up a little so I can see inside . . . thanks. Tomatoes, mayonnaise . . ."

Fun, Maggie thought with pleasure. She knew what he meant, because that was what she liked about him, along with everything else, of course. "Is there any lettuce left?" she asked, peering over his shoulder.

"Nope. We'll have to run into Zena tomorrow and pick some up." He backed up and looked around. "I did put the turkey away, didn't I?"

"Yeah, I saw you." As he renewed his search, she moved the candle closer for him.

"Hmm, I could've sworn I put it in the meat keeper drawer."

Her heart thudded. "Oh Lord," she whispered. "Not here, too."

"What?" he asked, craning around to look back at her.

Maggie hadn't realized she'd spoken the words aloud. "Oh, nothing."

"Ah, there it is," he said grabbing a package wrapped in white paper, then closing the door. "While I fix your sandwich, you can tell me what your 'nothing' was."

She folded her arms and leaned back against the counter. Watching him put the sandwich together, she tried to think of a way to explain. When the words didn't come, she opted for the obvious. "Do you believe in ghosts?"

"No." He handed her the sandwich and a napkin, then studied her for a moment. "Do you?"

"No, of course not," she said quickly, then took a bite.

"Don't you want to sit down?"

"I'd rather stand, thanks."

He leaned a hip against the counter and studied her. "Why'd you ask if I believed in ghosts?"

"It's just . . ."

"Just what?"

She took another bite, wondering how she could put it without sounding crazy.

"Go on. Say it."

Maggie swallowed, then looked at him. "Well, since I've been at Gran's, there've been an awful lot of strange things happening."

He folded his arms over his chest. "Like what?"

Maggie stared absently at her sandwich, then put it on the napkin and laid it on the counter. "I know this is going to sound ridiculous, but like the thing with the key, for starters. I mean, that was really weird. And since then, there's been numerous little things. I'm basically a very organized person, you know."

"Yes," he said, casually taking her hand in reassurance.

"Well . . . things have been getting misplaced."

"You've had a lot on your mind."

"I know, and a few of the times I've realized that, yes, I was responsible. But it's happened so much..." She worried his thumb with her own. "I mean really strange things, like a paintbrush would end up in a room I couldn't remember even being in that day. Masking tape has virtually been hidden. A gallon of paint I'd had in a room upstairs ended up in the downstairs entry closet. Putty knives, caulking tools—you name it, and it's disappeared at one time or another."

He brushed a kiss over her knuckles. "Even the best of people have been known to go through periods of absent-mindedness under stress. Maybe being in the house is upsetting you more than you realize."

"No! I'm very happy there!" She sighed and dropped his hand, then began to pace, frustrated that she couldn't make him understand. "How do you explain phantom phone calls and the doorbell ringing with no one there? And oh, there's something else," she said, whirling to face him. "Gran's scent...there are times when these things happen that I can smell Gran's perfume for a moment. How do you explain that?"

He pushed away from the counter and moved to her, taking both of her hands in his. "Logically. The answer to the first two things are children. As to the third, well, she *did* live there a very long time. Her scent has probably been absorbed by various things throughout the house. Her clothes, the curtains, the woodwork..."

"I guess you're right. It's just that...you know how most kids go through a thing where they worry about someone they love very much dying?" He nodded. "Well, Gran comforted me once by saying that if she died before I was grown and happily settled, she'd find a way to watch over me. And though I'm grown, I'm still not settled yet."

"How does watching over you equate with sabotaging your work?"

Maggie frowned. "It doesn't, does it? I mean, what I'm doing are things we'd planned together. You'd think if she could do anything, she'd be speeding me along." She shook her head, then looked down at the floor. "Lord, you must think I'm a nut."

He slid an arm around her waist and lifted her chin. "No. Not at all. Who knows? Maybe it *is* Bea. Many a time she did things I didn't understand." He kissed her on the forehead. "I'll tell you one thing."

"What?"

"She loved you very, very much. And if such things were possible, I think she would've found a way."

Maggie laid her cheek against his chest, accepting the comfort she found in his arms. "Of course," she whispered, "such things aren't possible. It must be my imagination working overtime, trying to compensate for losing her." She raised her gaze. "Thanks for listening, and not making me feel foolish."

"There's nothing to thank me for."

The flickering candlelight added to her fathomless gaze before she slipped from his embrace and started putting the things back in the refrigerator. What was wrong? he wondered. "Don't you want to finish the rest of your sandwich now?"

Her back was to him as she shook her head.

"Oh, ready for the ice cream, huh?"

She shook her head again, wiping the countertop.

He closed the distance between them and turned her around. "What's wrong?"

"Nothing, I just wish . . ."

"What?"

She turned her head away and whispered, "It's very wicked and demanding."

"Sounds promising." Jake laid a finger at her cheek, nudging her gaze toward him. "What is it?"

Her smile was as becoming as her embarrassment. She shook her head. "Never mind."

"If you're thinking what I think you're thinking—" he laced his hands loosely at the small of her back and pulled her to him "—you should know that I've been thinking of it since the moment you got out of bed."

"You have?" she asked, playing her hands through the hair at his nape.

"Can't you tell?" He lowered his head, pressing his lips to hers. "I don't know about you, but I find so much thought frustrating." Jake swept her up into his arms. "Why don't we go to bed and see if we can't figure out a way to help each other not be so frustrated?"

Maggie retrieved the candlestick from the counter. "Sounds like a noble cause to me."

Chapter Nine

Last night had been a mistake. A mistake he should never have allowed to happen.

Jake stood on the cool, wet deck, a mug of coffee in his hands, recriminations twisting in his stomach. The sky before him hinted at a new day. Pink on the horizon flowed into violet as morning pushed the dark of night upward. Yet what he saw before him was Maggie as he'd seen her only minutes ago—soft, sexy and far too vulnerable in sleep.

He pressed the heel of his hand against the bridge of his nose and smelled her scent on his shirt. Nameless emotions swirled with memories of last night, and he shook his head to dispel them. He understood nothing of what he felt. He only knew it had been wrong to give in to his need for her. A woman like Maggie deserved so much more than he could offer.

Now, like last night, it was the sound of the sliding glass door that heralded her approach. Jake cursed silently. He needed time to find a solution, time to figure out what he was going to do. Not having that luxury, he knew the best course to follow was one that wouldn't complicate things further. Steeling himself against the weakness of wanting, he tightened his grip on the mug as she stepped beside him.

"It's been years since I watched a sunrise. Of course, there are those who say they're impossible to see in L.A. anyway."

He felt her gaze on him and prayed she wouldn't touch him, as she added, "Have I come out at a bad time?"

Jake kept his eyes trained on the horizon, not wanting to risk looking at her. He shrugged. "Not if you like sunrises."

Anxiety stole over Maggie, as real as the chill penetrating her robe. Last night everything had felt so comfortable...so indisputably right. She'd awakened with a smile on her face and love in her heart. Though she'd been disappointed at his absence in bed, her smile had returned when she found him out here. But now...

Maggie took a measured breath, trying hard to remember that in many ways he was a quiet man. "May I have a sip of your coffee?"

When he gave her the mug without so much as a sideways glance, her anxiety mushroomed. She took a careful sip. Bitter and black, it was just what she needed. Not wanting to crowd him, Maggie shored up her defenses and handed him the mug. "Maybe I just better leave you alone a while." She walked away, heading for his room.

"If only you'd taken that attitude last night," she heard Jake murmur like a whispered lament.

It didn't matter that he probably hadn't meant for her to hear. What hurt was that he would even think it. Awash with pain, a well-honed protective instinct had her back straightening. Maggie redirected her steps toward her own room. "Well, you know what they say, Wilder." She opened the sliding glass door and stepped inside. "Better late than never," she said, then rammed the door into place.

Pain-pumped adrenaline sped the riotous beat of her heart. She slumped momentarily against the wall, suddenly unable to take another step as what he'd said sunk in.

He'd told her there were always regrets. Obviously, he'd meant it. Maggie pushed herself forward, torment curling inside her. Last night *had* been indisputably right. She'd gone to him willingly and wouldn't regret it!

This morning, however— Damn him! Damn, damn, damn him! When she walked out on the balcony she'd felt full of love's wonderment. Maggie jerked her suitcase from the floor and tossed it on the bed, fighting now against feeling cheap.

A moment later the glass door slammed against its metal casing and Jake stepped inside. *"What in the hell do you think you're doing?"*

She wouldn't look at him, couldn't allow herself to. Instead, she commanded a composure into her actions that she didn't feel, and walked over to the dresser where she'd placed her belongings. "I think it should be obvious," she said casually, opening a drawer. She scooped up her clothing and walked to the bed. "I'm packing."

"Why?"

Her laugh was little more than a disbelieving expulsion of air as she dropped the clothes in the suitcase. "Really, Jake," she said lightly. "I've never made it a habit of staying where I'm not wanted." She went down on her knees, looking beneath the bed for her shoes.

"Not wanted?" In the span of a moment he crossed the room and pulled her to her feet. She wanted to cry out against him and jerk away, but with more aplomb than she'd thought she possessed, she lifted her eyes to the anger in his.

"Not wanted?" he repeated, his voice rising.

Maggie couldn't fathom what drove him to act as if *she'd* offended *him.* Guilt? Pity, maybe? Wanting neither, she raised her chin, determined to keep what pride she had left by acting civilized. "It's my fault, I assure you, and nothing to scream about. I should've realized how uncomfortable one-night stands could be when dragged over an entire weekend."

"One-night stands?" he boomed.

"Is there an echo in here?" she asked dryly, then glared at the hand curled tightly around her arm. He loosened his grip, but didn't release her.

"Do you honestly believe I think of you like that?"

It was the tenderness in his voice that drew her gaze, and suddenly she didn't know what to believe anymore. The anger was still in his eyes, but there was something else there, too. She couldn't afford to assume it was pain; she couldn't afford to assume anything.

Confused, and desperate not to make a bigger fool of herself than she already had, Maggie looked at her suitcase. She'd started her exit, and wanted to pull it off before she had a chance to break down.

"Hey, it's okay," she said, easing from his grasp. The movement made her robe gape, and she clasped it together at her neck before turning away. "It's apparent you don't want a repeat performance, so if you'll excuse me, my gown is in your room."

Ten minutes. She only had to last ten more minutes. Then she would be packed, dressed and gone. And though it would cost a king's ransom, maybe she could offer a taxi driver a flat fee to get her home.

Maggie barely had the door to the hallway opened when Jake slammed it shut. All her pretense at composure fled as she whipped around, her eyes brilliant with anguish. He trapped her against the door, his hands on either side of her.

"Move," she demanded.

His jaw tensed as his eyes narrowed. "You're a fool, Flannagan. You know that?"

Maggie folded her arms and tossed back her head, refusing to free the tears pressing at her eyes. "I'd say you pretty well drove that point home out on the balcony."

"Forget the balcony!"

"If only I could," she bit back.

He winced. "All right, I handled that poorly. I didn't even mean to say it out loud, it's just..." He shook his head, then looked deeply into her eyes. "Don't you see, Maggie?" he asked softly. "You...you deserve a knight on a white horse, or at least a man who believes in happily-ever-after. And I...I can be neither."

"You're kidding!" Furious, she ducked beneath his arm and strode across the room, pointing outside. "I'm supposed to believe that that little scene was inspired by some misguided sense of conscience?" She laughed, planting her hands at her hips. "Look, Wilder, don't bother. I don't need your guilt feelings, okay? I sure as hell didn't ask you to be a knight, nor did I expect some fairy-tale end to the weekend!" She no longer tried to keep her voice down, but let it soar free and loud. "And what's it to you, anyway? I don't recall appointing you my fairy godmother!"

"Maybe you didn't, but it doesn't seem to matter," he said, his voice as loud as hers. He stalked toward her, wrath shining in his eyes. "I love you, dammit! I want the best for you, and it's driving me crazy knowing that I'm not it!''

"You *what*?''

He gripped both her arms and pulled her close until they were almost nose to nose. "I said I love you!''

"Well, I love you, too,'' she tossed back, "but it doesn't make me stomp around and scream like an idiot!''

His eyes closed and his grip slackened. "*Now* what's wrong?'' she demanded.

His eyes opened slowly and her heart absorbed what her mind had not. She didn't know what to say, she only knew his tender gaze compelled. Maggie caressed his cheek and felt her defenses melt as he pressed a kiss against her palm. His smile was ironic as he slipped his arms around her shoulders. "For two people who didn't want any complications, I'd say we've sure mucked everything up.''

Maggie pressed her cheek against his chest. "Are you sorry?''

He lifted her chin with his fingers. "That I love you?'' When she nodded, he kissed her nose. "No. It just scares the hell out of me.''

"Why?''

"Because there doesn't seem to be a way to keep from hurting you.''

Incredibly touched by his concern, she couldn't disagree with him. She only knew what she'd accepted last night. "The biggest hurt comes from unfulfilled expectations. I've experienced that and so have you.'' One by one, she began undoing the buttons on his shirt. "Where we're lucky is that we both have the realities firmly in mind. You don't want marriage, and frankly, neither do I.''

"But you said—''

"Eventually, sure, after I've had the time to find myself—pardon the cliché.'' She stripped his shirt from his shoulders and placed a lingering kiss over his heart. "That's what I intend to do in Pacific Grove." She smiled up at him. "Think, Jake. Until I know who I am, how can I know what I want? So please, spare yourself the hair shirt over what I need."

"Is that what I was wearing?"

"Mmm-hmm." There was vulnerability behind the humor. She saw it in his eyes, felt it in his fragile hold. Maggie framed his face with her hands. "I love you, Jake Wilder." Wonder filled his eyes, ripping away any guards she might have kept to protect herself. "I love you very, very much."

Jake picked her up and cradled her in his arms, looking at the rumpled twin bed meaningfully. "Too confining."

She traced the shape of his mouth with her fingertip. "I agree."

He glanced down at the floor. "Too hard."

"Rug burns can be nasty," she said, nibbling on his ear.

Jake carried her to his bedroom. "What do you say, Goldilocks? Is this one . . . just right?"

She smiled wickedly and teased his upper lip with her tongue. "I'd say it's . . . very much just right."

Their gazes caught and held. Smiles faded. Maggie felt cocooned in the tenderness of his eyes as he laid her on the bed, then stood. Morning's light stole softly into the room through the partially opened drapes, casting a halo around him.

Her lover. Her love. Never had his shoulders looked so wide, nor the breadth of his chest so impressive. Her fingers curled against the sheets. The hair that played across his chest was seductively soft. Her gaze lowered where it grew crisper, tapering into an entrancing line, exposed by each snap he freed from confinement. Impatience was a sweet ache inside her as he pushed his jeans down powerful thighs, then stood before her—proud, aroused, magnificent.

Maggie lifted her arms and he came to her. Last night their lovemaking had been filled with a passionate urgency. No less passionate, but gentled, she luxuriated in the freedom of slow kisses and the pleasure of simply being held.

As he pressed kisses down her neck and began nudging her robe aside, Maggie grabbed his shoulders. "No," she whispered. He lifted his head, obviously puzzled. She kissed the frown between his brows, then, guiding his shoulders, rolled him to his back. He lay still, watching her almost warily as she stretched out next to him on her side and teased his calf with her foot.

It struck her that he'd been given so little in his life that he didn't know how to receive. Though she wasn't foolish enough to think a woman had never touched him, she knew no one had touched him as she would. Wanting nothing but to cosset him in the love she felt, she began lazily trailing her fingertips in a line from his thigh up to his chest.

Time lost meaning as Jake submerged in a world filled with sensation. She taunted him with the lightest of touches and seduced with the flick of her tongue. From the inside of his wrists to the back of his knees, no place remained untouched. His blood sped, muscles tensed, while defenses built through the years crumbled under the caress of her hand, the kiss of her lips.

Love. Such a simple word, such an elusive emotion...until now.

No longer able to wait, Jake pulled her to him on a groan. Discarding the robe, he plundered the sweetness of her mouth and called her name out loud when she took him into her. Suddenly he couldn't seem to get close enough. He wanted to drown in her, lose himself in her, be reborn in her.

It was possible, he thought. With her, anything was possible. Their hips moved in rhythm while he used his hands and mouth to drive her higher. Then at the moment he felt her every muscle straining, he tore his lips from hers and watched her eyes. He saw the love there, as pure and strong as the passion she gave. The power of it sang through him as together they reached the highest pinnacle and took the final plunge.

It might have been hours or moments that they lay together afterward. Jake didn't know, didn't care. It was more than the pleasure of sated passion. More than the echo of excitement that still whispered through his blood. He shifted and held her tighter, pressing a kiss to her temple. Serenity swept through him and he trailed his hand lightly, possessively, down the curve of her back. He loved, and was loved in return.

"Mmm," Maggie murmured. "I don't believe I've ever felt so languid, so content—" she lifted her head and looked down at him "—so happy in my entire life."

His gaze—blue and deep—spilled another wave of warmth through her that stole her breath away. "When you look at me like that, I swear, I go all weak inside."

A defined dark brow arched. "Like what?"

"Like you know everything about me... The first time you looked at me like that, it made me nervous."

He stroked her hair, smoothing it out over her shoulder, and she sighed in response. "When was that?"

"That first night. I was in your robe and you came in the living room, griping at me for not taking a longer bath."

He smiled. "God, but you looked sexy."

"Sexy? I looked—"

"*Very* sexy. *Very* inviting. I think from the first moment I saw you I was between a rock and a hard place, wanting to help... and simply wanting."

Maggie grinned, finding it difficult to believe, yet enjoying the thought. "Really?"

"Mmm-hmm." He brushed a kiss against her lips. "You're a very beautiful woman, Maggie."

She ducked her head. "If anyone in this bed is beautiful," she murmured, "it's you."

Maggie gasped at the speed with which she found herself on her back. Jake loomed over her, his expression dark and fierce. "*You* are beautiful. Outside, inside, upside down and backward. I don't just say things, Maggie. If I say it, I mean it, and I want you to believe it!"

He looked angry. Actually, truly angry. She hadn't been fishing for a compliment, she'd simply been saying what she felt was true. But now, seeing his scowl, another defense inside her melted. For him she felt beautiful, *was* beautiful.

A glow built inside her until she felt near to bursting from it. She smiled slowly and raised a hand to his cheek. "Okay, I am beautiful. Now quit frowning."

"Really?" he drawled, as if he didn't quite believe her.

She gave him a haughty look, full of the power of her newfound beauty. "Really." Though his frown dissipated, the intensity of his gaze remained. "Now what?" she asked.

How could he tell her everything he was feeling when he didn't fully understand it himself? The concept of love was too new, too fragile, and over it all was the specter of a future without her. He pushed back the reality and concentrated on now. The emotion, the joy, was more than he'd ever believed possible, and he didn't want it spoiled.

Jake traced her lips until they curved slightly, producing the dimple, then kissed it. "I love you, Maggie," he whispered.

The brilliance of her smile reached the farthest corners of his heart. "And I love you." She kissed him lightly, then lingered, stirring needs inside him.

Jake broke the kiss, but nuzzled her cheek. "If you don't stop this, Flannagan, we'll never get out of bed."

"Would that be so bad?"

Before he could answer, the rumble of her stomach made them chuckle. "You're quite the insatiable woman, in more ways than one." He rubbed his nose against hers. "C'mon, lazybones." He rolled out of bed. "Daylight's burning and we've got a lot to do."

Maggie propped herself up on her elbows, loath to leave the bed despite her hunger. "We do?"

Jake pulled on his jeans. "There's the matter of breakfast and, though I showered and shaved while you were still asleep, I could keep you company while you showered."

"That sounds promising."

"I also thought we could pack a picnic lunch and go out on Mac's boat. Maybe do a little skiing."

She laughed. "To be honest, it's been a few years...."

He sat on the edge of the bed and helped her into her robe, bestowing a kiss on her breasts before bringing the silken edges together and tying the sash. "It's like riding a bicycle. I promise."

"Then what?"

Jake stood with a sigh, wanting nothing more than to gather her to him and hold her forever. "Then we come back and make mad passionate love until we die of exhaustion."

Maggie promptly scooted from the bed and made a beeline down the hall, looking back over her shoulder.

"Speed it up, Wilder. Daylight's burning and we've got a lot to do."

Maggie stood on the rocky shore of the secluded cove. Water lapped softly at her ankles and the sun warmed her face. A month ago she wouldn't have thought herself capable of feeling so at peace. Logically, it made little sense to her to feel so now. There was the work on the house to complete, Pam and Kathie waiting for her arrival at the inn...

She marveled at how none of it seemed to matter. For the moment there was no past, no future, no demands...just herself and Jake.

"Homesick for the ocean?" Jake wrapped his arms around her waist, drawing her back against the warmth and solidity of his bare chest.

Maggie rested her arms atop his. "Surprisingly, that hadn't crossed my mind. I was thinking."

"Of what?"

Maggie watched a sailboat edge into view, far in the distance. "Before I saw that boat, I was thinking how easy it was to feel like we were the only two people in the world."

"I know." He nudged her hair aside and brushed a kiss at the curve of her neck. "I've had to remind myself about a hundred times in the past couple hours that we're not."

She rested her head against him. "Me, too. I really like this place. How'd you find it?"

"With you." He smiled, liking the sound of that. "I've never been here before, but with eleven hundred miles of shoreline I figured we ought to be able to discover someplace."

Need rose inside her with dizzying speed. She wanted to turn to him, hold fast and never let go. She fought the temptation, knowing things would be hard enough when it came time to leave without making matters worse.

Worse? The sudden threat of tears burned her eyes and sped her heart. Wasn't love supposed to make things easier instead of more difficult?

Determined not to spoil what time they had together, Maggie cleared her throat and forced her mind to a less confusing subject. "Uh, I'm surprised you haven't bought a place of your own here."

"I've thought about it, but I've been too busy. If I did, I'd want to build it in an area like this where there weren't a lot of people around. I'd probably buy a boat, too. A—"

She tilted her head back and looked up at him. "If this is a buildup so you can make a crack about my lack of skiing ability, you're going to be very sorry."

"No, I said I wouldn't tease you anymore, and I meant it. All I was going to say is I'd probably get a sailboat."

Maggie turned at that and put her hands on her hips. "You sail?"

"It's been a while, but yes."

"Why didn't you tell me?"

"I just did."

She fumed. "I meant, why didn't you tell me yesterday when I—" His slow smile had her lips wanting to curve. She glanced heavenward, then gave up the struggle. "You're a very frustrating man."

Jake put his hands around her waist and pulled her close. "The word is frustrated. Let's get in the boat, open the throttle and get home."

"Why wait?" She placed a kiss on his chest and snuggled against him. "We've got a blanket."

"Because, my little lust bunny, there's a fishing boat rounding the bend."

"Lust bunny?" she said, pulling back. "*Lust bunny?* If I'm a lust bunny, what does that make you?"

His grin was outrageous. "A very...happy...man." He kissed her then until her knees went weak, then clasped her hand and headed for the boat. "Or, at least I will be, once we're back at the house."

The weekend had been magical and idyllic. Even when Jake called his son twice, Maggie had been cushioned from reality by their relative seclusion. They'd shared long walks, whispered words of passion, laughter and love itself, all the more precious for its time limitations. Maggie swallowed hard against a feeling of melancholy and stared out the car window.

Jake had told her northeastern Oklahoma was called Green Country and it was easy to see why. Endless stretches of meadows and hills were dotted by occasional herds of cattle and horses. Wildflowers grew in abundance, splashing the verdant countryside with color. The scenery was the same they'd passed on the way to the lake, but suddenly it seemed important to memorize it.

Jake rested his hand on her shoulder and she started slightly. "You okay?"

"Fine," she said, coming up with a smile.

He looked back to the road, but left his hand where it lay. "You're being awfully quiet."

"I'm just a little tired, I guess." A bittersweet warmth shot through her, from both the massage he started on her shoulder and his glance of shared intimacies.

"Me, too. Now I understand what Mac has always meant by needing a day to recover after a weekend of relaxation." He pushed back the hair that fell against her cheek. "Why don't you take a little nap? You've got plenty of time before we get to Mac and Brenda's."

The nerves she'd ignored all morning gripped her stomach. She took a measured breath to combat them, then spoke calmly. "Mac and Brenda's?"

He stroked his thumb lazily against her collarbone, a poignant reminder of the easiness they'd shared. "Yeah. After we pick up Christopher, we can either go out and grab a bite, or get a pizza delivered to the house." He grinned, his eyes straight ahead. "I've really missed him, you know? I was thinking it might be nice if the three of us could go to a movie tomorrow night, since he didn't get to go to the lake."

She'd hoped the return to reality would be softened by the long drive. Instead, she felt as if they'd just run into it headlong, no less tangible than a brick wall. Maggie laced her fingers together. "I don't think that would be a good idea."

His hand stilled. "Which?" he asked quietly. "The movie or dinner?"

She gathered her strength, then looked at him. "Both."

His smile looked a little stiff when he glanced at her. "C'mon, Maggie. After this weekend, I know you have to eat or your stomach yells."

Dammit! Why was he making it so hard? Muscles in her neck tensed with the knowledge that she had to make things perfectly clear, and wishing she didn't. "I'll eat at home alone, and I'd prefer you dropping me off before you get Chris."

Remote. The change had taken no longer than a blink of an eye. He lifted his hand from her shoulder and returned it to the steering wheel, leaving her bereft. "Of course. Whatever you'd . . . prefer."

Maggie's stomach lurched at the way ice all but dripped off his final word. She knew he was hurting, but dammit, so was she! Somehow there had to be a better way.

Moments passed and she fidgeted in the seat, reminded of the time when Brad had broken their engagement. He'd told her about Sharisse, said there wasn't really anything for them to talk about, then had taken her home. She had been so stunned, she'd accepted his decision without question. Though this was a different situation, the deafening silence was the same. She couldn't take it the rest of the way home . . . *wouldn't* take it.

"Pull over," she demanded, pointing to a shaded place up ahead. The car continued on its steady pace and she looked at him. "Don't you raise that damn eyebrow at me! Pull over!"

Muscles flexed in his jaw as the brakes squealed in protest and he angled off the road. Before he could cut the engine, she had her seat belt off, the door open, and was getting out. Tall grass tickled her bare legs as she headed toward a barbed wire fence. Resolute, she looked back over her shoulder and found him still sitting in the car.

Maggie turned toward him. "Would you *please* get out?" she asked, raising her voice to be heard above a passing truck.

She had begun to wonder if he was going to sit there indefinitely, when he complied. He walked around to the passenger side and leaned back against the door. "Now what?" He crossed his feet at the ankles and jammed his hands in his pockets.

Frustration spawned fury and she marched to within a foot of him. "'Whatever I'd *prefer*?'" she mimicked. "Damn you, Jake!"

Jake shrugged, trying hard to loosen the tension that had him strung tighter than a fraying bowstring. "*Prefer* was your choice of words," he reminded her. "Not mine."

"I didn't—" Her voice broke and she looked away for a moment, then raised her chin. Her struggle for control tore at his own. "I didn't say it the same way you did."

No matter how she couched it, the bottom line was she wouldn't see him anymore. It hurt, even more than he'd imagined. "Pardon me," he said slowly. "I was merely trying to go along with what you want."

"Dammit!" she cried, stiffening her arms at her sides. "It's not a matter of what I *want* or what I *prefer*. It's simply the way it has to be!"

Ingrained lessons allowed his eyes to remain indifferent, despite the rage inside him. "I see."

She pushed at his shoulder. "You don't see a damn thing! For God's sake, stop and think about Christopher!"

Jake stood straight and felt his control slip a degree. "What about him? He likes you."

"Precisely! And if we start doing things together, he'll like me even more."

"Would that be so damn bad?" he asked tightly.

"Not now. Not while I'm as close as next door. But what happens later after he's gotten used to seeing me?" She started pacing. "He's vulnerable now, Jake. And though the two of you are doing well, you've got to know that he still misses his mother. Then here I come. The three of us spend time together. Affection grows and dependency develops, then wham! I leave for California." She stopped in front of him. "He doesn't need that kind of fluctuation," she said passionately. "You've built something good between the two of you. He can and should depend on it. So why introduce what would amount to a mother substitute when you know already that I'm going to leave?"

Jake stared up at the cloudless sky. She was right, and he knew it. She spoke not only from concern for his son, but from experience as well. Still, it didn't make their predicament any easier to swallow.

His gaze returned to hers. The torment in her eyes reminded him that Christopher wasn't the only one in peril if she allowed herself to get too close to the boy. "Oh hell," he said gently, caressing her cheek.

His unexpected tenderness was almost Maggie's undoing. She covered his hand with her own. "I don't *want* to quit seeing you—"

"Then don't." Jake slipped his other arm around her shoulders and pulled her to him, holding her tightly.

Maggie relished the warmth of his embrace, but knew it couldn't last. She lifted her face to his. "I have to. Besides everything I've already said, I wouldn't feel right knowing I was taking valuable time away from Chris."

Realizing all her objections centered around his son gave Jake an idea. "Who says you have to take time away from Chris?" Puzzlement filled her eyes. "You eat lunch, don't you?"

"Usually," she said slowly.

"Well, if it fits your schedule, you can come by my office and we'll go to lunch together. Or if you're bogged down, I could always bring lunch to you. Chris is at the sitter's then, so you wouldn't be taking any time away from him."

The show of her dimple was like a flag of hope. He tightened his hold on her, relief pouring through him that he'd bought them a little more time together.

"Christopher also goes to bed at eight-thirty and is asleep by nine. He's a very sound sleeper and wouldn't know if you came over for a visit after you quit work for the evening."

She was crazy to consider it, Maggie thought. She had work to do... yet he hadn't suggested she drop everything at his convenience, but at hers. She recalled the hurt she'd experienced only minutes ago, then acknowledged how good it felt to be in his arms now and knew there was nothing further to think about. Maggie smiled in acceptance, then went on tiptoe to seal the arrangement.

Chapter Ten

"Are you about ready to call it a day?" Mac asked, peering over Jake's shoulder.

Jake shifted his gaze from the master sheet on his right to the computer keyboard. "Since when do we close up shop in the middle of the afternoon?"

"We don't. It's after five."

"Hmm?" Jake typed the zip code, then checked the address against the list.

"I said it's after five." Mac eased into the chair across from the desk. "Ten minutes after to be exact."

Comprehension dawned, and Jake cursed explicitly as he rose from his chair. "I was going to quit at four and pack that guitar for—"

Mac gave him an indulgent smile and held up his hand. "It's done and on its way to Amarillo, even as we speak. I also got back to Carver about the violin appraisal, and made our reservations for the Southwestern Vintage Instruments Exhibition next month.''

Feeling a twinge of guilt, Jake sank back into the chair and swiveled it a quarter turn, a grin tugging at his lips. "Do you feel like you've been deserted?"

"I feel—" Mac propped his feet on the desk "—intensely grateful. Not only because Maggie helped us choose which computer and software to get, but because she's helping you learn how to use it." He nodded toward the computer. "Thank God you understand how that thing works, because I have serious doubts about my own aptitude."

Jake had to laugh. "Saying I understand anything concerning a computer is a gross exaggeration. At this point I'm little more than a trained monkey. Maggie shows me what to do, and I do it."

"Speaking of Maggie . . ." Mac slipped the pencil from behind his ear and began tapping the eraser against his upper lip. "How much longer is she going to be here?"

The change in conversation made Jake uncomfortable and he turned to the computer. Her departure was something he didn't like to think about, and he sure as hell didn't want to discuss it with anyone.

"Well?" his friend prompted.

Jake concentrated on the work before him. "It's hard to say. She decided to strip the woodwork in the kitchen instead of paint over it, and she's thinking about replacing the curtains. The wallpaper she ordered is also supposed to be in later this week."

"Then she'll be through?"

"Who knows!" he fired back, then immediately regretted it. The clickety-clack of the keyboard stopped as he took a deep breath for patience and stared at the screen.

"She did mention that she's thinking about stripping and revarnishing the floor downstairs, but it's not definite."

"I've heard of painting a few walls and sprucing a place up a bit before you try to sell it, but wouldn't you say she's getting a bit extreme?"

Jake pinned Mac with a sharp look. "It was her grandmother's house, Mac. Before Bea died, she and Maggie had planned—"

"Hey, relax, I'm not criticizing her." Mac ran a hand through his thinning, sandy hair. "Has she put the house on the market yet?"

Jake frowned and turned to the screen. "No." When seconds went by without Mac's saying anything, Jake glanced back at him and found him smiling. "If you've got something to say, say it, but wipe that silly grin off your face."

"Well, as long as you've asked for my opinion..." Mac took his feet off the desk and sat forward, tapping his pencil on the closed computer book. "For a woman who was so all-fired determined to spiffy up a house and get back to California ASAP, she sure shows signs of staying put."

"So it's taken her a little longer than she planned. That doesn't mean—"

"That's not all there is to it, and you know it," Mac said, no longer teasing. "I've known you a long time, Jake. I've seen you with lots of different women and I've seen you married, but in all that time I've never seen you look at a woman the way you look at her. More important, I've never seen a woman who made *you* look so happy." He pointed the pencil at him. "You can look as incredulous as you like, but for the past week and a half you've come back from lunch all but glowing."

Jake cursed succinctly and began moving the cursor through the commands to close down. "You've been reading Brenda's romance novels again, haven't you?"

Mac rose from his chair. "Not necessary," he said smugly. "I've just had to watch my best friend." He tossed the pencil on the desk. "Sorry if I upset you. Make sure you lock the front door. I'm leaving."

"Mac..." Jake switched off the computer and stared at the black screen. "I can't allow myself to think she might stay," he admitted.

"Yeah, I know."

Jake heard the front door close and rubbed the heels of his hands against his eyes. Restrictions. They'd been back from the lake for nine days, and he'd been sick of the restrictions for the past eight. He had to monitor what he thought, what he said, when he saw her, when he held her.

It could be worse, he thought as he stood and slipped his suspenders over his shoulders. She could be gone and he wouldn't have to monitor a thing. The thought was less than comforting.

Ten minutes later, Jake's mood hadn't improved. He veritably stormed around the side of the baby-sitter's house to the backyard. His son was on the jungle gym. "Chris. Come on. Let's go."

Chris climbed down the maze and ran toward him, a smile on his face. Almost mystically, some of the tension that had built inside Jake dissolved.

"You're late and I have so much to tell you!"

Jake lifted the boy into the air and received a somewhat sticky kiss. "Sorry, champ. I got all involved in that stupid computer and lost track of time."

"That's okay, I'm just glad you're here now." Chris twisted in Jake's arms and waved goodbye. "See you in the morning, Mrs. Stephenson."

"Bye, sweetheart."

"Remind me to pay you tomorrow, Mrs. Stephenson," Jake added. "I'm taking Friday off and he won't be here."

"Okay. See you then."

By the time they reached their own front porch, Jake had heard—in more detail than he cared to—how Melanie Clifton had thrown up her chili dog all over Mrs. Stephenson, and Tommy Porter had pooped in his white shorts. Jake grimaced. Full-time fatherhood had provided many a revelation—the most unappealing one being a small child's absolute fascination with any and all bodily functions.

"Can I unlock the door?"

Jake handed Chris the key, but his gaze wandered to the old, white Victorian house next door. What was Maggie doing now? he wondered. When she picked him up for lunch earlier she'd been wearing a pair of white cotton slacks and a nautical red-white-and-blue shirt. Her braid had been decorated with matching ribbons. Though he'd acted like a perfect gentleman, his thoughts had strayed to what she'd looked like the night before, wearing nothing more than candlelight.

A tug on his hand brought his mind back to his son and they walked inside. "You're getting real good at unlocking the door. We may just have to get you your own house key," he said, rumpling the boy's hair.

Christopher's eyes sparkled. "On a key chain and everything?"

"Everything." Jake pointed at the paper pinned to his son's shirt. "What's that?"

Chris undid the note and gave Jake the folded paper. "It's about my makeup day for gymnastics."

Jake glanced at the note and nodded. "I'm going to change before I fix dinner. Remind me to write 'makeup day' real big on the calendar."

Chris nodded in agreement, but was frowning. "Jake..."

"Yeah?"

"Why do I have to wear makeup?" he asked earnestly.

Jake bit the inside of his cheek to keep from laughing and hunkered down to his son's level. "It's not that kind of makeup. Remember when you didn't get to go to class last week because your teacher was sick?" The boy nodded. "Well, this week you'll go an extra time to make up for the day you didn't get to go. Understand?"

"Oh. So I don't have to put junk on my face?"

"Nope."

"Good," he said with a big sigh. "Can I have a cookie?"

"You can have two if you'll drink a glass of milk."

"Deal." He gave Jake a quick kiss before running toward the kitchen.

Jake laughed softly as he went into his bedroom and stripped out of his long-sleeved shirt and jeans. Fatherhood. Not all his problems were as easy as simple explanations of words, but they weren't as bad as he'd imagined before Chris came.

He opened his drawer and drew out a black polo shirt and a pair of khaki shorts, then put them on. As fathers went, he decided, he wasn't doing a half-bad job. He caught his reflection and tried to remember a time when he'd ever been able to talk to his father about anything as exciting as a kid throwing up on someone else. Unable to think of a single incident, Jake decided he wasn't merely doing half-bad, he was doing a damn good job.

A smile was still on his face as he headed toward the kitchen. "Hey, Chris, what do you think we should have for dinner? Goulash? Or spaghet—"

The milk carton sat on the counter, alongside a full glass of milk. "Chris?" he called. "What have I told you about not leaving the milk—"

His foot bumped something and he looked down. At the sight of Babbit on the floor, a frisson of fear shot up his spine.

"Chris?" Jake walked through the house, his stomach knotting with the silence. He checked the bathroom and Chris's bedroom, and found them empty. He stopped in the living room. "Chris, this is no time to play hide-and-seek. Front and center."

He checked on the front porch, his pulse starting to race. "Christopher James," he called. Every horror story he'd heard about children being kidnapped came to mind as he ran back through the house, trying to tell himself he would find the boy messing with the birdbath or on the swing in Maggie's yard.

He slammed out the back door and down the steps, then stopped abruptly. The birdbath was undisturbed; the empty swing hung eerily still. "Christopher James! If you can hear me, you'd better show your face now!" Jake turned in a slow circle, looking for movement of any kind as his heart thudded rapidly. When his gaze fell on Maggie's house, he started running. She knew kids. She would have an idea where he'd gone.

He didn't bother to knock but burst into her kitchen. She faced him, her hand at her heart, her expression startled.

"He's gone. You've got to help me find him. Please!"

Jake's face was pale beneath his tan; his eyes, desperate. "He's here," Maggie said quickly, crossing the room.

"He's what?"

Maggie put her arms around him to soothe, and felt the tremor of relief go through his body. "He said you told him he could have two cookies. I thought it seemed a little strange that you'd send him over here, but—"

"Yeah, I said he could have two cookies, but I meant two of ours." He cursed under his breath. "God, but that was terrifying."

"I can imagine," she said, stepping back. "I'm sorry."

He glanced over at the nook. Two fans were set in separate windows, drawing the stripper-tainted air outside, but there was no sign of his son. "Where is he?"

"Well, he was here just a moment ago. He must've wandered into the living room while my back was turned, probably to get away from the smell."

"Thanks," he said, brushing a kiss against her cheek before striding from the kitchen. "Christopher James, where are you?"

Hands on his hips, Jake stood beneath the arch between the dining and living rooms, his gaze darting around. Maggie walked up beside him and pointed to the closet door that stood ajar. He crossed the living room and flung the door wide open. "What the hell are you doing in the closet?"

She peeked over Jake's shoulder and saw Chris scramble to a standing position. He knew he was in trouble, she thought. His eyes were wide with wariness. He held up something. "Look what I found," he said.

Maggie recognized the faded, striped drawstring bag as the one she'd kept her marbles in as a child. "Where was that?" she asked.

He pointed to a small shelving unit at the side. "Under that shelf."

"That still doesn't answer *my* question," Jake said pointedly, folding his arms over his chest.

"I just wanted to look around." Tears welled in the boy's eyes. "The door was open and the light was on, and it smelled so good, I wanted to see what was in here." He stared down at the bag. "This was all I could find."

"Listen here, young—"

"Wait," Maggie whispered. She put her hand on Jake's arm. "Let me ask him something." Jake stepped aside and she crouched in front of Chris. "What do you mean, it smelled so good?"

"It reminded me of that basket in Grandma Larson's bedroom." He looked up at Jake. "You know, the one with all the dried up purple stuff."

"Lavender?" Jake asked.

"Uh-huh. It smelled like lavender."

Dazed, Maggie stood and backed up until she ran into the couch. When she sank down on its arm, she saw the look of concern on Chris's face.

"I'm sorry," the boy said. "I'll put it back."

"No, you keep it," Maggie said. "I have a feeling my grandmother wanted you to have it."

"Can I keep it, Jake?"

"I guess, but you're still in trouble for leaving the—"

"But you said I could have two cookies and we didn't have any, and you said one time that Maggie always did..." His breath ran out and so, apparently, did his courage. He looked down at the floor. "I didn't think it would hurt anything," he mumbled, sniffling.

It would have been easy to pull his son to him and tell him everything was okay, but Jake knew what he had to say would have more impact if he waited until later to hug Chris. He knelt down and lifted his son's chin. "Never, never leave the house or yard without permission. You know why. We've talked about it, remember?" Chris nodded solemnly. "Now that you take the time to think, do you see where you were wrong?"

"Yes, sir."

"All right. Go to the kitchen, sit at the table and wait for me. And don't touch the fans," he added. "I need to talk to Maggie for a minute."

A solitary tear trickled down the boy's face. "I'm sorry I made you mad."

Jake wiped the tear from his son's cheek. "You scared me, Christopher. Rules are rules for a reason. In this case, it's a rule to keep you safe because I love you. Okay?"

Chris threw his arms around Jake's neck and hugged him. "I love you, too."

His point made, Jake gave in to his heart and hugged the boy in return. "Now scoot," he said, kissing Chris on the forehead. "I'll come get you in a couple of minutes."

"Yes, sir."

With Chris's departure, Jake rose and studied Maggie. Her eyes were focused on the closet and her arms were wrapped tightly around her waist. Recalling their conversation in the kitchen at the lake that first night, he didn't have to be in her mind to know what was running through it.

He lifted her chin. "I know what you're thinking, but there's got to be a logical explanation."

She stood like a shot. "Fine!" she replied in an agitated whisper. "Give it to me! The closet is empty, except for my jacket." She gestured toward it with her hand and met his gaze with defiance. "I cleaned it out two weeks ago."

Jake stuck his head in the closet and took a deep breath. Though he couldn't smell lavender, he did find a sweater hanging in the corner behind Maggie's windbreaker. He took it off the hook and handed it to Maggie. "Here's your culprit."

She stared at it with disbelief. "I packed this."

"No," he said patiently. "You obviously saw it and meant to, but it got pushed to the back and you forgot it." If looks could kill, he would have been six feet under. Strained patience glowed in Maggie's eyes.

"For the record, let me assure you that I did *not* overlook this sweater. But for the sake of argument, let's say you're right and I did. Can you smell lavender?"

He took the sweater and put it to his nose. "Yes."

"Sure," she said with a smirk, grabbing the navy cardigan. "When you stick your nose in it! Chris smelled it from outside the door."

Jake shrugged. "It rained this afternoon. Dampness can bring out a smell sometimes so that it lingers in the air."

Maggie rolled her eyes, her grip tightening on the sweater. "Again, for the sake of argument, let's say I buy that, though I don't. Tell me," she said, watching him closely. "How did the closet light get on?"

"Chris must've turned it on."

Her smile was slow and triumphant. "First of all, he can't reach it. Second of all, he said the door was open and the light was on."

"You must've left it on then."

"I haven't been in the closet today."

Jake thought of her Wednesday schedule. At lunch this afternoon she'd even mentioned that she felt as if she was meeting herself coming and going. Surely that was the answer. He smiled, touching her cheek. "Maybe you were, and you just don't remember," he said softly.

She swatted his hand away. "Maybe *you* were here, and *you* turned it on!"

"Don't be silly."

"Well, my explanation makes as much sense as yours!" She turned and threw the cardigan on the couch, then faced him, angrily folding her arms. "Dammit, Jake," she whispered harshly. "Quit being bullheaded! I'm not senile. I packed that sweater and I cleaned that closet, including under the shelf!"

Bullheaded? *He* was being bullheaded? "Fine," he said, dipping his hands into his pockets. "Bea finds the spirit world a little chilly and pulled out the sweater to keep herself warm. And let's not forget, she lured Chris to the closet to find the marbles she'd hidden for him."

"Don't patronize me," Maggie warned, turning away.

Jake grabbed her arm before she'd taken her second step. "Look, I'm sorry. It's been a hell of a day, and I just had seven years scared out of me thinking my son had been kidnapped. As far as the closet goes, it's not that I think you're senile. I just can't help but feel there has to be a logical explanation."

Her anger faded as quickly as it had flared. "You're right. It has been a hell of a day. I scraped my knuckles twice, gouged a three-inch slash in the wood..." She pressed her lips together as he tenderly examined her hand. "And to top it all off, I got another damn letter from Brad!"

"*Another* letter?" He lifted his gaze to hers. "When did you start receiving letters?"

She hadn't meant to mention it, as she didn't like dwelling on the subject of Brad. Maggie slipped her hand from Jake's, studying her nails and the damage she'd done to them in the past few weeks. "After I hung up on him three times."

"Doesn't that guy get the hint?" Maggie looked up at the sound of jealousy in Jake's voice. "How many letters have you gotten?"

"Oh, I don't know." She ran a hand through her bangs and glanced off to the side. "Three, four..."

"What's he saying?" he demanded.

His incredulous gaze had Maggie folding her arms again. "Who knows? I don't open them. I send them back!"

"You do?" A smile blossomed on his lips.

"That's what I just said, isn't it?" she snapped, determined not to let him get around her with that idiotic, pleased grin.

"I'm sorry. I keep managing to get you angry when it's the last thing I want you to feel." Maggie's determination faltered as he undid her arms and coaxed them around his neck. "Will you forgive me?" he whispered against her throat. He slid his hands down her sides, teasing her breasts in the process and making her head swim. "Hmm?"

"Yes, but—" She lost her train of thought when his hips brushed provocatively against hers. "I...I didn't go in that closet today."

He nibbled on her ear. "I believe you."

"And I don't care what—" He moved his hands again, one to her lower back, pressing her to him, while the other strayed to her breast. "Uh, what what's-his-name has to say."

"That's nice," he murmured against her mouth.

"Nice," she echoed, relaxing into him. The kiss was rich and tender and slow. She kept thinking that in time he wouldn't be able to make her so breathless, so dizzy. Yet the more they kissed, the more quickly it seemed her control fled.

Maggie broke the kiss suddenly, her eyes wide. "You're forgetting Chris!"

He smiled. "No, I'm not. He's sitting at the kitchen table and wouldn't dare move."

She pulled back when he started to kiss her again. "You're speaking awfully confidently for a man who not ten minutes ago was terrified because he couldn't find his son."

"He—"

"Ja-ake," the boy called from the kitchen.

Jake sighed. "Yes, Chris."

"I'm hungry."

"I know how he feels," he whispered, then gave Maggie a final kiss before they headed into the kitchen.

Maggie walked behind him, smoothing her shirt and willing her pulse to steady.

"How about some goulash or spaghetti?" Jake asked, approaching his son.

Chris looked longingly toward Maggie's Crockpot on the counter. "I like real soup better."

Jake picked the boy up and set him on the counter. "I'm afraid you'll have to settle for—"

"Do you like vegetable?" Maggie asked.

Chris turned toward her, smiling. "It's my favorite."

Maggie hesitated only a moment, then glanced at the large pot. "I've got to take some soup over to the Irvings, because they've got colds and don't feel well. But even after I do that, I'll still have enough for an army." Her gaze met Jake's. "Would you like to stay for dinner?"

"Could we, Jake? Could we?"

Jake's eyes turned serious. "You're sure?"

She wasn't sure about much of anything lately, but what harm could there be in one evening? She lifted her shoulders. "What's a little soup among friends?"

The next evening Maggie stopped rubbing stain into the baseboard to glance up at the small television she'd placed in the middle of the kitchen floor. The high-pitched tone foretold a weather bulletin. She eyed the dark, rain-pelted windows. Last night the breeze had been the perfect balance between cool and warm, and she'd been playing marbles on the living room floor with Jake and Chris. Well, she was on the floor again, but she was alone and the temperature had dropped from seventy-five to thirty-eight in three hours.

A flash of lightning was followed quickly by a deafening peal of thunder. Maggie capped the stain and crawled over to the television to turn up the volume.

"Tornadoes have been spotted aloft in the line of thunderstorms moving northeast from southern Tulsa to Broken Arrow. Be prepared to—"

A crackle of thunder shook the house, plunging it into darkness. Maggie's heart beat strong and fast, and she froze, willing the electricity to come back on. Moments passed, accentuating the keening of the wind and the driving force of the rain as it hit the panes of glass.

Maggie rubbed her arms and sat back on her heels. "First things first," she said, then stood. Remembering a flashlight in the left-hand drawer, she was appreciative when the momentary brightness of lightning allowed her to zero in on the drawer without difficulty.

The flashlight was the large, heavy-duty kind and Maggie pushed the red button forward, but got no results. She shook it and tried again. Even taking the batteries out and rearranging them didn't help.

"Now what?" The flashlight didn't work, she'd seen no extra batteries about the house, and she knew both radios were run by electricity alone. Candles, she thought with elation, then frowned. She'd packed the candlesticks last week and thrown the half-burned candles into the trash.

"Dammit!"

She tapped her chin with the useless flashlight. "Think, Flannagan. *Think!*"

Laughter bubbled from inside her. Jake might have batteries, and if not, Maggie knew for sure he had candles! She smiled and felt her way to the entry closet for her jacket. Ever since they'd made love by candlelight that first night, he'd continued the practice and called it tradition. Surely he would have a spare.

Maggie slipped into her jacket and opened the front door, immediately wishing it was a full-length coat. Out on the porch, she flipped the collar up, then noticed lights were still on in all the other houses. "Gran, if this is your idea of a joke, I'm not laughing," she muttered, dashing down the stairs.

Cold rain stung her face, and she flinched against the lightning and roar of thunder. As a child she'd been fascinated by the one tornado warning she'd been in. The sky had tinted everything an eerie shade of greenish yellow, and the wind, after blowing furiously, had grown ominously still. By day, there had been a touch of excitement to the danger. At night, and now that she was older and knew more, it was a different story. She didn't care for what the shroud of darkness might conceal.

Her tennis shoes and socks were soaked before she was halfway across the yard, and the wail of a loud, weather-warning siren spurred her to run even faster. She slipped going up Jake's stairs and cursed as she scrambled upward, knowing she wouldn't bother with knocking. She flung back the screen door just as the front door opened.

"Maggie! I just tried to call you—"

Wet and shivering, she went into Jake's arms as the siren droned on. He took a step back and closed the door while she absorbed the feeling of being safe. She looked up. The touch of his hand against her face was warm as he pushed away the hair plastered to her cheek.

"Got a spare battery or two?" She smiled, holding up the defunct flashlight. "It doesn't work."

"Forget the flashlight. I was just coming to get you. Chris and I have set up the basement just in case and—"

Maggie shook her head. "I can do the same at Gran's, I'd just like a little light to do it in. And if you have a radio I could borrow that—"

His brows lowered. "Don't be ridiculous! You'll stay with us."

"No, I—"

"Was last night so bad?" he asked, unzipping her jacket.

Why did he always have to phrase things like that? "No, last night was lovely, and you know it. I enjoyed being with you both, and while I don't regret it, I just don't think it's very—"

"Under normal circumstances, I could see your point, but there are tornadoes skipping around out there from hell to breakfast that void any point you could make."

Maggie opened her mouth to argue, but sneezed twice instead. Jake took her flashlight and tossed it on the couch, then stripped her jacket from her. "You're going to go to the bathroom and get out of your wet things while I dig up something dry for you to put on. Then you're going to come out and sit in front of that fire and get warm." While he hung the coat in his closet, he called out, "Chris, bring three cups instead of two. Maggie's come to our party."

Maggie heard the hurrah from the kitchen and felt Jake's hands come down on her shoulders from behind. He propelled her through the living room. "Anyone ever tell you you're bossy?" she asked.

"Only you."

She stopped at the bathroom door and looked over her shoulder. "Shouldn't we be going down into the basement or something?"

"Not yet. Don't worry. As I said, the basement's ready, but it's usually not necessary. I've got the television on and the radio tuned to an all-weather station to keep track of the storm. Now scoot," he said, giving her a nudge, "before you catch pneumonia."

Maggie had barely stripped out of her wet things when she was surrounded by darkness for the second time. Within moments Jake was at the door, clothes and a lit candle in his hands, a wicked grin on his lips. Laughing, she closed the door, then dressed to the sounds of Christopher's practicing on the piano. Jake's red cashmere sweater was warm and welcomingly soft against her bare skin. His black sweatpants, however, presented a problem. Thanks to the drawstring waist, she was able to keep them up, but could do nothing about their comical length pooling at her ankles. Red argyle socks adorned her feet.

With a wry smile for her appearance, Maggie left the bathroom. The scene that greeted her at the piano warmed her more than the promise of the fire in the living room. Three candlesticks stood atop the baby grand, and Jake was seated next to his son. Chris's playing was less than perfect, but he smiled proudly at his father at the piece's end and gave him a kiss. Golden light flickered against their dark hair, pointing up their resemblance, and Maggie recalled Jake thanking her for helping him with his son. Seeing them now she knew he would have gotten to this point, with or without her help. She knew, too, that the love he'd felt deprived of as a child had been given to him as a father.

Maggie clapped and Chris jumped up and shuffled over to her in his footed pajamas, his eyes dancing with excitement as he took her hand. "Isn't this neat-o?" he said, leading her into the living room. "It's just like before Thomas...Thomas...?" He frowned and looked back at his father, who had followed them.

"Edison," Jake whispered.

"Yeah, like before Thomas Edison vented lights. C'mon," he said, tugging her hand. "We gots cocoa and chipolate cookies and Jake's gonna read stories." He glanced up at her, his eyes sincere. "You'll like it. He's the bestest story reader...even better than Mommy."

"Oh, he must be good then."

"Is Maggie gonna spend the night?" Chris asked.

"No, I—"

"I think she should," Jake said, "to be on the safe side."

"Me, too. Please, Maggie? Please?"

Entreating young eyes looked up at her. A pushover at heart, she nodded.

"Oh boy!" Chris led her onto the blanket, carefully sidestepping the tray with cups of cocoa and cookies on it. "You sit there, Jake. And you sit there to get warm, Maggie," he said, pointing to the place between his father and the fireplace.

"Where are you going to sit, champ?" Jake asked, lowering himself to the floor.

"In Maggie's lap so we can both see the pictures."

Maggie gave Jake a sidelong look as she sat cross-legged, whispering, "Seems your son inherited your bossy genes as well as your blue eyes and black hair."

Jake shrugged as Chris picked up Babbit and settled in Maggie's lap. "We gots to be—"

"Have to be," Jake corrected.

"Oh, yeah. We have to be quiet to hear the story, and if he stops, we still gots...have to be quiet for him to hear what the radio says."

"Oh, okay." A smile twitched her lips as she reached for her cup.

Jake watched Maggie with his son. Did she know how right they looked together? How he'd longed to have her here with them, sharing an evening? He'd thought he'd gotten close to his wish by their all being together last night. This was even better.

Firelight shone through her bangs, setting the red in her hair ablaze. Lord, but she was beautiful, though not the artificial, exactly perfect kind of beauty. Maggie was "real" beautiful, and for tonight, she was his. Maybe he wasn't the sort of man cut out for marriage. Still he couldn't help but feel that for this one evening, it was as if they were family...and it felt very, very right.

"You can start now," Chris said, munching on a cookie.

Jake picked up a book and launched into Chris's favorite story. By the time Jake got to the first, "Fe-fi-fo-fum," he noticed Chris's eyes were growing heavy. Reaching the part where Jack steals the goose who lays the golden eggs, Jake saw Chris was comfortably slumped and snuggled against Maggie's chest.

"He's gone," Jake said quietly.

She smiled, fingering the child's short curls. "For about the past five minutes."

"Here, let me take him and I'll put him to bed."

She shook her head. "May I?"

"Sure." He helped Maggie to her feet, then walked into Chris's room. After pulling down the spread and setting a flashlight on its end to act as a night-light, he watched Maggie lay his son in bed.

Chris's eyes opened sleepily as she started to remove his arms from around her neck. He smiled and pulled her close, kissing her cheek. "G'night, Maggie."

She brushed his hair from his forehead and kissed him there. "Good night, Chris." She stepped back. "Sweet dreams."

"Don't let the bugs bite."

"Bedbugs," Jake corrected, tucking the covers around his son.

Chris nodded as he yawned. "I think I'm real lucky."

Jake sat on the bed's edge. "Why is that?"

"I got two daddies to keep me safe. You, and Daddy Evan."

Jake felt the tug on his heart. It was the closest Chris had ever come to verbally recognizing him as his father. "Yep, you're really lucky, and we're lucky to have you." Jake kissed his son, then stayed low for a hug.

"I love you, Daddy. Don't let the bugs bi—bedbugs bite."

Acceptance washed over Jake like a flood, stealing his breath. He held his son tightly and waited for the tears that had come to his eyes to pass. "I love you, too, Christopher. Very much."

Before they left the room, Chris was asleep again. The hinges on the door squeaked as Jake closed it and he and Maggie walked silently into the living room. Jake sat on the blanket and had Maggie sit in front of him, her back to his chest. They watched the fire and listened to the sound of the ebbing storm, the crackle of burning wood and the endless banter of the weatherman. Contentment seeped into Jake like the warmth of the fire. His son had called him Daddy, and the woman he loved was in his arms. Could any man ask for more?

"It sounds as if the danger is over. I better be—"

"You can't go. Sure, the brunt of the storm may have passed, but the danger's not over." Maggie scooted around and sat facing him. "Besides, you told Chris you'd stay and . . ." He undid the clip at the bottom of her braid and started loosening her hair.

How could such a small thing make it difficult to breathe? "And?" she asked.

The ribbons that had been entwined in the braid fell to the floor as he spread her hair over her shoulders. "And his father is really counting on your staying."

His gaze was temptation itself. "I really don't think we should—"

Jake cut off her protest with an achingly gentle kiss. "I've gone crazy tonight watching you," he said, tracing the V neckline on the sweater with his finger. "Knowing you had nothing on underneath was arousing as hell."

How could she have chill bumps when her body was burning? "Shouldn't we go to your room in case Chris—"

"Later." Jake lowered her to the floor and lay on his side next to her, determined to take it slowly. There was something special about this evening, something magical that filled him with a crazy combination of desperate longing and a need to relish the moment. He bent his head and teased her breast through the sweater.

Maggie gasped and lifted his head. "He could wake up from a bad dream or—"

"He did twice, at the beginning." He inched the sweater upward. "He's the kind of child who stays in bed and calls for you to come to him." Firelight danced over the creaminess of her skin with prurient delight.

"But—"

He kissed the frown from between her brows then gazed deeply into her eyes. "Trust me, Maggie. I wouldn't do this if I thought there were even the smallest chance he'd come out here. Besides, his door sticks and squeals when it opens. We'd hear him before he saw us." He traced the shape of her lips with a fingertip. "Let me love you, here and now," he whispered, his breath feathering her lips.

On a sigh, Maggie drew his mouth to hers.

Chapter Eleven

He'd had less than four hours' sleep. He should have been exhausted. Instead, he felt invigorated...and not from his shower. Jake slid his fingertips soundlessly over the piano keys as he passed, then stopped at the doorway. Leaning against the doorjamb, he watched Maggie.

Bacon sizzled as she laid it in the hot skillet. Coffee was perking, filling the air with its aroma. She'd donned her now dry, paint-decorated white T-shirt and jeans, and was singing softly, keeping time with an intriguing sway of her hips. The sight of her in his kitchen warmed him. This was how a day should begin.

Other beginnings from years ago floated through his mind. The long, formidable table, orange juice in crystal, eggs Benedict on china, ornate silver rings holding Irish linen napkins, and above all, the restriction of "speak only when spoken to."

Happy to be in this kitchen with this woman, Jake stole quietly behind her and wrapped his arms around her waist.

She gasped in surprise, then laid her head back against his chest. "What would you have done if I'd screamed and awakened your son?"

"Told him women can be awfully skittish in the morning." He nuzzled her neck. "What're you doing up so early?"

"Nine isn't early, and you better watch what you're doing. Chris could come in any moment."

He nibbled on her ear. "When you don't get to sleep until nearly five, nine is damn early. As for Chris, he usually sleeps a good twelve hours. And as for watching what I'm doing—" he cupped her breasts and teased them with his thumbs "—I much prefer watching *your* response."

Maggie turned around, her lips curving despite the stern line she tried to keep them in. He smelled of soap and shampoo and undeniable masculinity. He'd tossed a pink shirt over his jeans, but hadn't bothered to button it yet. Her fingers itched to follow the swirl of hair on his tanned, muscled chest, but knowing that Chris could walk in at any time kept her hands resolutely on his shoulders. "We can't be doing—"

He covered her mouth and kissed her until she leaned pliantly against him. "Mornin', Maggie," he whispered across her lips.

Maggie fought the weakness she felt and drew back, fingering the roughness of his beard. "You're arrogant, and—" How strange it was, she thought. He wasn't doing any more than simply looking at her, yet heat kept flowing through her as if he were doing much more. "And you forgot to shave."

His grinned. "That's not what you're supposed to say."

She kissed the dark stubble on his chin. "Morning, Jake."

The telltale squeal of a door had Maggie's brows rising. "Twelve hours, huh?" Jake gave her a shrug and a swift kiss before heading for the coffee cups.

Fully dressed and eyes bright, Chris scooted into the kitchen. "You're up a bit early, too," Jake said, lifting the boy into his arms. "Aren't you, champ?"

"The bacon woke me up." He looked away from Jake to eye the skillet and Maggie. "Daddy only fixes a big breaskiss on Sundays. You oughta sleep over more often."

Jake nodded enthusiastically behind Chris's back. Trying not to laugh, Maggie turned to the skillet. "Unfortunately, I can't, but as long as I'm here, would you rather have eggs, or pancakes?"

Hope widened the child's eyes. "Could I have both?"

"Think you can handle both?" she asked. Chris's nod was as enthusiastic as his father's nod had been. "Are scrambled eggs okay?"

"They're my favorite." He looped his arm around Jake's neck. "Daddy and I are gonna see a movie today. Wanna go with us?"

"That sounds like fun, but I've got work to do."

"Pleeease?" he begged. His eyes, Maggie predicted to herself, would be the downfall of many a girl in the future. "Movies don't take too long," he added.

She paused, listening to her own internal debate. "Well, we'll see."

"Tell you what," Jake said, giving Chris a kiss on the cheek. "While Maggie fixes breakfast, that gives me time to run over and check her house. Do you think you could go out and take care of the birds all by yourself?"

"I'll bet I can!" The boy scrambled from Jake's arms and was out the back door in two seconds flat.

When the door slammed, Maggie tilted her head a bit. "Sounds pretty good, huh?"

Jake turned to her. "What? Pancakes and—"

"Daddy," she said softly.

His smile warmed her from the inside out. "Sounds damn good." He leaned forward and brushed his lips over hers, then started buttoning his shirt. "I shouldn't be long." He'd taken two steps away from her before he backed up and took her in his arms, bending her over backward as he kissed her deeply. When he stood her upright, she felt light-headed. "Make that, I *won't* be long," he said, striding from the room.

The smile on her lips couldn't be denied as she tended the bacon and started cracking eggs into a bowl. The sun shone brightly in the window and she looked across the yard to Gran's. The house was coming along beautifully and in no time...

Maggie's smile faded as she realized how close she was to finishing her work there, unless she redid the floor... She wished she could paint the outside of the house. A soft blue-gray, maybe, with white for the gingerbread trim. Unfortunately, she had to watch her money, not to mention the time factor involving Pam and Kathie.

She took a wire whisk from a drawer and started whipping the eggs. "I could call them and ask how things are," Maggie reasoned aloud.

"Call who?" Chris walked up beside her.

"I didn't hear you come in."

"I was quiet 'cause I didn't want to scare any birds away." He went up on tiptoe, straining to see on the counter. "Whatcha doin'?"

"Scrambling the eggs. Want to help?"

"Can I?" he asked eagerly.

"Drag a chair over here to stand on, and I'll let you do that while I take the bacon out of the pan."

Maggie had always found working with children pleasurable. They approached the most mundane of tasks with awe and laughter. With Chris, there was a generous helping of both. Together they made the eggs, cleaned the pan and started the pancakes. What she lost in time and efficiency, she gained in enjoyment.

Maggie drizzled batter for four sets of eyes and smiles before pouring the usual circles. "Since you're such a good helper, I'm making you some special pancakes."

His face beamed and he laughed in delight as she turned the creations over, revealing happy faces. Still standing on the chair, he leaned over and hugged her neck. "I love you, Maggie."

Stunned, she stood motionless. She'd been afraid something like this might happen. Maggie just hadn't thought it could happen so easily. She cared for Chris, and because she did, she knew she couldn't let the situation develop any further.

Chris pulled away, distress clouding his eyes. "Are you mad at me?"

"No." She shook her head and touched his cheek. "Not at all, sweetheart. You surprised me, that's all." She fiddled with his hair. "Women can be kinda silly about things like that sometimes."

He nodded. "Yeah, that's what Daddy Evan says."

Maggie handed him a filled plate and smiled. "Go ahead and start eating, and I'll fix Jake's pancakes."

For the next few minutes she was glad small children had a tendency to rattle. With a minimum of effort on her part, Chris kept the verbal ball in play while she worked to pull her composure together. She wanted nothing more than to bolt the moment Jake came back, but she knew she would have to sit down and go through the motions of eating.

Dear God, what was she going to do? Chris didn't *really* love her. At least, not in the way that she was worried about. His avowal had served as a warning, however. A reminder that he was the type of child who could form attachments quickly, and if she wasn't careful he would be hurt when she left Broken Arrow.

Her eyes closed, remembering how hurt Jonathan and Amy had been. How they hadn't been able to understand her leaving. She glanced over at Chris, who was sitting happily at the table, and promised herself he wouldn't give her departure more than a moment's attention.

Maggie retrieved another plate, slipped the pancakes onto it and turned off the electric skillet. The sound of the front door closing drew her gaze. Her heartbeat sped with the grim look on Jake's face as he walked toward her. Her fingers tightened on the plate's rim. Was something wrong at the—

"You have company," he said flatly, entering the kitchen.

"Company? Who—"

"Brad and his kids."

"No!" The plate slipped from Maggie's fingers and fell to the floor. The crash jarred her and she knelt immediately, beginning to pick up the pieces. "I'm sorry. I'm sorry. I'm—"

Jake hunkered down in front of her and stilled her hands. "Leave it. I'll clean it up."

Maggie put down the pieces and stared at the mess, only vaguely aware of the voices around her.

"Chris, take your plate into the living room and watch *Sesame Street* or something. And close the kitchen door behind you."

"Is Maggie okay?"

"She's fine, just go."

"Yes, sir." A moment later she felt the touch of a small hand on her shoulder. "It's okay. He's not mad."

She smiled weakly, but couldn't look at him. "I know," she said quietly. "It just makes me angry when I break things."

Maggie waited until the door closed before she stood and looked out the window. Brad, Jonathan, Amy...could they really be at the house? The clatter of broken pieces as Jake dropped them into the trash had her turning toward him. "Are you sure it's them?"

"I didn't ask for his ID, if that's what you mean," he said tersely. He swung his gaze to hers. Minutes ago it had heated her blood. Now those same eyes were distant. "He introduced himself, and I remembered him from pictures Bea had shown me." He folded his arms and leaned against the wall. "Did you know he was coming?"

"Did I know?" Maggie's laugh was mirthless. "Is that why you look so griped?" Her hands went to her hips, his audacity raising her temper. "You think I knew he was coming and just hadn't told you?"

The lift of his shoulder was negligible. "I don't think anything. I simply asked you a question."

"You're damn right you don't think!" She took a step toward him, reminding herself to keep her voice down. "Hell, Jake. It was only two days ago that I told you I'd returned a letter to him unopened!"

When he still held himself aloof despite her reminder, realization widened her eyes. "Surely you don't think I knew he was coming all along and was trying to hide it."

"No, of course not!" He raked a hand through his hair.

She moved a step closer. "What *do* you think?"

"Hell, I don't know!" He hadn't thought, he'd only reacted to what he felt. First jealousy, then fear, as he'd imagined Brad coming back into her life and taking her away. Needing to touch her, he closed the distance between them. He raised his eyebrows in apology and fingered the ends of her hair. "What are you going to do?"

"The only thing I *can* do." Her eyes closed as she rubbed her temples, and he noticed that her hands were trembling. "Go over there."

She opened her eyes and lowered her hands, clasping them together. "So, am I going home to electricity, or is it still off?"

Jake rested his hands on her shoulders and accepted the change in subject. "Everything was working fine. I checked the fuses to see if one was loose, but none of them were."

"Figures," she murmured. "Thanks for going over." She gestured to the counter. "There's your breakfast, sans pancakes."

"Would you like me to go with you?"

"No." She touched his cheek, and though she smiled, he saw the worry in her eyes. "I need to handle this myself."

"Maggie…" Jake wanted to ask her what she felt about Brad's arrival. He wanted to remind her that he loved her. Something. Anything. He shrugged. "Thanks for breakfast."

"Sure."

He stayed in the kitchen until he heard the front door close a couple minutes later. He walked into the living room and stood beside his son, watching Maggie from the window.

"Is she gonna come back to go to the movie with us?"

"No, she has company." Two children ran out of the house to greet her. Jake moved away, not wanting to see any more.

"I know. Maggie thanked me for helping with breas-kiss and told me why she was leaving. But gee, Daddy, those kids look nice. Couldn't all of us go to the movie?"

Jake slumped on the couch, rubbing at the pain behind his eyes. "No, I don't think so."

The next thing Jake knew, Chris was crawling up on his lap. "Don't be sad, Daddy. We can still have fun."

"I'm not sad," Jake said, conjuring a smile for his son's sake. "I just have a headache."

"We can stay home," Chris said earnestly.

Surprised by his son's consideration, Jake knew he couldn't allow his upset to interfere with keeping a promise. "Nope. We're not staying home." He lifted Chris's chin. "I'm going to take some aspirin and we're going to go have a ton of fun. Okay?"

Chris grinned as he closed his fist and held up his thumb the way Jake had taught him. "Okay!"

Maggie hadn't felt so much apprehension since she first approached the house so many weeks ago. As she started up the steps, Jonathan came flying out of the house, shouting her name, followed closely by sweet-faced, three-year-old Amy. A smile broke past Maggie's apprehension, and tears started running down her cheeks as she lifted up Jonathan in her arms, then knelt to include Amy in the hug.

"Hey, guys, let's give the poor woman a chance to get in the house, okay?"

Brad Taylor. Though she could detect changes in the children's appearance since she'd last seen them a little more than three months ago, Brad was the same. The crease in his casual slacks was as sharp as a knife, his golf-playing tan was perfect, his dark brown hair unruffled despite the breeze, his smile suitably friendly. She'd often wondered how she would feel if she ever saw him again. Now she knew.

Maggie felt...nothing. She stood with Jonathan on her hip as Brad picked up Amy. "This is quite a surprise," she said evenly.

"I take it you sent my last letter back unopened?"

"If you're speaking of the one that arrived on Wednesday, yes."

His brows rumpled in disappointment. "I was hoping the postmark might make you curious."

"The postmark? I don't even remember noticing it."

"Evidently not, or you might have opened it." His smile was easy. "I wrote you from my brother's in Arkansas to tell you I'd be by. The kids and I are between flights, so we'll only be here a couple of hours."

"I see," she said, setting Jonathan on the porch.

Brad opened the front door. "Shall we go inside where we can talk?"

Nothing had changed. Not only did he look the same, but even in a situation where he shouldn't have been in command, he took charge anyway.

She smiled, walking past him. "Inside or out, it won't make any difference," she informed him airily.

Maggie had to give Brad credit. Once they were in the house, he didn't try to push, but let her sit and chat with the children for a few minutes. Jonathan talked nonstop and looked as if he'd grown two inches since February. The baby roundness of his face was already giving way to an older look. He gave her several drawings that he'd colored with care and tied a red ribbon around. Together they went into the kitchen and mounted the artwork on the refrigerator with magnets.

Amy followed them everywhere, vying for attention by showing off her ponytail and proudly lifting her skirt to show her ruffled, big-girl pants. Accepting the bittersweet emotions involved, Maggie allowed herself to be led to the couch for a game of I-got-your-nose.

Brad sat quietly throughout, watching her with the children. After a few minutes, Maggie's curiosity about the visit got the better of her, and she served the children some cookies and turned on the television to a kid's program. Once they were settled, she took a steadying breath and faced Brad.

"Shall we go in the kitchen and have a cup of coffee?"

He rose from his chair and smiled gratefully. "I'd love some."

Nerves. She'd rarely seen Brad display any. The fact that he kept playing his thumb over his index finger piqued her curiosity more.

While she put the pot on the stove to make instant, he sat at the table. "I met your neighbor, or rather, I should say I introduced myself. He didn't extend me that courtesy," he muttered, then paused, clearing his throat. "Who is he?"

Maggie almost laughed, visualizing the meeting—Brad's hand-pumping congeniality versus Jake's stony countenance. She grabbed the jar of coffee and glanced over her shoulder. "A friend."

"A friend?"

The tinge of disbelief in his voice had Maggie's blood pressure rising as she faced him. "Look, Brad, I'm not the one who showed up on your doorstep without an invitation. If you have something to say to me, say it, but leave my personal life out of it. It's none of your business."

He held up his hands. "You're right, I apologize. I guess I just felt . . . it surprised me when he came to the door instead of you." He paused and shifted in his seat, studying the table as if something were written on it. "Sharisse and I were married March third—"

"Congratulations." Maggie crossed the kitchen and retrieved two cups.

"We filed for divorce three weeks ago," Brad said quietly. "This time, the split was mutual." He rubbed his jaw. "You know me, Maggie. I don't take failure easily. When she walked out on me the first time, you, better than anyone, know what a shock it was." He shook his head. "God, how I loved her then. She was so beautiful, and for a time, so loving. When she left, I tried to cut her out of my heart."

Maggie's astonishment at his speech doubled when he walked to her and clasped her upper arms. "Then you were there, always so caring, so gentle. I loved you, Maggie. Maybe not the way I should have, but I did."

"Brad—"

"Please, let me finish." He shook his head. "When Sharisse came back, I got confused. She dazzled me, just as she always had. Feelings I'd never resolved came back. I felt torn between the two of you, and in the end, I told myself it would be best for the children if they had their natural mother back." He caressed Maggie's cheek. "I was a fool to try and recapture the past. In doing so I gave up the best thing that had ever happened to me." He paused. "I still love you, Mag—"

She laid her fingertips against his mouth. "No, Brad. Don't say that." Her heart ached for what he was going through. "I . . . I appreciate the problems you had. I even understand them. But what I felt for you died months ago."

He took her hand in his. "Couldn't we try again?"

"Recapture the past?"

"No! A fresh start this time, for both of us."

"I'm sorry, Brad." She squeezed his hand. "It's just not possible."

The whistle of the kettle provided a perfect excuse for her to move away. She fixed their coffee, then sat down at the table across from him.

Brad fiddled with the handle on the cup. "I can't say I'm surprised. You sounded pretty definite the one time you talked to me." His gaze met hers. "I am sorry for the hell I put you through. Can you forgive me at least?"

To Maggie's amazement, her heart felt lighter for their talk. All the hidden animosity she'd felt had dissolved. "I think I forgave you a long time ago, but just hadn't realized it."

He smiled and took a drink of his coffee. "Think we can be friends?"

"I don't see why not."

He glanced around. "The house is looking great."

"Thanks. As you can see I'm still working on the woodwork in here and the wallpaper's supposed to be in today. After that, I'm through." Her gaze drifted to the rooms beyond. "Unless I decide to strip and revarnish the floor down here."

"I was surprised there wasn't a For Sale sign in the yard. Have you already sold it?"

"No..." She circled the rim of her cup with her finger. "I, uh, meant to put it on the market immediately, but I've been so busy that I haven't gotten around to it."

He raised a brow in disbelief. "Maggie Flannagan, project manager extraordinaire, who could handle several deals at once without missing a beat? How could *that*

Maggie Flannagan be so busy that she'd let such a major detail go unattended?''

Maggie laughed at his incredulous expression and leaned forward, propping her chin on her hand. "I've changed a bit. I've slowed down and tried not to get myself bound up in rigid schedules. After several years of nothing but, it's been a refreshing change."

A knowing grin slanted his lips. "You've decided to stay, haven't you?''

"No!" she denied quickly, sitting straight. "Of course not. I told you what my plans were the last time we spoke. And if you learned anything about me in all those years we worked together, it's that I always follow through."

"Ah, but as you said, you've changed."

"I said I've changed *a bit* . . . not totally."

"May I ask you something as a friend?"

"You can ask," she warned with a small smile. "But I won't guarantee an answer."

"Does the man next door have anything to do with your refusal to reconsider being with me?''

"Absolutely none," she said truthfully. "If you'd asked me that question back in early April, my answer still would've been the same."

"Does he have anything to do with your still being here?''

"Of course not!" Agitation set her knee to bobbing as her mind spun. "As I told you, I—I've invested in the bed-and-breakfast and...and...quit smiling at me like that!" She glared at him, not the least bit amused.

"Sorry," he said, covering her hand with his. "It's just . . . well, will you allow me one bit of advice, friend to friend, if I won't say another word about it?''

It? What was *it*? she wondered. He'd paused dramatically, as always, making her wonder what in heaven's name he could say that he hadn't already. Seeing the sincerity in his eyes, she nodded, trying to be patient.

"Because of me and what I put you through, you're vulnerable as hell. Please, take care of yourself, and be it now or in the near future, be very careful about love on the rebound." He smiled. "End of speech."

"Thanks for the concern," she replied, stealing her hand from his. "But it's not necessary," she added firmly.

"Okay." He glanced at his watch. "I know I've imposed on you by popping in like I did, but we've only got a little more time before we have to get back to the airport. I promised the kids we'd get something to eat before the plane took off, so would you like to come to lunch with us? My treat."

"Would you settle for—" she rose and checked the refrigerator, happy to focus on something else "—a grilled ham and cheese sandwich?" She looked over her shoulder at him. "I've even got crunchy peanut butter for the kids."

"I hate to put you out."

"Nonsense." She pulled out the cheese and ham. "Besides, it'll give me a little more time with Jonathan and Amy."

"You know, you're really a very special lady."

She felt a tug on her heart, but not because of Brad. "Yeah," she murmured, thinking of Jake. "So I've been told."

The rest of the visit went smoothly. Even when it came time for goodbyes, they weren't as heart-wrenching as they'd been before. Though Jonathan and Amy would never be hers, now that she and Brad were on better terms, she knew she would at least be able to keep in touch with them.

After they were gone, Maggie went out to pick up her long awaited wallpaper, then purposely centered her concentration on finishing the woodwork in the kitchen and stripping the old paper from the walls. Bone-weary and emotionally exhausted, it was eleven when she entered the welcome darkness of her room and changed into a silky nightshirt.

As if he were a sentry stationed on her bed for the sole purpose of making her face the questions she'd refused to listen to all day, the bear, Cuddles Malone, sat atop her pillow. Maggie sighed in resignation and, with Cuddles in tow, moved to the window seat.

Did Jake have anything to do with her still being in Broken Arrow? She stared at the stars dotting the midnight-blue sky, puzzling over Brad's question. Though the odd things that had happened in the house *had* slowed her progress, she'd added to the delay by doing more than originally planned. Part of the reason was her love for the house, the one place she'd ever considered home. The other reason, she admitted slowly, *was* Jake. Though she'd lied to herself as well as to Pam and Kathie, she wouldn't do it now. She had enjoyed being with him . . . even before their relationship had turned physically intimate.

Brad's warning about love on the rebound came back to her, quickly followed by something similar Jake had said. Maggie looked down at Cuddles, restlessly stroking his fur. She had told Jake she loved him. She'd both felt it and believed it strongly. But did she really?

She stared at the bear as if expecting an answer. If she hadn't just come off a bad relationship, would the way Jake made her feel have been so intense? And what did it really matter? Either way it was a relationship that could go nowhere. She was leaving, and Jake wasn't interested in a real commitment. So why did she hurt so badly?

Maggie thought of the other things Brad had said, recalling in particular his comment about her leaving details unattended. He'd been right. It wasn't like her to let something as important as listing the house slide. Lord, she thought, clutching Cuddles close to her body, had she pussyfooted around so long because she was afraid to take the next big step in her life? Or was it something as simple as not wanting to part with the house?

A light breeze stirred the fragrant scents of evening and her gaze drifted outside. Heaven knew she'd always been happy here. Even with the sadness of Gran's passing, she'd been happy to be here. Not only because of the house or Jake, but she'd made some good friends. She'd also enjoyed working at the thrift store, and she loved the town.

Suddenly it seemed she had as many questions as the sky had stars. Unfortunately, she had no clear answers.

Questions didn't matter. She'd planned her life, her fresh start. A start she couldn't begin fully until she reached California. Weeks ago she'd taken the first step by having enough faith in her ability to break away from the safety of a corporate structure and invest in herself. Did she have any less faith now?

"No," she whispered. "No," she repeated, this time with more conviction as she stared at Cuddles.

Maggie took a deep breath of resolution. It was time to move on before things with Jake and Christopher got any more complicated. Leaving. The thought of it made her throat constrict. Despite her rationalizations, she knew it would be hard for her to go; her departure might even be a little hard on Jake.

"Now's not the time to get maudlin, eh, Cuddles?" She clung to the fact that both she and Jake had known this time would come. It might be a little strained when she first told him, but hadn't he always been supportive? She closed her eyes, able to imagine Jake giving her a hug.

"Why, he'll be glad for me and wish me the best of luck." She smiled, ignoring the tears that ran down her cheeks. "He'll probably even promise to stay at the inn if he ever gets out our way.

"We're going to be fine, Cuddles. We really are."

Twenty-seven hours had passed since Maggie left. Twenty-seven hours had gone by without talking to her. Twenty-seven hours that she hadn't been with him, but with—

Jake frowned, setting his concentration to the task of unknotting a guitar string. He wouldn't think about the time. He wouldn't think about her, he decided, yanking the string through the bridge. A protesting metallic zing told him he'd pulled too quickly.

Damn her, he thought, throwing the string on the floor. Why hadn't she called? Surely she hadn't allowed Mr. Freshly Pressed to worm his way back into her life! Jake reached for a new string, reminding himself that he had no say in whom she saw or talked to. In another few weeks she would be gone and—

Jake looked toward the door, the sounds of giggles and tennis shoes slapping against the concrete breaking into his thoughts. A moment later Christopher and Timmy pressed their noses against the screen.

"Timmy wants to know if I can eat lunch with him. Please, Daddy, they're having hot dogs."

"Please, Mr. Wilder," the other boy added. "Mommy said it's okay."

Jake couldn't help but laugh at their mashed faces. "Sure. Don't forget to say please and thank-you."

"I won't."

They disappeared from the door, their whoops of joy fading as they—"

"Hi, Maggie!" Jake heard Chris say. "Daddy's in the living room and me and Timmy get to eat hot dogs."

Nerves made Jake's skin crawl and his muscles knot. His gaze steady on the door, he felt dread and anticipation curl inside him, followed quickly by longing as Maggie came into view. Her shorts and shirt befitted the summer day; her braid curved over her shoulder. Jake bit back the questions he wanted to fling at her as she raised her hand to knock, saying instead, "Door's open. Come in."

Maggie swallowed her trepidation and walked inside, telling herself everything would be just fine. The smile she'd put on her face eased to amusement. The coffee table had been scooted across the room. Jake sat on the couch, a guitar across his lap and four others in stands around him. Strings littered the floor, reminding her of a Jackson Pollock abstract. "You sure look busy."

"Not as busy as you've apparently been," he muttered. He watched as she picked up a string from the floor and played it through her fingers, obviously unaware of the edge in his voice.

"Boy, have I ever. I finished the woodwork in the kitchen, and only have to put up the wallpaper." She lifted her gaze to his.

"Is *he* still there?"

Acid splashed into Maggie's stomach. Things weren't going as she'd imagined. "You mean Brad?"

"No, the postman," he said dryly.

Maggie wrapped the thin coil of nylon around her finger, wanting to set things on the right track. "Look, I'm sorry I didn't call you last night but—"

"You're under no obligation to me." He laid the guitar on the couch beside him, fighting to keep his voice calm.

"No strings. No regrets. Isn't that what you said?" The wounded look in her eyes was the hardest thing he'd ever faced. Her chin rose as the look faded.

"That's exactly what I said," she replied, letting the string fall from her fingertips. She turned, heading for the door.

Jake bolted to his feet, knowing he'd pushed her away. "Where are you going?"

"Back to the house. I didn't come over here for you to jump all over me!"

"What did you come over for?"

She stopped at the door and faced him. "To tell you I'm leaving Tuesday!"

Jake marveled at his control. He felt as if she'd just rammed him in the solar plexus, yet he was able to stand, quite amazingly, without letting her know she'd scored a direct hit. He stuck his hands in his back pockets. "I've got to give him credit. He works fast."

Arms stiffly at her sides, her hands clenched in fists, she walked toward him. "*He* doesn't have a damn thing to do with my leaving! They came by for a visit and were gone two hours later!" She exhaled sharply. "I've got a life waiting for me in Pacific Grove. Remember?"

Knowing that Brad wasn't involved in her decision should have made Jake feel better, but it didn't. He stared at her, paralyzed by the confusing tangle of emotions he felt.

"Oh, forget it!" In exasperation, Maggie threw up her hands. "I thought you'd care and want to know. Evidently I was wrong."

Before she could turn away, Jake caught her arm. "I'm...sorry, Maggie." He dropped his hand to her wrist, circling it loosely. "I *do* care. I guess I'm a little grouchy because I didn't sleep well."

Because she wanted so desperately to believe that the scenario she'd imagined last night could happen, Maggie smiled slowly. "I didn't sleep too well myself."

"Tuesday, huh?"

She nodded, cursing the tightness in her throat.

"When does the moving van arrive?"

Her hand sought his and she cleared her throat. "There won't be one quite yet. There's a certain charm to Gran's, and the furniture is part of it. I, uh, thought the house might look cozier and more appealing if I left it behind until someone..." Maggie lowered her gaze. "Until someone buys it."

Apparently the words were as hard for her to say as they were for him to hear. Jake had had trouble imagining that house without Bea living there; without Maggie, it would be worse. "Is there anything I can do to help?"

"No, thanks anyway."

Though she'd expected a bit of sadness, Maggie wasn't prepared for this overwhelming sense of melancholy. Lifting her gaze, she studied his face: the cut of his jaw, the enviable long, dark lashes, the arrogance of his nose, his eyes, which had always seen more than she'd wanted him to.

Maggie hadn't planned for this to be goodbye, but she realized suddenly that to continue seeing each other would only prove more hurtful. His grasp tightened as did hers, and she knew he'd come to the same conclusion.

"Will you tell Christopher goodbye for me?" she whispered, unable to speak any louder.

Jake nodded, wanting to absorb everything about her so he could let her go. Her life was planned, as she'd said, and it didn't include staying in Broken Arrow or being with him. The moment seemed endless and yet too short as they looked at each other. Commanding his muscles into action, he pressed a kiss to her cheek. "So long, Maggie," he said softly. "I hope you'll be happy."

"You, too, Jake."

One by one, their fingers opened and their hands reluctantly relinquished their hold. Tears were in her eyes. Still her dimple twinkled valiantly before she walked away.

He watched her from the window, everything inside him crumbling as she crossed the yard and went into Bea's house. He'd lived within boundaries all of his life, but it wasn't until now that he acknowledged it. With Maggie, he'd stepped outside them. Too late he discovered the pain of having done so.

Pain. He'd protected himself from it for so many years that he'd thought himself invincible. If this was what love did to people, they could have it. To him it was a Pandora's box that promised pleasure, but ultimately left one broken and bleeding. Not being a masochist, it was a box Jake promised himself never to open again.

Chapter Twelve

When did you get back from your walk?'' Kathie asked, strolling into Maggie's office. "Haven't you heard all work and no play makes Maggie a drone?''

Numbers on the computer screen blurred, and Maggie closed her eyes. It was no longer September in California, but May in Oklahoma. Jake stood before her on Gran's porch, his blue eyes sparkling with the same taunt. The vivid image brought with it yearning, and Maggie quickly opened her eyes, pushing away the remembrance.

She glanced up at her friend and managed a dry look. "Drones don't take walks on the beach.''

"Sure they do.'' Kathie stole Cuddles Malone from the top of a file cabinet and flopped on the worn cloth sofa. "It's just that they work like crazy beforehand so they feel they've earned it, then start again the moment they return to make up for the time they've lost.'' She craned her neck, her gaze skimming the top of the desk. "I swear, I've never seen anyone keep so busy in all my life. What are you doing now?"

"Logging today's receipts and expenditures into the general ledger." At Kathie's exaggerated sigh, Maggie smiled. "It only takes a few minutes a day, and it makes things easier at the end of the month."

"Are you almost through?"

Maggie looked back at the sheet of paper, then resumed typing. "Uh-huh."

"Good. Ray and I are going to a movie, and Bill said if you'd go, we could make it a foursome. It would be a lot of fun."

"Well, I do have a few more items on my list—"

"Forget the list, Maggie. You've worked hard all day, so there's no reason why you shouldn't go."

No reason, Maggie thought. No reason at all. She'd told herself that dozens of times, trying to get enthused about the prospect of dating. She had yet to succeed.

"Thanks for the invitation," Maggie said, turning over the sheet to start on the next one, "but I can't. I've really got to —"

"You always have something to do," Kathie said. She glanced down at the bear. "You know, Cuddles, I don't think she's very happy here. What do you think?"

"He thinks you're crazy." Maggie swiveled the chair to face her friend. "Ask me. I love it here! I love my job, working with you and Pam, meeting new people... You know how much the inn and being so close to the ocean means to me."

"Yeah, I know." Kathie worried the bear's ear. "Still, I'm concerned about you, and so's Pam. It's not just that you're working hard, I mean, we all do. But you keep yourself buried in it."

For a moment Maggie wavered on the brink of telling Kathie about Jake, but logic prevailed. If she didn't talk about him, she would get over him sooner—or so she told herself.

Maggie tapped the desk with her finger. "Remember how many piles of paperwork there were when I came? I had a lot of catching up to do. And now I have a lot of ideas I want to implement, or at least check for feasibility. That's all it is, Kath." She mustered a smile. "Why, once I'm firmly entrenched and have done my share of the work, I bet you'll start harassing me about being too lazy."

"You don't smile much, Maggie. And you laugh even less." Kathie raised her hand as Maggie started to object. "Don't get me wrong. You're wonderful with the guests. You smile every time someone comes to the desk out front. You even laugh at the worst jokes ever told. But it's the in-between times that—"

Pam stuck her head around the doorway. "Sorry to interrupt, but you have a call on line two, Maggie."

"Thanks." Maggie glanced at Kathie. "Look, I appreciate your concern. But you're worrying over nothing, I promise. I'm always obsessive with a new job at first, but once I'm settled in . . . *really* settled in, you'll see. I'll be ready to—" Maggie grinned "'—party hearty.' Now you'd better go and not keep Ray waiting, and if Bill is still interested in going out once I have everything the way I want, then I'll be happy to go out with him, or anyone else for that matter. Okay?"

Kathie looked unconvinced as she stood and set the bear on Maggie's desk. "Try to make it before the year 2000."

Maggie rolled her eyes and picked up the phone. "See, I'm smiling," she said as Kathie left the room. Maggie punched the blinking button. "This is Maggie, may I help you?"

"Hi, this is Sheila with Gunderson Realty. My call is of the good news/bad news variety, with the emphasis on good."

Maggie sat very still, hoping to slow the suddenly rapid beat of her heart. "Well hello, Sheila. Let me guess. It rained so much today, Gran's house is now on Grand Lake?"

"How'd you know it rained?"

Not wanting to admit how she'd kept track of the weather in Oklahoma since arriving, she opted for a white lie. "I've become a morning-show addict, they always tell what's happening across the country weather-wise."

"Oh, I see. Well, it *did* rain all day, but your house is still intact. I also just received a contract on it. That's the good news."

Maggie's chest tightened, and she picked up Cuddles and clutched him to her. "Well that's...good news, all right."

"However, the contract came in low by ten thousand. The buyer apparently wants to carpet throughout and make a few changes. I suggest that we counter. Also, there's a little matter of..."

Though Sheila continued talking, Maggie ceased to listen. Carpeting? Some idiot wanted to cover up those beautiful floors? True, they did need to be refinished, but still... And if they were going to commit that sacrilege, she shuddered to think what the other "few changes" might entail.

"Maggie?"

"I'm sorry, Sheila. What did you say?"

"I'll go ahead and send the contract for you to look over, but in the meantime, I wanted your okay on the plumber as long as it's not—"

"Plumber?" Lord, what had she missed? "I'm sorry, I got distracted. What's this about a plumber?"

"The toilet sprang a leak and water seeped through the floor. The living room wall has sustained some minor damage. Naturally, I've turned the water off to prevent more problems, but I need your okay before I call—"

"No! Don't!" *Minor* was a relative term, Maggie thought. There was only one thing to do. "I'll, uh, fly out there tomorrow and—"

"Oh heavens, that's not necessary. I'll be more than happy to—"

"I appreciate that, Sheila, but the house *was* my grandmother's, and frankly, it'll make me feel better if I come take care of it myself."

"Okay, if that's what you really want."

"It is."

"If you'll give me a call after you've made your reservations, I'll be glad to pick you up at the airport."

"Thanks, I'll call you right back."

Maggie hung up the phone and immediately started jotting down the need-to-do items as they raced through her mind: call the airline, check the calendar, give Pam the bills that were due to be mailed out, start packing.... Still writing, she reached for the Rolodex with her free hand. A small part of her heart lifted at the prospect of returning to Oklahoma. Maggie squelched it immediately, glaring at the bear as if he'd spoken aloud. "I know what you're thinking. But I'm going to check on the house, not because I want to see—"

"Uh-oh," Pam said, leaning against the doorjamb. "It must be bad news if it's got you talking to a stuffed animal."

Maggie set Cuddles aside, disconcerted because he suddenly seemed to be smiling. "I—uh, finally got an offer on

the house, but it's ten thousand too low. Even worse,
Sheila said that the upstairs toilet leaked and did a bit of
damage to a wall." Maggie fingered through the card file
until she found the airline she wanted, then looked up. "I
need to assess the damage and get it fixed. I hope you and
Kathie won't mind my leaving."

"No, of course not." Pam slipped her hands into her
pockets. "I'm surprised Sheila didn't offer to take care of
it for you."

"She did. But, well, I'll feel better doing it myself. Don't
worry, though, I'll only be gone a couple days, and I'll
have everything taken care of here before I go."

"No problem. We can hold the fort."

Maggie picked up the phone and punched in the airline's number, her gaze settling on the bear. "You're
wrong," she whispered, turning the bear's back to her.

Maggie stood at her grandmother's front bedroom
window, absently watching Sheila. As was the woman's
habit, she was sitting in her car preparing for her next ap-
pointment. "Don't feel bad about the offer, Maggie,"
Sheila had said. "The name of the game in real estate is
offer/counteroffer."

Maggie turned from the window to get a postflight cigarette. Sheila had felt optimistic about ending up with an
offer closer to the original asking price, so why did each of
Maggie's steps seem weighted with concrete? Why did the
threat of tears press against her eyes?

"Cheer up, Flannagan," she said, trying to forget how
the moment she crossed the threshold, she'd felt as if she
was home. "You put the house on the market to sell it.
You should be happy."

She glanced at the mirror over the dresser, absently
smoothing her pink slacks, then fussing with the short

sleeves of her pink-and-white sweater. By the time her gaze made it up to her face, she had to admit she looked anything but happy. Groaning, she grabbed a cigarette and lit it, then started pacing.

"So the stupid woman wants to carpet the floors? That's not my concern." Like a child writing a task on a blackboard, she mentally repeated that line of thought over and over again. Halfway through her cigarette, she told herself she believed it.

"It's not like I'm losing everything, right?" She flicked her ashes, eyeing the antique bed and its wedding-ring quilt. "I'll still have the furniture...." When her mind betrayed her by wondering if the bed would ever look right anywhere but in this room, she shook her head and headed for the flowered chaise longue by the front windows.

"Be positive, Flannagan! That bed will look wonderful wherever it is!"

Her determined steps faltered then stopped, her gaze straying to the view out a side window. The descending sun shone brightly on the house next door, and for the first time since arriving, she allowed her thoughts to settle on Jake without cutting them off.

No longer denied, the ache of emptiness penetrated her thoroughly battered guard. Maggie gripped her sides; silent tears rolled down her cheeks. Why did her mind still retain vivid memories of that last moment when their hands had slowly untwined? Even now she could all but feel the touch of his palm against hers as it slid inexorably away, taking with it all that had made her feel warm.

Maggie wiped her face and sniffed, sagging against the window frame. How was Jake doing? she wondered. How was Chris? Were the two still getting along as well? Were they in the kitchen even now, fixing dinner? Her heart twisted as the questions took an unwanted turn.

Was Jake involved with someone new? Had he even missed her?

She stood straight and turned away, reminding herself that Jake was no longer her concern. At least, he shouldn't have been. Realistically, she'd known it would take time to get over him. Out of sight, out of mind. It should have worked. As yet, it hadn't.

But it would. *By God, it would*, especially if she would quit staring at his house and concentrate on keeping her mind occupied. Grabbing the ashtray and pack of cigarettes, Maggie stalked to the chaise, pausing long enough to pick up a piece of paper sticking out from beneath the flowered seat. She sat down, kicked off her flats, then put her feet up. Occupy your mind, she repeated mentally, crushing the cigarette in the ashtray.

Whom was she trying to kid?

Maggie set the ashtray and cigarettes aside and idly rolled the paper in her hands. The truth was she didn't have to be looking at Jake's house to think of him. In the past three months even the radio had become her enemy by playing old recordings of Jake's group, seemingly whenever she turned it on. And how many times had she been walking along the beach in Pacific Grove, only to have her heart skip a beat when she saw a tall, dark-haired man? How many times had she awakened from a sound sleep, sure that she'd felt Jake's touch and heard him call her name in a tortured whisper?

Eyes wide open, Maggie allowed the truth of what she felt to wash over her. She loved Jake. Not because she was on the rebound, not because she was vulnerable, but because it was so. And now that she knew...

Her heart lifted and fell within a beat. Knowing she loved him made no difference at all, except to make her more miserable. She knew his views on marriage, and she couldn't settle for less. Not that she had to worry about being faced with the choice after the way she'd left in June.

Maggie smoothed the curling edges of the blue paper, viewing the hurried printing through misty eyes until one word stood out: Changes. As the words came into focus, her eyes widened and her mouth gaped in horror. Not only would the floors be covered by carpet, the woman wanted to get rid of the clawed bathtub and pedestal sink in the bathroom, knock out the wall between the other two bedrooms, and enlarge the kitchen at the expense of the nook and back porch!

Impotent fury twisted inside Maggie and she wadded the paper and threw it across the room. She was losing everything, *everything* that had meant something to her! First Jake, and now her... rather, her grandmother's home.

She lit another cigarette and stood, envisioning the results of the proposed remodeling. "Oh Gran, the woman's not planning a few changes," she whispered. "She's going to destroy your house!"

A light scent of lavender permeated the air. Maggie frowned in confusion and looked down at the cigarette she held. "What...?"

Her gaze lifted and she turned, searching the room. "Oh Gran, you truly *are* here," she said, her mouth curving in wonderment. "You meant for me to keep the house, didn't you?" She combed her fingers through her hair, trying to absorb the reality that her "fresh start" from Gran hadn't been the money she would make from the sale, but the house itself.

"And Jake...the key that wouldn't fit for me, but would for him. The broken refrigerator, assuring our getting to know each other. The power failure..." A tear trickled down her cheek as the final piece fell into place. "It doesn't really matter how much you may have had a hand in, I understand. Jake was part of my legacy, too. Wasn't he?''

The doorbell rang and Maggie cursed. What could Sheila want now? Had she forgotten something? Impatient and wanting to be alone, Maggie got as far as the chaise to yell out the window. "Door's unlocked. Come on in, I'm upstairs.''

She glanced over at Jake's house and sniffed. "I may have screwed that up, Gran. But your house isn't sold yet.''

Maggie stooped beside the chaise, dousing the cigarette in the ashtray, then hurried to the dresser. Peering closely in the mirror, she wiped smudges of mascara from beneath her eyes and fluffed her hair, not wanting Sheila to see she'd been crying.

The faint lavender smell that had yet to fade increased ever so slightly, and Maggie turned around. Jake stood in the doorway, more heart-stoppingly handsome than ever. His slacks were gray, his shirt white, his suspenders a burgundy paisley, and his expression—guarded. Maggie gripped the dresser behind her, not trusting her legs to keep her standing. "Hello, Jake.''

Minutes ago Jake had caught a glimpse of her, and after ninety-three days of feeling numb, he'd experienced a stirring of sensations. Now that he was face-to-face with her, emotions flooded through him—love, anger, happiness, frustration. A vision in pink, her hair loosely curled and tumbling over her shoulders, she was beautiful. Damnably beautiful, he thought, as the longing he'd tried to deny ripped through him.

Jake lifted the jacket he held at his side. "I...happened to be walking home when I saw you get out of the car with the real estate lady.'' He hung the jacket on the doorknob. "You left that at the house last time you were there.''

"Thanks." She pushed away from the dresser. "How's Christopher?"

"Fine. He's at the movies with Brenda and the boys."

"And you, how have you been?"

How had he been? *How had he been?* She'd made him love her, then blithely skipped back to California leaving him bleeding, and she dared to ask how he'd been? Frustration took precedence as he moved into the room, thrusting his hands into his pockets to keep from reaching for her.

He raised a brow. "Why are you here?"

Maggie clasped her suddenly trembling hands behind her back. There was an edge to his voice she couldn't quite name. Skepticism? Caution? Hope, perhaps? Did he *really* care one way or the other why she'd come? Logic kept her own hope on a short leash, reminding her not to jump to any conclusions. "Sheila, my real estate agent, called me yesterday about a leak in the bathroom. You know how old this plumbing is, and I—"

"That's it?" he asked incredulously. "That's the reason you flew all the way from the West Coast?" Maggie swallowed hard as he shook his head and looked around the room. This time it wasn't necessary to guess what was in his voice—it was definitely irritation. "Your agent could've gotten you a plumber."

"I know, and perhaps it was foolish, but I didn't want to trust Gran's house to just anyone. Besides, I wanted to see for myself—"

"Have you sold the house?" His question sounded more like an accusation, and she followed his glare to the contract she'd left on Gran's bed.

Defensive, she stood a little straighter. "I have an offer. It came in ten thousand too low because the buyer has some changes in mind, but—"

"*Changes?* What's to change?"

"Lots, apparently," Maggie murmured, pointing to the wadded note.

He frowned and picked up the paper from the floor, then read it. Like the storms of spring, his expression darkened dangerously. "Luckily you're under no obligation to sell, since they didn't meet your asking price." The coolness of his voice belied the intensity in his eyes. "You aren't accepting the offer, are you?"

"I'm not wild about it, but Sheila says—"

"I don't give a tinker's damn what Sheila says!" he exploded. Maggie's grip on her fingers increased as he closed the distance between them, brandishing the outrageous note. "How can you even consider the offer, knowing, seeing in print, what will happen to the house?"

Any hope that she'd entertained about Jake's having come to see *her* vanished. How, she wondered, could her heart shatter anew when it was already in pieces? She slipped her arms around her waist, telling herself it was best this way. Before he came she had been on the verge of trying to figure out how to keep the house. Now, at least, she knew it was impossible. To live here, with Jake next door, would only be asking for a future of continuing heartbreak.

"The way I see it, beyond countering to get their offer up, I don't have a lot of choice." Maggie lifted her shoulders, then let them fall, striving for nonchalance despite his anger. "Remember, I live in California. I can hardly spend time sitting around here, screening prospective buyers on the basis of what they intend to do with the house, now can I?"

Jake threw the note to the floor, then backed her up against the dresser, planting a hand on either side of her. "Call your damn real estate woman and get her over here," he said through gritted teeth. "You can flatly reject your other offer. *I'll* buy the house. That way, you can fly back to California tomorrow."

If it hadn't hurt so much, the thought of his buying Gran's house would have been laughable. Maggie forced a disbelieving smile to her lips. "You'll buy the house? That's the most absurd thing I've ever heard. You've still got boxes that you've never even unpacked from your last move, so what in heaven's name do you want this one for?"

"*I'd* preserve it," he said with a deadly calm. "*I'd* take care of it properly and not sell it off to strangers." Maggie rolled her eyes and his narrowed. "*I'd* fill it with children as it was meant to be . . . as Bea wanted!"

The painful reminder hit home, but Maggie laughed in defense. "All on your own?" She touched her tongue to her upper lip. "That would be a neat trick."

His hands left the dresser to grab her shoulders and pull her against him. "It wouldn't have to *be* on my own if you'd quit running away and marry me!"

Stunned, the cocky smile left her face. Had she heard him right? He'd once told her he wasn't cut out for marriage. Yet here he was, flinging a proposal—of sorts—at her . . . to get the house? She looked up into his incredibly dark blue eyes and absorbed the feeling of his body pressed to hers. For ninety-three days she'd yearned to be in his arms again . . . but not like this. Not as a means to an end. That fate could be so cruel made her shake her head.

"Let me get this straight. You'd actually marry me to get this house and fill it with children . . . to please my grandmother?"

Jake grinned slightly and took a step back, releasing his hold. He'd been just as stunned as she by the proposal. Lord knew marriage had never entered his mind before . . . or maybe it had been there all along and he'd been too afraid to admit it.

"Your grandmother was very special to me, Maggie, but don't be ridiculous. I'd marry you because I love you. The house," he said, gesturing with his hand, "I can get, with or without you. The only reason I hadn't bought it yet was that as long as it remained unsold, I felt like a part of you was still here, and that you might return one day."

Maggie took two tentative steps, led by her heart, wanting desperately to be sure. "Was that a proposal then?"

"Do you want it to be?"

Maggie opened her mouth to say yes immediately, but looked away as practicality and logic stole her voice. Though he'd said he would marry her because he loved her, she couldn't forget how firmly opposed he'd been to marriage only a few months ago. Anguish wound inside her. Loving him as she did, how would she react if in a year or two he decided he'd been right to start with. Guilt chimed in, reminding her of her responsibility to Pam and Kathie. Responsible adults didn't enter into business agreements, then renege on them.

Torn between the dictates of her heart and mind, she raised confused eyes to his.

She was doing it again, Jake thought. Mental list-making. Opting to let it work *for* rather than against him, he smiled and stepped around her to check her purse. Sure enough, he found what he was searching for. He retrieved a pad and pen. Seeing his name scribbled repeatedly in the margin of the top sheet of paper gave him the courage to go through with the plan he'd just formulated. He flipped the pages until he found a clean one and handed her the pad and pen. "Have a seat," he said, nodding to the chaise.

Baffled, she did as he asked, but slowly. "What are you—"

Raising his hand to stop her, Jake sought the safety of distance by walking to the bed before facing her. He leaned against the wrought-iron-and-brass footboard. "Our entire relationship has been based, in a way, on pretense. First of all we pretended to ourselves and to each other that we could simply be neighbors, friends at most. Once we became lovers, I think we both pretended tomorrow would never come. It did, of course, three months ago. Now, thank God, we're finally to the tomorrow that's today." He dipped his hands into his pockets. "I think it's time we looked at things in black and white." He couldn't help but smile at her puzzlement. "You'll like this part. I want you to make one of your infamous lists."

"What?"

"You can put a header at the top...call it pros and cons." He paused, waiting for her to do it. "Go on. P-R-O-S—"

A grin pestered her lips and she bent her head to write. "I know how to spell."

"On the Pro side," he said, "I love you." She glanced up. "You can write that in capital letters because I've never said those words to any woman but you."

Skepticism raised her dainty brows. Jake smiled and held up his hand like a Boy Scout. "That's the honest truth. I never said it to Claire. I told her I was crazy about her, which I was. And there was a time when I thought it might be love, but never being sure, I didn't say the words. As it turned out, I cared for her, respected her deeply, liked her a lot, but I didn't love her...except, maybe, as a dear friend."

Jake took a deep breath, knowing the next few minutes would be the most important of his life. He'd let her walk away from him once. If she did again, it wouldn't be because he hadn't tried to keep her. "I've been a loner most of my life, Maggie, and content to be so. It wasn't until you left that I discovered what it was like to be lonely. I love you, Maggie Flannagan—body, mind, heart and soul. I always will."

He rubbed the muscles that had gripped his neck like a vise. "Now, I need to know...do you love me?"

Was the man blind? Maggie wondered. "Oh, yes," she assured him. "And I get to put that in all caps, too." A shadow of doubt crossed his eyes. "True," she went on, "I did tell Brad I loved him, because I thought I did. But when I compare that to what I feel for you...well, it's very clear to me that what I felt for Brad was affection. Affection enhanced, not only by my compassion for his situation after Sharisse left, but by my love for his children.

"It's *you* I love, Jake. A love that's worthy of all caps and bold type."

"I can live with that." And he wanted to, forever. Jake moved his hands to the footboard, grasping it tightly. It took every bit of his control to keep from walking across the room and taking her into his arms. His grip turned white-knuckled, for he knew that once he held her, he would never let go. "So," he said, nodding to the list. "What do we have so far?"

"Two facts on the Pro side. JAKE LOVES MAGGIE and..." She finished printing, then showed it to him. "MAGGIE LOVES JAKE."

Could he ever hear those words enough? "Sounds like an unbeatable combination to me," he said, smiling broadly. "Now on to the next fact. Christopher. Once Claire and Evan get back from London and move to Texas, Chris will be with me during part of every summer and some holidays. I know he thinks the world of you, but ... where would *you* list him? Pro or con?''

''Definitely pro. You know I think he's a wonderful boy.'' Maggie added his name to the list, no longer afraid to let the love she felt for Jake shine brightly in her eyes. ''What next?''

''I'd say the inn.''

''Yes,'' she said slowly as she came to her feet. ''What about my obligation to Pam and Kathie?''

When she stood, Jake's stomach lurched. He walked to the window and looked down at his house. ''The way I see it you have two options. One is to continue working there. Personally, I left California with a bad taste in my mouth. If you're there, however, I'm sure it'll be a different story, and I could commute as need be. The other option is ...'' He faced her, swallowing to combat the sudden dryness of his throat. ''You could give them the benefit of your financial help and business know-how, commute when you wanted and live here.''

She moved to the dresser, nibbling on her lower lip as she frowned. ''But I was going to use part of the money I made from the sale of the house to finance my partnership. If I live here, I obviously won't be selling.''

Jake shrugged. ''I could give you the money.''

''No,'' she said firmly. ''It wouldn't be right.''

''I disagree, but I understand.'' His muscles tensed with the problem, and he started pacing. He couldn't get this far, only to fail. Halfway to the door, he turned toward her and found she'd moved to the end of the bed. ''Why not sell the house, or at least half interest of it, to me?''

''But Jake, if we decided you *did* propose and I accept, it wouldn't be necessary. It would be your home as surely as it's mine.''

That she felt that way gave him hope. Maggie was standing not five feet away, and suddenly he didn't have the strength to go on without touching her. He walked to within a mere inch of her and allowed himself the luxury of curling a strand of silky hair around his finger.

"I don't know what it is about this house, Maggie, but from the moment I saw it, I was drawn to it. Not because it was Victorian. Frankly, if it were simply the style of house I liked, I could build one. What I'm talking about isn't as tangible as four walls. It's..." He searched for the words, resting his hands atop her shoulders. "You asked me at the lake if I believed in ghosts, and I told you no. While that's true, I do feel it's possible for a place to retain an emotional atmosphere of its inhabitants. I felt something when I saw this house, and it was reaffirmed when I walked into it. As surely as my parents' home was cold, there's a lot of warmth and love here."

He stared down into eyes that were deeply green and understanding. "I'd like to be a part of that, and if I contributed a share of the cost, I feel I truly would be." He raised his brows in question. "So, what do you think?"

"I like the idea of living here, yet still keeping my end of the bargain regarding Pam and Kathie." Like, hell! Maggie loved it and him even more somehow, knowing how much the house meant to him. She added the inn to the Pro side of the paper, then tossed it and the pen over her shoulder. Smiling, she slid her hands up his chest, then linked them behind his neck.

"Some men," he started, "don't like their wives working." He slipped his hands to the small of her back as he pulled her body to his. "I'd want you to do whatever you wanted. If it's volunteering at the thrift shop, getting a challenging job—" he couldn't resist rubbing his cheek against hers, just for a moment "—or even coming to the rescue down at Strings for Sale..."

"Ah-ha," Maggie murmured, savoring the thrill of his touch. "The truth comes out. You don't want me for myself, but for my business expertise."

Jake drew back, knowing full well that with their bodies so close she could feel what a lie that was. "What can I say? The computer likes you more than it does me."

He caressed her cheek as her dimple dented beguilingly. "There's one last thing I should add," he said. "Especially since it's guaranteed to go on the Pro side. Bea."

"Gran?"

"Mmm-hmm." He kissed the puzzled line between her brows. "Though I wasn't named as one of the beneficiaries in the will, Bea told me that she'd left me a legacy. Naturally, I asked her what she meant. She wouldn't tell me, but she smiled and said that there would come a time when all I had to do was look to see it. I'd all but forgotten that conversation until that evening when I came home to find you on my doorstep." He smiled. "I can't tell you how many times she said we'd be perfect for each other."

"A smart woman, my Gran," she said, playfully tangling her fingers in the hair at his nape. "I realized today that she hadn't been sabotaging my work this summer. That was her way of giving me time to fall inescapably and irrevocably in love with you."

As she laid her cheek against his chest, he kissed the top of her head. "That's a nice thought, Maggie. But don't you think it's a bit fanciful?"

Her gaze met his, rather smugly, he thought, and she ran a fingertip down his nose. "Take a deep breath and tell me what you smell."

He shook his head tolerantly. "Now, Maggie..."

"Humor me. Please?" Maggie pulled away, but not out of his arms, glad she'd forgotten her perfume in her rush this morning. He sighed, then inhaled deeply. She smiled in satisfaction as the awareness registered on his face.

"Okay, so I can vaguely smell lavender, but it doesn't prove a thing. She lived here for most of her life and—"

"The room didn't smell like this until I realized that the buyer intended to ruin the house. Then when you showed up, it grew a little stronger." Maggie cupped his face in her hands. "Don't you understand? She's here, now, watching over me until I'm happily settled." She smirked. "So for heaven's sake, quit making us wait. Are you going to propose to me properly or not?"

"I don't know... You said you had to find yourself. Did you?"

"Yes. I'm right here . . . waiting impatiently!"

Months ago she'd told him what she wanted in a man. He grinned, recalling it as he held her hands to his heart. "Maggie, I must be the man for you," he said, matter-of-factly. "Not only do I love you, I also think you're the neatest thing to come along since peanut butter. Will you marry me?"

"Oh, Jake!" Maggie smiled, feeling her love grow impossibly stronger. "Yes—"

His mouth slanted over hers, tempestuous in his claim, as if he were trying to make up for all their empty yesterdays, before gentling in a promise of glorious tomorrows.

His eyes were intense when he lifted his head. "I wish Bea really *was* here so we could thank her for bringing us together."

No sooner had he spoken than the subtle scent gained strength, as if they'd just walked into a field of lavender. Jake's eyes widened and he touched his cheek with his fingers. A moment later, Maggie felt a soft warmth brush her cheek. She covered the spot reverently with her hand as her eyes misted with understanding.

I love you, Gran. Goodbye.

Jake turned his head, looking around the room. Then, without so much as a breath of wind from the open window, the bedroom door closed and the fragrance dissipated.

Gran had kept her promise, Maggie thought, wiping the tears from her eyes. Jake still stared at the door, and she caught his noble chin with her fingertips, bringing his stunned gaze back to hers. Her heart full of love and joy, she stroked his chin.

"You wanted to thank her?" Maggie touched her lips to Jake's and whispered, "I think we just did."

* * * * *

Silhouette Romance®

AWARD OF EXCELLENCE

LONG, TALL TEXANS

Diana Palmer brings you the second Award of Excellence title
SUTTON'S WAY

In Diana Palmer's bestselling Long, Tall Texans trilogy, you had a mesmerizing glimpse of Quinn Sutton—a mean, lean Wyoming wildcat of a man, with a disposition to match.

Now, in September, Quinn's back with a story of his own. Set in the Wyoming wilderness, he learns a few things about women from snowbound beauty Amanda Callaway—and a lot more about love.

He's a Texan at heart... who soon has a Wyoming wedding in mind!

The Award of Excellence is given to one specially selected title per month. Spend September discovering *Sutton's Way* #670... only in Silhouette Romance.

RS670-1R

FOUR UNIQUE SERIES
FOR EVERY WOMAN YOU ARE . . .

Silhouette Romance

Love, at its most tender, provocative, emotional . . . in stories that will make you laugh and cry while bringing you the magic of falling in love.

6 titles per month

Silhouette Special Edition

Sophisticated, substantial and packed with emotion, these powerful novels of life and love will capture your imagination and steal your heart.

6 titles per month

Silhouette Desire

Open the door to romance and passion. Humorous, emotional, compelling—yet always a believable and sensuous story—Silhouette Desire never fails to deliver on the promise of love.

6 titles per month

Silhouette Intimate Moments

Enter a world of excitement, of romance heightened by suspense, adventure and the passions every woman dreams of. Let us sweep you away.

4 titles per month